If she didn't act, she'd regret it

Chloe steadied her gaze on Riley, his smile broader with each step she took toward him. She stopped inches away.

"Hello there," he said softly.

"It's my birthday. And when I blew out my candles, I promised myself the next time you walked in here, I would..." She trailed off.

He looked her over, slow and easy. Every place his gaze touched came alive to him. Then he kissed her.

She wanted more. She wanted this. She wanted it all. The new Chloe was going to kiss this man until she was finished with him. Kiss him and then some. When she slid against him, he groaned and his eyes lit with fire. He grabbed her backside to stop her movements.

"This could get hot fast, Chloe."

"Exactly what I had in mind," she said, thrilled by her boldness.

"You sure this is what you want, Chloe?" he asked.

"This is my birthday. And this is my wish," she said. "Please take me to bed."

Blaze™

Dear Reader,

Believe it or not, this book made me a better cook! To understand Chloe's passion for cooking I had to do some research, of course. I discovered how much better freshly chopped garlic tasted than the stuff in a jar. And fresh herbs? Yum. What aromas, what flavors. So that was a cool benefit of the book, beyond bringing together a man and woman who needed each other.

It was so rewarding to match Chloe with Riley, the tough-guy cop who needed her optimism like water in the desert. Who could be better for a man who believed he didn't have much heart than a woman who has nothing *but* heart? And Riley helped Chloe free herself from the family obligations that kept her from living her own life, going after what she wanted—in bed, too. Now, that was fun to write. Especially the handcuff part.

I hope you enjoy how these two work out their differences as much as I did writing their story. Now I can't wait to get a reservation at Chloe's restaurant when she finally opens it. Something tells me Riley will be in the kitchen doing prep work. What do you think?

I'd love to hear your thoughts on this love story. Write me at dawn@dawnatkins.com. Keep track of upcoming projects at www.dawnatkins.com.

Best,

Dawn Atkins

HER SEXIEST SURPRISE
Dawn Atkins

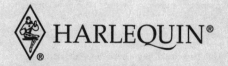

HARLEQUIN®

TORONTO • NEW YORK • LONDON
AMSTERDAM • PARIS • SYDNEY • HAMBURG
STOCKHOLM • ATHENS • TOKYO • MILAN • MADRID
PRAGUE • WARSAW • BUDAPEST • AUCKLAND

ISBN-13: 978-0-373-79436-2
ISBN-10:   0-373-79436-3

HER SEXIEST SURPRISE

ABOUT THE AUTHOR

This is award-winning Harlequin Blaze author Dawn Atkins's twenty-second published book. Known for her funny, spicy romances with a touch of mystery, she's won a Golden Quill for Best Sexy Romance and has been a several-times *Romantic Times BOOKreviews* Reviewers' Choice finalist. This year she was a finalist for a *Romantic Times BOOKreviews* Career Achievement Award for "Best Love and Laughter." She lives in Arizona, where, inspired by this book's heroine, Chloe Baxter, she tries out culinary experiments nightly on her hapless husband and teen son. So far, they've survived.

Books by Dawn Atkins

HARLEQUIN BLAZE

To Amy and Laurie for never letting go

ACKNOWLEDGMENT

Heartfelt thanks to Carol Jennings for sharing her culinary-school expertise with me over that leisurely lunch.

Carol, your courage in the face of the challenges that began that very day moves me beyond words.

1

HOLDING HER BIRTHDAY CAKE high, Chloe Baxter backed through the restaurant pass door, grinning in advance at how delighted her friends would be when they tasted what she'd made.

She whirled, then froze, startled by the sight of Riley Connelly in a nearby booth. She'd missed his arrival and so had Sadie, her fellow hostess, who'd threatened to drag him to the birthday celebration if he showed at Enzo's tonight.

He'd showed all right, and he'd stopped Chloe dead. The pass door whapped her on the butt and she jolted forward, looking ridiculous, no doubt.

Riley flashed a grin, knowing and sexy and so *kissable* that Chloe melted like the candles she would soon blow out.

Jeez, Louise, the man merely smiled and she dissolved? She should get out more. She should get out, period. And she should certainly get laid.

She smiled back, hoping her face didn't look as hotly red as it felt. She had such a crush on the man.

Walking toward her party table, Chloe felt light-headed. Part of that was the champagne Enzo insisted they tap from the bar's stock. She rarely drank, but in honor of her birthday, she'd downed an entire flute of the bubbly gold.

At the table, everyone exclaimed over her cake, which she set at her place, midtable, right across from the booth where Riley, who mouthed happy birthday to her, sat.

She nodded her thanks, wishing she were bold enough to do something—anything—more than smile and nod at the man.

At least Sadie had been too busy lighting Chloe's candles to notice Riley and mortify Chloe by inviting him over. Sadie said he was hot for her, too, but Sadie exaggerated everything about sex, including how much Chloe needed it.

Chloe dropped her gaze to her cake, where twenty-five candles sent up hopeful little flames.

Twenty-five. A quarter of a century and what did she have to show for it?

Not much. Her hostess job and her own car. But she still lived at home to look after her father. She rarely dated, even more rarely had sex, and she'd saved only seven thousand dollars toward her dream of culinary school.

At least now that her sister Clarissa was finally settled with her husband in California, Chloe could sock away more cash. All she needed was time and no disasters. She lowered her face to wish for that, the candles warming her cheeks.

"Not yet! Don't wish yet!" Enzo's wife, Natalie, waved at Chloe from down the table. "Enzo! Give it to her." She tugged her husband's sleeve.

Enzo pulled an envelope from the dinner jacket he always wore when he appeared at his beloved restaurant, and passed it down the row with a somber nod.

"We know your dream is cooking school," Natalie said as the envelope reached Chloe. "So practice on us!" Natalie was ten years younger and far livelier than her husband.

Puzzled, Chloe tore the envelope flap.

"We want you to be our cook!" Natalie burst out.

The card inside offered a too-generous salary for cooking for the Sylvestri family. "This is too much just to cook," Chloe said.

"So we add some light housekeeping." Natalie beamed at her. "I *finally* talked Delores into retiring. It was frozen foods and takeout every night. Come save us, Chloe. Will you? Please?"

"But…my job here…" she said, stunned by the offer.

"We'll fix the schedule," Enzo said. "No trouble."

"Save your money and you'll be in cooking school before you know it," Natalie added. "That was your wish, right?"

Exactly. "I don't know what to say…"

"Say yes and blow out your candles."

How could she turn them down? The Sylvestris had treated the Baxters like family since the Chicago days. "Yes," she said softly. "Thank you so much."

Everyone applauded.

"Now make a new wish," Natalie commanded.

"Okay," she said, leaning down to the glowing cake.

"Wish for Riley," Sadie murmured. "Quick, before he escapes. Last chance for a b-day lay."

Chloe glanced up to see Riley putting his wallet away, ready to leave. He caught her gaze and saluted her before he turned to go.

"He's getting away," Sadie said. "Go get him."

"Forget it," she said. She couldn't chase after the man. Not even for a date, let alone sex.

But that would sure be…exciting. Different. Kind of crazy. When was she ever crazy? Never. She did the practical, responsible thing at every turn. She looked down at her candles, melted to stubs in hot puddles, the flames flickering fiercely, fighting going out with all their waxy might.

Maybe it was time to try something different. Something wild and fun and just for her. Why not, now that she had a quarter century under her belt?

Yeah. So, instead of a wish, she made herself a promise: *The next time Riley Connelly walks through that door, I'll ask him out.*

She blew out all twenty-five candles to cheers from her friends. Now came the best part—serving her cake. "This is called the Surprise Cake," she announced to the group. "It's ten cakes in one. Every piece is different so we can pass them around and share."

Chloe cut through the butter-rich frosting, passed out the pieces to oohs and aahs and waited for her friends to taste.

"Ooh, cinnamon-nut?"…"Yummy, cherry cobbler!"… "Taste this. Is it raspberry cheesecake?"…"Mine's peanut butter and…toffee? Yeah, toffee, yum."

So it went as everyone nibbled and exclaimed and passed their plates to nibble and exclaim again. Chloe was thrilled. This was why she cooked—to give this delight, made even more special when it was for people she loved.

After her guests declared themselves stuffed, she opened her gift—a set of top-of-the-line knives they'd all pitched in for. "Thank you so much," she said, tears welling. "This means so much. And, Natalie and Enzo, the job will be amazing."

Just as she sat down, the door opened and a man entered. *Riley?* Could it be? She blinked away the happy tears to be sure. Yep. It was Riley striding to the hostess stand, where Glenda handed him a cell phone. He must have left it in his booth.

The next time Riley Connelly walks in the door…

Was fate testing her resolve? How could she act with her party still going on? Next time. That was what she'd meant.

Dammit, no. She'd made a promise and the smoke had barely cleared from her candles before she was negotiating it away. She stood so fast her chair scraped the floor.

Everyone stopped talking and looked at her.

"Thank you, everyone. This has been great, but I need to…I have to…get my wish," she said, her face flaming, knowing everyone would watch her now. But if she didn't act, she'd regret it. It was past time to get on with her life.

She steadied her gaze on Riley, who looked puzzled, but waited to see what she wanted, his smile broader with each step she took toward him. She stopped inches away.

"Hello there," he said softly.

"It's my birthday…"

"I gathered that."

"And when I blew out my candles, I promised myself the next time you walked in here, I would…"

What? *Ask you out?* Not dramatic enough for her birthday high, for Riley's magical reappearance, for the hopeful crowd behind her. She'd already leaped off the cliff. Now it was time to fly. "Just…this." She rose on her tiptoes and planted her lips on his.

For a second, she feared he'd break it off, but after the briefest hesitation, he tilted his head, deepened the kiss and pulled her into his arms.

His mouth was warm and firm, and he tasted of rich, dark coffee, and she was so glad she'd taken the leap.

Her friends roared and whistled, which finally made her laugh and she broke away. "Thank you," she whispered.

"No, thank *you,*" he said, his smile wicked. He still held her at the waist.

Unsure of her next move, she was relieved when Sadie bustled over with her purse. "Go on. Have fun. We'll pack up your gift and whatever's left of that incredible cake."

"Are you sure?" she said.

"Yes!" the entire group said in unison. Their laughter trailed her and Riley out the door, as though they were new-lyweds off on their honeymoon.

Once outside in the sudden quiet of the spring night, Chloe became painfully aware she'd just kissed a man to whom she'd never said more than "Booth or table?" and "Your server will be with you in a moment."

"Thanks for going along with me," she said, stepping off the sidewalk between two cars. "It was out of the blue and a crazy sort of dare and I've had champagne and—"

Riley cut her off with a kiss, pulling her into his arms and taking his time, exploring her mouth as comfortably as if they'd been lovers for years.

She relaxed into the moment, not wanting it to end. If this were a movie, the director would cut to a bed and their naked bodies in golden lamplight. There would be no tense seconds, no awkward fussing with zippers and clasps and discussions of prophylactics and blood tests.

She leaned back.

Honk…honk…honk…honk…honk. The car alarm she'd set off brought her back to reality. She was no screen star embracing the man of her dreams. She was Chloe Baxter, talented cook with a problem father, a flaky sister and a cranky cat. Her goofy birthday promise had her making out in a parking lot like a hormone-crazed teenager.

Riley laughed good-naturedly, not a bit thrown by the honking. "My house is close and I promise no alarms will go off." When she hesitated, he added, "It's reasonably clean, I swear. For a guy."

"It's not that. It's just…"

"Your mama told you not to go home with strange men. I get that. But you know me, Chloe. I'm at Enzo's all the time. I'm harmless, I swear." He crossed his heart. "If I misbehave, my dog will pin me to the ground and gnaw my nuts off." He looked so sturdy and sweet and trustworthy, she could only laugh.

"You in?" he asked, his eyes twinkling in the moonlight.

"Let me see…" She rose on tiptoe to kiss him again. His lips were strong, yet soft, his kiss slow and urgent, and she went boneless with desire. "I'm in," she breathed, hoping the kiss would prolong her courage.

Riley seemed to sense her doubts. "You call the shots, you know. You're the birthday girl. We can have a beer, watch TV, play cards or, hell, do you like *Guitar Hero?*"

She laughed, feeling surprisingly comfortable with the man.

"Or we could hit a bar if you'd rather."

"No. Let's go to your place." Something about this man and this moment made it right. She felt different. New. Ready for anything. Well, not *anything.* And not *entirely* different. Just enough for tonight. She shivered in anticipation.

"You cold?" Riley asked, running his hands up and down her arms as if to warm her.

"Just excited, I think."

"Good, then. Let's go." He gave her his address and she followed his vintage red Mustang the few blocks to his house, her heart pounding, her toes and fingers tingling, her stomach fluttering with a million butterflies. The champagne buzz was gone, so it had to be nervous excitement she felt.

Riley held her door for her, then led her up the walk, a gentlemanly arm around her shoulders.

At his front door, she stopped. "This isn't like me, you know. I'm usually cautious and careful and, I don't know…"

He waited for her to figure it out.

"Boring," she said, realizing it was true. "Utterly dull."

"You're sure not boring me," he said, kissing her again, soft and coaxing and warm and sure.

When he opened the door, they were greeted by a barrel-chested dog with wispy black-and-white fur—an oversize Chihuahua on stilt legs who galloped around them, barking.

"This is the guy who's supposed to knock you to the ground if you get fresh with me?" she teased.

"Oh, you don't want to get on his bad side," he said, bending to the dog's level. "He's ferocious, aren't you, boy?"

She bent down, too, glad of the distraction. The sudden intimacy of being in Riley's home made her feel awkward.

"This is Idle," he told her.

"Nice to meet you." She patted the dog, who was remarkably ugly but had the warmest eyes. "He's sweet."

"He's usually shy with strangers, but he's taken with you. So am I." He leaned over the dog to kiss her.

Her lust surged again, telling her she wanted more from this man, this night, though she wasn't sure how much.

He helped her to her feet, holding both her hands, then led her to the sofa. "Would you like coffee to clear your head?"

"My head is clear. Or reasonably clear." She laughed, still

a little uncertain how she'd gotten here. "I only had a little champagne really."

"A beer then?"

She stayed away from alcohol as a rule. She'd tested herself in high school to be certain she didn't have her father's disease, deliberately getting drunk to see if a craving commenced. She'd thrown up lemon Schnapps until she could hardly crawl. Even now, the smell of lemonade gave her a twinge.

"How about juice?"

"I've got orange." He headed to the kitchen to get their drinks. His dog followed him with his eyes, then stayed put. She patted him, trying to slow her thrumming pulse. What would happen? Would they just make out? Or do more? Have sex? Could she see herself going that far?

She shivered and looked around. This was a guy's place. No real decorating, generic furniture, though the brown leather sofa was remarkably comfortable. The cream walls held art posters—a race car, a beach scene, a sepia print of a black jazz band. Shelves had books, DVDs, CDs and video games for the consoles that shared space with a fancy stereo and a plasma TV in the entertainment center. The cocktail table had car magazines and *Popular Mechanics*. But it was neat, as he'd said.

Riley brought the drinks in plastic tumblers and sat close beside her, handing her hers.

She sipped, then smiled, nervous again. "Your dog is so friendly. Nothing like my cat. She's feral. I named her Pepper Spray because if you get near she hisses and spits. Mostly she hides. I only know she's around by the shredded curtains and the empty food bowl."

"How did you end up with her?"

"She's a rescued cat. My friend has a shelter and couldn't find a home for her."

"So you took her?"

"Yeah. Every few nights, she tears around the house like

she wants to escape. I don't know what it takes to convince her she's safe."

"Maybe find a farm that needs a mouser and get yourself a friendlier one."

"She's family." She shrugged. "I love her."

He studied her, as if puzzled by that admission. "So, I didn't count. How many candles were there?"

"Twenty-five. I can't believe I'm that old."

"That's not old. Try thirty-two."

"Wow, old." She laughed. "Just kidding. I guess I feel like I've been waiting for my life to start."

"Why is that?" He leaned back, ready to listen. He was easy to talk to. Maybe it was the kissing or her long-held crush, but she felt as if they'd sped through the usual getting-to-know-you steps and landed in more intimate territory.

"I don't know," she said. "Family obligations. I have a younger sister who's struggled, and my father has had problems."

"So you helped them out?"

"Yes. I was happy to do it, but the years slipped by and I'm twenty-five and it's time for something new. Something less cautious, careful…"

"And boring?" He grinned.

"Exactly. That's why I kissed you. The old Chloe wouldn't have had the nerve. The new Chloe goes for what she wants."

"Nice to meet you, New Chloe." He tapped his glass against hers. "You can call me Lucky."

"Lucky?"

"Lucky I left my cell phone at Enzo's."

"Okay. Nice to meet you, Mr. Lucky."

He looked her over, slow and easy. Every place his gaze touched came alive to him. He set down his glass and kissed her—softly, not pushy, asking her if she wanted more. Her heart raced and everything in her rose to meet him. She felt freer than she'd ever felt in her life. The Sylvestris had made her dream of cooking school possible, so why couldn't she have more?

She wanted more. She wanted this. She wanted it all. The new Chloe was going to kiss this man until she was done with him. Kiss him and then some.

Her mouth on his, she leaned against him until he was lying on the sofa and she was on top of him, the hard length of him beneath her. When she slid against him, he groaned and his eyes lit with fire. He grabbed her backside to stop her movements. "This could get hot fast, Chloe."

"Exactly what I had in mind," she said, thrilled by her boldness.

"You sure this is what you want?" he asked.

"This is my birthday. And this is my wish," she said. It was the real wish, the one beneath her desire to talk to the man. She wanted to feel her own power in her own life, she wanted passion, she wanted fire. "Please take me to bed." The words surprised her, but rang with truth. The new Chloe was ready to fly.

SWEEPING A TREMBLING Chloe into his arms, Riley bent for another taste of her sweet mouth before starting to his room. Talk about lucky. As usual, he'd gone to Enzo's to track the action. Two hours and a birthday wish later, he was carrying the hot hostess he'd fantasized about to his bed.

Even luckier, because of the clump of Idle fur on the pillowcase, Riley had changed his sheets yesterday. Did he still have condoms in his nightstand? Was he *that* lucky?

Idle whined from behind them. The warning made Riley stop. "You're sure you're sure?" he asked her.

"Absolutely," she said, her eyes clear and smart. She wasn't drunk, just high on her decision. She'd cast him as the star in her birthday play, so he couldn't disappoint her.

Bullshit. He'd watched her for months, imagining her naked, her soft mouth on his, her husky voice saying his name.

Now that he'd kissed her, seen the need in those hot green eyes of hers, well, how could he pass that up?

It was lust and something more. She was so sweet and

eager and *new*. She tugged at him, reminding him of a softer time in his life.

"Did you forget where your bed is?" she asked, wagging her legs to get him moving. "Or did you change your mind?"

"No way." It had been a long time since he'd wanted anything this much. He'd forgotten this whirlpool of wet heat and need. Or maybe he was different with her, too.

Was it immoral? Unethical? Against regs? At the moment, with her clinging to him, kissing him while he stumbled down the hall, he didn't give a damn. Blind with lust, he ripped down his spread, aimed them at the mattress and landed them on their sides.

Chloe's lips never left his, even as she kicked off her shoes and he ditched his own. Her tongue moved restlessly inside his mouth and she caught quick breaths, as though if she stopped, she'd lose her nerve. She smelled like sugar and oranges and something else—a season…spring—and warm rain.

Her hand worked at his zipper and he went at her buttons, sliding her blouse off her shoulders to kiss the tops of her breasts above the white lace of her bra.

"That feels…so…good," she said, reaching to unclasp her bra in the front, watching his face as she did, offering herself to him, brave and vulnerable at the same time.

"You're beautiful," he said, cupping her breasts, which trembled in his hands, the nipples tightly aroused. He took one into his mouth, tonguing the tight bud while Chloe squirmed and moaned, fighting her way into his pants, intent on his cock.

She shoved at his jeans, her nails scraping his skin. He smiled against her mouth. No one had gone at him this way in a long time and he liked it.

"Allow me," he said, tearing off his clothes, then tackling her skirt. She lifted her hips to help him and soon she was down to white panties, through which he could see her soft hair. When he tugged off the thin fabric, she gasped, then smiled, wiggling against him.

What next? He wanted to kiss and lick and stroke her everywhere at once. First, he had to make sure they were protected, so he reached beyond her to the nightstand, praying what condoms remained hadn't passed their use-by date.

Grasping a loose foil square, he checked. Score. He waved it at her.

"I'm on the Pill," she said. "And healthy. If you are, too, maybe we don't need that."

"Sounds good." He tossed the condom onto the nightstand and smiled down at her. They'd slipped into an easy familiarity that made sex seem the natural next step.

She ran her hands down his arms, and he slid his hands across her ribs, along the curve of her hip to her thigh, enjoying her warmth, the shakiness of her breath, her smooth skin. Then he reached his target. Watching her face, he gently brushed the unbelievably swollen softness of her folds.

She gasped and cried out, lunging at him, lifting her hips, asking for more. Blood pounded in his cock. "You're so wet," he breathed, letting his fingers slide in and out with silky ease.

"I know. I can hardly believe this is happening," she said, her eyes shining with a trust he wanted to be worthy of. She took little gasping sips of air, swept away on sensation.

"Me, either," he said. He prided himself on being rational, self-sufficient and in control, but all that was out the window at the moment.

She stroked his cock with diabolical fingers, arousing him nearly blind. Everything he did made her moan and writhe, as though she hadn't been touched in a long time. As though she didn't expect to be touched again for even longer. They were like hungry animals together.

"We've got all the time we need," he breathed in her ear, thinking they should slow down before something snapped, but Chloe was having none of that.

"Did you forget who the birthday girl is?" She shot him a

look full of fire and determination and gripped his cock with both hands like she expected to steer him somewhere.

Anywhere you want, babe, he thought, while she straddled him on her knees, then lowered herself, sending him deep into her tight, wet heat. Damn, that felt good.

"Oh. My." She blinked, startled, it seemed, to find herself in this position.

"You feel good," he said to reassure her, squeezing her butt cheeks with both hands, lifting and lowering her slowly.

"Mmm, I do. I do feel good."

He brushed her clit with a thumb and she shivered and began to wriggle in a slow circle. "Slow is nice, too," she said, smiling in soft surprise.

"Slow is great." Slow gave him time to memorize how she looked above him, her breasts swaying, lips swollen and parted, eyes dazed with arousal, time to enjoy being buried to the hilt in her warmth.

She swiveled her hips, making him want to pump into her, catch the wave of release, but he resisted, forced himself to stay slow and easy, to let it build.

He stroked her clit, enjoying her cries and moans, the way she threw her head back in pleasure, the way her body responded to him. She sped up and so did he. She was close… closer.

She made a little sound and her eyes flew open as she stiffened, then shuddered into a climax. He held her hips, steadying her, then released himself, flying free of everything but her body. They shook for long seconds, moving, making sounds, shivering and bucking. When she was finished, she fell onto his chest. "That was great," she panted. "Thank you."

"No, thank *you,*" he said as he had when she first kissed him, chuckling as he wrapped his arms around her. He was Mr. Lucky, all right. Lucky he'd gone to Enzo's for dinner. Lucky he'd left his phone. Lucky Chloe had her eye on him.

It was no doubt a bad idea to sleep with a hostess at the

Chicago mobster's restaurant. Supposedly, Enzo had retired from his vending-machine business when he moved to sunny Arizona with his second wife and kids, but wiseguys always kept their beak in, Riley knew.

He himself had been part of busts with other Sylvestris—fraud with a charitable trust, drug smuggling at a strip joint and a knitting shop, of all places.

Surely the sweet woman in his arms knew nothing of her boss's evil deeds, despite the fact that the man had been smack-dab in the middle of her birthday dinner. Just this once, Riley would hope for the best.

2
___

WHEN CHLOE OPENED HER EYES, she found herself looking between Riley's fingers like they were the bars of a cell where she'd been locked away by the slut police.

She'd just slept with a man she knew nothing about except that he preferred booths to tables and was great in bed.

She'd been wild, too, carrying on like a porn star, except none of her moans had been fake. Remembering, she got a queasy stomach and a pounding head she couldn't blame on champagne.

She'd made that birthday promise, right? Except it was to ask him out, *not* to screw his brains out. She'd gone too far. Having more fun and being free did not equal mindless sex with a near stranger.

How mortifying. She gently lifted Riley's hand from her face to check the old-fashioned alarm clock ticking noisily on his nightstand—3:00 a.m. She had to get home.

She hoped her father hadn't waited up for her. He'd only made a cameo at her party, since she'd insisted he go to his favorite AA meeting. He went to bed early, so hopefully he hadn't noticed she hadn't returned. She should have called. It had been the champagne, the birthday candles. And the man.

Oh, the man.

There he lay beside her, naked, tan and muscular, half-covered by white sheets that smelled of laundry soap and the spicy cologne he wore. She sighed. If she had to go wild and throw herself at a guy, at least she'd snagged a good one.

He'd made her slow down and enjoy what they were doing. *Are you sure?* he'd asked her more than once. He'd even offered her coffee to clear her head. Surely he hadn't thought she was drunk. There had been no stopping her. The new Chloe had broken free, seized her sexual power, gone for it.

The old Chloe woke up mortified by her actions, worrying about her father, wondering what Riley thought of her. Did he think she was a slut? He wouldn't say so, but she might read it in his eyes and she couldn't bear that. How could she face him at Enzo's again? She had to escape before he awoke.

The new Chloe would have teased him awake with a blow job. The old Chloe had to get out fast.

She slid out of bed with great care. The still-sleeping Riley reached for her, so she pushed a pillow over and he settled into a cuddle. For a sec, she wanted to crawl back into bed with him, but what was the point? She'd had her new Chloe moment. Enough for now. She grabbed her scattered clothes, then got on her knees to hunt a missing shoe.

She'd kicked it across the room, under the bureau. When she stood, her fingers brushed a small, framed photo. Leaning in, she recognized Riley wearing a police uniform. Riley was a cop?

Wow. She looked over at his sleeping form. He hadn't mentioned what he did for a living. Actually, she hadn't asked.

She'd never dated anyone in law enforcement. Sadie considered herself an expert. Drawn by the sexy uniform, she'd gone through what she called her law-and-order phase, but gave up when the guys turned out to be "macho, uptight, emotionally stunted commitment-phobes."

It was wrong to generalize, despite her father's bad experiences with the law, and she knew cops came in all flavors, but Riley didn't seem to fit the mold. He'd been so easygoing, gentle and warm. And such a good listener.

She tiptoed to the door, clutching her clothes to her bare chest. Idle jumped from the bed and followed, tags rattling. "Shh!" she said, and the dog tilted his head at her, curious.

"Where you going?" Riley's voice was scratchy with sleep.

"Home," she said, embarrassed to be sneaking out naked.

"Come back here." He patted the sheet beside him. "We're still celebrating your birthday."

Desire shivered through her. More would be nice. They could try new things, more positions, go slower….

No. She'd had a great time. She should be content. She backed up and banged her shoulder against the doorjamb.

"Careful there."

"I'm fine," she said, pulling the door closed.

"Chloe?"

She peeked in again. "Yes?"

"Happy birthday."

She smiled. "You made it that way. Thanks."

"Anytime."

Anytime? He wanted more, too? How could it be that good again? It had been the right mood, the right man, the right moment. She'd made a memory. That was plenty enough for her.

She wiggled her fingers goodbye.

For just a second, in the warm spring night, she missed new Chloe, who might dance down the street singing. New Chloe wouldn't have turned down more sex with Riley.

But reality now weighed on her shoulders. She checked her cell phone. No missed calls. No messages. Whew. Her father didn't know she'd stayed out this late. She didn't want him to worry about her. She worried enough about him.

He'd been quiet lately, which was odd in such an affable man, and he seemed troubled. What was up? He never complained, feeling guilty for all the trouble he'd been over the years.

It had been unusual last night and yet freeing to not be the person who watched out for her father and Clarissa, the one who thought two steps ahead, anticipated problems, pushed for solutions.

Not that Chloe minded taking care of her family. She'd been proud to take on the role when their mother left. Unable

to cope with Mickey Baxter's drinking and fresh-start promises, she'd taken off when Chloe was ten, Clarissa six.

Their mom visited a couple of times, but after a while they
had to settle for weekly postcards—thoughtful and loving messages, but not the same as seeing her in person. Chloe longed
for her tight hugs, reassuring smile and loving encouragement.

As an adult, Chloe realized her mother had been wracked
with guilt, making the visits pure torture. At the time, Chloe
had felt like a burden, a weight and a worry. Taking charge of
the house gave her a way to be useful, to feel valuable.

Lately, though, she'd become impatient with her sister,
whose financial struggles had drained Chloe's savings and
delayed her dream, and her father, whose good sense could
be snuffed out like her tiny birthday flames with the merest
puff of temptation. She tried to support, not enable, both of
them, but sometimes it was tough to tell the difference.

Having wild sex with a man she hardly knew had been a
way to rebel, she guessed. Here on out, she'd choose more
productive actions. Though she might not need to rebel.

Her sister, married last year, seemed settled in Ventura and
her husband finally had a solid job. Chloe's father, sober for the
ten years they'd been in Phoenix, seemed to have his gambling
under control and spent less time with questionable friends.

As long as her family remained stable, her new job with
the Sylvestris meant she was all-systems-go for a bright future.

When she opened the door, the roar of sports from the TV
startled her. Had her father fallen asleep in the lounger?
Rounding the corner, she was hit by the smoky aroma of
whiskey and the gulping snores her father only emitted when
he'd been drinking.

Sure enough, beside the lounger, an empty quart of Wild
Turkey gleamed evilly in the gray flicker of *World Wide Wres-
tling* on TV.

Not again. Not after all these years. Chloe's heart sank.
She had miserable memories of him like this. She'd hated

when he drank, hated helping him to bed, seeing him so weak and sad and helpless. Something was wrong, just as she'd suspected.

Going closer, she noticed how much older and frailer he seemed, his hair a wispy gray, his face drawn and wind-burned. He was only forty-five. Her heart squeezed tight in her chest.

Whatever it is, we'll fix it, she promised the sleeping man. She touched his thin shoulder. "Dad?"

"What? Huh?" He jerked upright, eyes wide. "Oh, Chloe. It's you. So late." He groaned, rubbed his face and dropped back to the headrest, staring up at the ceiling.

"What is it, Dad? What's wrong?"

"Nothing," he said, his eyes telling a different story. "Everything's…fine."

"Not exactly." She held the liquor bottle before him.

"It was a mistake. I slipped." His mouth went grim.

"You had a reason. Tell me what happened."

"I can handle it. Don't you worry about me."

"Tell me what it is and we'll fix it together."

He stared at her, swallowing hard, his fingers picking at the fabric of the armrest. "It's just something with Sal, that's all. I will handle it."

"Sal Minetti?" Sal was Enzo's nephew. He was bad news and his friends were even worse. Enzo complained about him a lot.

"I'll work it out. Don't give it a thought." Her dad reached for her hand, but his was trembling.

"Tell me what happened, Dad," she said levelly.

Tears slid from his eyes and he shook his head slowly back and forth, the way he used to when he'd lost too much at the track or had to be picked up from a bar, too drunk to drive. He was ashamed, tortured by his failure.

He'd never been drunk at work or spent grocery or rent money, but they'd also never had spare cash and Chloe had become expert at creating arty looks with thrift-store buys.

He'd assuage his guilt with ridiculous extravagances—a

fancy boom box, a giant stuffed giraffe, a top-of-the-line mountain bike. He tried. He loved them. He just had…limits.

"Talk to me."

"Sal asked me to drive for him," he said shakily. "He and his buddies, Carlo and Leo, wanted to go to this strip mall in Glendale. So, no problem, I drive 'em. They're quiet, which should tip me off…" He swallowed again and eyed the ceiling.

"So they tell me to pull around back, they need to talk to a guy, and they get out with backpacks. Next thing I know they're running to the car, backpacks jammed. They robbed a jewelry store. They had some guy fox the security system and I dunno what all, but it's not on the up-and-up. That I know."

"You didn't get caught, right? So you're okay?"

He shook his head, miserable. "No, but they want me to keep driving. 'Special assignments,' Sal calls it."

"You have to tell him you can't do it."

"You don't say no to these guys."

"They can get somebody else, Dad."

"But, see, that's it…." He swallowed hard, as if gathering courage. "See, Sal helped me out with a shortfall. If I do this, I'm covered."

"More gambling?"

"An investment idea went south."

Anger stabbed at her. Why was her father so vulnerable to something-for-nothing schemes? At least it hadn't been illegal gambling. She fought to focus on the problem at hand.

"We have to talk to Enzo, Dad. He'll stop Sal."

"Absolutely not." He lunged forward, his eyes wide. "If Enzo finds out, I don't want to know what Sal might do, who he might hurt."

Sal had threatened them? She couldn't imagine. He didn't seem violent, but she only saw him flirting at the bar. Her father looked petrified. Maybe someone above Sal was the danger.

"Then the police," she said. "If Sal's doing crime, he should be arrested." What about Riley? Her heart leaped with hope. Riley would help her. He'd been so kind and generous.

"Not with my record."

"It was a few days in county for drunk and disorderly. And in Chicago, they conned you as much as they did, those business owners, who were crooks, too."

"It's enough, trust me. Cops only care about the rules."

"We'll get an attorney to protect you."

"With what money? No. Just let it ride for now. I told you I'll handle it. I will."

"This won't just go away." She lifted the bottle again. "And *this* makes things worse."

"I know. I lost my strength. I had so much hope, see, and I wanted you to be proud. It was for your school. I wanted to surprise you on your birthday. Instead I screwed up again." His eyes were red and desperate.

"Just don't drink, Dad. That's the gift I want from you. And use good sense. No quick deals, no easy money. Think before you jump. If it looks too good to be true, it *is* too good to be true." She was babbling the same advice she always gave and he somehow failed to heed, but she had to do something with her frustration. "It'll be all right, Dad. I know it will."

First, she'd talk to Riley. Thank God she'd met him. He wasn't a hard-ass like the highway patrolman who gave her a speeding ticket outside Blythe. That guy hadn't cracked a smile when she'd asked if his day was going better than hers. He just lectured her like she was an idiot and slapped the ticket into her palm. Riley would be sympathetic.

Maybe all he had to do was put out the word and this could go away. It felt strange to ask for a favor from a man she'd only known naked, but when it came to family, you did what you had to do. That was something the old Chloe knew cold.

THE DOORBELL WOKE RILEY. Seven o'clock, according to his clock. Who could it be? He'd told Max and the squad he intended to sleep all weekend as a reward for solving the Sanchez case.

Climbing out of bed, he noticed gray light through the window and the drip of water. More spring rain. A good thing, since it had to hold them through the broiling Arizona summer. But hearing it made him want to curl under the covers for a morning snooze. With Chloe.

Too bad she hadn't stayed. Not his typical response. He liked waking up alone and peaceful. But the sex hadn't been typical and neither had the woman.

He'd have made her breakfast. Oatmeal anyway, but he'd have made it special. Didn't he have a banana? Then some leisurely sack time, after which they could read the paper from the terrace, watch the quail boss their newborn chicks around, smell that great wet-desert smell. Someone had explained it was only creosote and dust, but to him it smelled healthy and pure and made him glad to be alive.

Idle clattered to the door as Riley stepped into jersey shorts and fished out a T-shirt.

The doorbell rang again and Idle barked. "Hang on," Riley shouted. *Where's the fire?* He wanted to sink back into bed and conjure up Chloe's moves and cries. She'd intrigued him, charged him up, made him feel new.

Leave it alone. He couldn't see her again, not with what he was doing at Enzo's—gathering leads, watching who ate with whom and what they said to each other, then passing it on to the Phoenix FBI's Task Force on Organized Crime. They considered him a resource and often picked his brain.

Besides, he liked things simple and Chloe was not a simple girl—taking care of her family the way she'd described told him that. Last night was a one-time deal. She clearly wanted it that way. Much better. No complications. No disappointment. One hot memory to call up when needed.

At the door, Idle whined and quivered, waiting for him to open it. He never acted this way, not even for Max.

"Settle down," he said, leaning to the peephole.

He was startled to see Chloe standing there, chewing her lip, wet hair plastered to her cheeks, holding a rain-peppered sack with purple flowers sticking out. What the hell? She'd brought him groceries? And flowers?

Idle whined again. "You smelled her, huh? Like spring." He grinned as he threw open the door.

"I'm back," she said with a shy smile. The wet-desert smell billowed in with her own scent, filling his head. They stood staring at each other, her eyes flitting here and there, his doing the same. Damn, she was pretty.

And nervous, he noticed. Hmm.

Idle squealed with delight.

"Hello, buddy." She leaned down to pat him with her free hand. "I brought breakfast," she said, looking up at him.

"You didn't need to—"

"I wanted to," she said, then ducked her gaze. "The kitchen is this way?" She set off, not waiting for a reply.

He followed and watched her put down the sack and take out the flowerpot. "Just for color," she said, blushing pink, then hurried to empty the sack of eggs, glass containers with herbs and oil, a bottle of maple syrup, sliced ham, mushrooms and a waffle iron. "I figured you like a hearty breakfast, so I thought Belgian waffles with ham crisps. The batter's ready. I just need twenty minutes to bake the crisps. That okay?"

She was babbling to cover her tension.

"I can wait." He moved closer. Was she embarrassed about returning?

"Good." From the bottom of the sack, she lifted a white chef's apron. When she looped it over her neck, her hands shook. Something was wrong.

He tied her strings, then turned her to face him. "How come you're all of a sudden my personal chef?"

"I wanted to make up for leaving so fast." But her face went pink and her eyes flicked up and left, signifying a fib. She reminded him of a suspect with something to hide or confess.

"What's wrong, Chloe?"

"Wrong? Nothing's wrong." She blinked, flushed full red, and stepped away from his hands.

"You're red and trembling and you won't look me in the eye. What's up?"

"Okay." She sagged, sheepish. "I do need your advice."

"*My* advice? About what?"

She studied him. "Maybe we should talk after breakfast."

Uh-oh. "Breakfast can wait. What advice do you need? And why me?"

"I, um, noticed your photo. You're a police officer, right?"

"Detective," he corrected, dreading what came next. Maybe she just needed a speeding ticket fixed. Not that he would do it, but he wanted it to be simple and small, something that wouldn't make his sleeping with her an even worse idea than it already was.

"That means you investigate crimes, right? That's great."

Uh-oh. "Let's sit down." He led her to his couch and sat beside her. Noticing her goose bumps and damp hair, he wrapped the throw his squad mate's wife had made for him around her shoulders.

She didn't seem to notice. She just looked at him, her big green eyes muddy with worry.

"Exactly what crime are we talking about?"

"Okay…" She took a deep breath and spoke in a rush. "Say someone got dragged into a robbery—just driving the car, with no knowledge of any theft—how much trouble would that person be in? And could they get out of it by talking to the police?"

"You mean how would they be charged? That depends…." The familiar hum started in his brain as he got ready to sort lies from truth, meaningless details from crime-solving gold.

"On what?"

"Who's involved, their prior arrests, the seriousness of the crime, what the D.A. wants. Just tell me what happened."

She stiffened at his tone. Too terse. He took her hands and softened his voice. "Just talk to me, Chloe. I can't help you if I don't know the whole story."

"Maybe I can go hypothetical? So it doesn't get official?" Her lower lip quivered. He'd scared her and she didn't trust him. Why would she? They'd been different people last night, both of them, lost in lust. This morning, he was a detective and she was either an informant, an accessory or, worse, a suspect.

"If you want," he said. "Give me the hypothetical."

"So, *hypothetically,* this person—it's a man—he's a driver for another man and this other man's nephew asks the man to drive him somewhere. As a favor because he—my guy— owes the nephew. So my guy drives and the errand turns out to be a robbery—"

"Was the victim present for the crime?"

"No. It was a jewelry store after hours. Is that good?"

"It's better. That makes it burglary, not robbery. There are several classes with varying severity. Were weapons present?"

"Weapons? I don't know. My person didn't have one. He just waited in the car to drive them back."

"That makes him—minimum—an accessory."

"Even unknowing and innocent? That sounds bad."

"Like I said, that depends. Go on." There was obviously more to the story.

"Okay…" Her voice was shakier now. "Now the bad nephew wants the driver to keep driving for similar jobs and my person is afraid to say no." She stopped, her face full of fear. "Can you help me, Riley?" she said. "My person, I mean?"

He couldn't promise much. "Who is it, Chloe?" A relative, no doubt. Riley had seen it before. He'd sat down with parents whose son stole from neighbors to fund a meth habit, a single mom with a daughter turning tricks to buy designer clothes, a wife whose husband had embezzled from his job to cover gambling debts. They'd all seemed sad and bewildered and lost. It got to him every time. What had they done to deserve this? How could loved ones hurt each other so badly?

"It's my dad, Riley," she said softly. "And the guy, the bad nephew, is Sal Minetti."

Enzo Sylvestri's nephew. Adrenaline shot through Riley. "I see." His mind raced, but he hid his reaction, needing as much information as he could gather first.

"My dad's a good guy. He tries. He was just doing a favor. He's too generous. And Sal wants him to drive more and he's afraid to say no. He can't be arrested, can he?"

"He could, yes, but if he comes clean, if he helps the case against the rest of the crew, sometimes the D.A. will deal."

"So if he talks to the police he'll be okay?" Chloe lifted her big eyes to him like he was the Savior himself.

"Like I said, it depends." What could he tell her? The law was the law and he'd been around long enough to know that what a man confessed to was usually the first load of dirt he'd shoveled under the carpet. "Do you have a lawyer?"

"Do we need one?"

"There are public defenders, but they're run pretty ragged. Not much time per case. Some are better than others…."

"So, it's serious? He's in big trouble? You can't make it go away?" Water gleamed in her eyes. She was about to cry? Shit.

"Let me talk to my lieutenant. If they're working on a case on Minetti, there might be wiggle room." There would be interest, he knew. Hell, *he* was interested.

"That would be great. I mean, I know my father will cooperate. With you on our side, helping us…"

"All I can promise is to talk to my boss."

"That's great," she said.

No, it was terrible. He should get her father down to the station now, while he was scared, before he clammed up and demanded an attorney, but Riley already cared too much about Chloe.

"So, it's settled, at least. Let me fix breakfast."

"That's not necessary, Chloe."

"But it's fun. I love to cook." She blinked at him, startled that he'd even question the idea. She was up and in the kitchen before he could object. He followed, wishing he'd kept his big mouth shut.

You made promises you couldn't keep and you ended up in big trouble. Or someone else did.

3

RILEY GROUND BEANS and started coffee, watching Chloe swirl
through his kitchen like a fragrant fairy. She plugged in the
waffle iron, banged a sauté pan onto the stove and slapped
down butter with the efficiency of a TV chef.

"Looks like you know what you're doing. Do you cook a
lot?" Despite everything, he was pleased to have her in his
kitchen making him breakfast.

"I'm practicing for culinary school." She laid slices of ham
into a cupcake pan, then began whipping eggs.

"So you're looking to become a chef?"

"I love making people happy with food." She grinned,
her drying hair forming soft curls against her cheeks. "Eventually I hope to own a restaurant, though I know that's a
tough business."

He realized he was ogling her. "Can I help with anything?"
he asked to distract himself.

"Chop these mushrooms and scallions maybe? Very fine,
please. Then, could you set the table?" She grabbed a knife
from his rack. "These are good knives. You must cook some,
too."

"When I have time, which isn't often." He'd eaten far too
much pizza, takeout and convenience-store burritos of late.

"You work too much?"

"Probably. More overtime than my lieutenant wants, that's
for sure." He shrugged. "Leads dry up fast if you don't push
when you have them."

"So you're dedicated." Her stirring slowed as she studied him. She was thinking that meant he'd move heaven and earth to save her father, he'd bet. "That doesn't surprise me about you."

"Why not?"

"Because of how you were…with me." She blushed again. "You paid attention. You had a lot of…focus." Her spoon slowed, as if she were remembering them in bed. Her eyes glowed like they had their own burners.

"I had you naked. Who wouldn't focus?"

A shiver moved through her. "Riley…" she said softly.

"Yeah," he said, backing away. Sex was out now. His body registered disappointment with a low-grade ache.

She turned to pour the batter into the waffle iron. The promising sizzle and the smell of sweet dough had him salivating like Idle, who sat at attention, hoping for spillage.

"God, that smells good," he said.

"I hope it tastes as good." She busied herself mixing what he'd chopped into the egg mixture, dashing in herbs and oil, then layering the ham into each cupcake space. He couldn't take his eyes from her flying fingers. Or her tight backside and softly swaying breasts. The scene was like a dream—breakfast aromas and a warm, enticing woman in his kitchen.

Idle whined desperately.

Chloe laughed. "Maybe you can have a bite, Idle," she said. "Did he get that name because he idolizes you?"

He laughed. "It's *Idle*. Like an engine. He was in a cage in a suspect's house, so skinny and weak I thought he was dead, but when I got close he vibrated with this low buzz like a car in Neutral. It was all he could manage."

"How sad." Idle stared up at her as if she was some kind of doggie saint.

"The way he's looking at you at the moment, maybe I should spell it the other way. I know how you feel, boy," Riley added.

She lifted her gaze to his.

He was leaning in, going for a kiss, kicking himself the whole way, when the timer dinged. They both pulled apart like boxers at the end of a round.

Chloe turned back to her cooking and he busied himself setting the table with the white plates and cheap silverware he'd bought when he got into the Academy. He dressed up the table with Chloe's purple flowers in their pot. Not bad…

"If this meal turns out as good as I think it will, I'll use it at my new job," she said.

"You're quitting Enzo's?"

"No. I'll still be there. My birthday gift from the Sylvestris was an offer to be their cook and housekeeper. They're paying me too much, but it's really to help me with culinary school. How could I say no?"

"That's generous of them." What was she doing getting so hooked up with a mob family? Not safe and not wise.

"It's the kind of people they are. Our families go back a long way. My father worked for Enzo's dad back in Chicago."

"Really? How'd you all end up in Phoenix?" He needed to learn what she knew before he said more.

"Ten years ago, Enzo had a heart scare and retired so he could spend more time with his family—Natalie's his second wife and the kids were little. We came out two years later. My dad drives him around and does odd jobs. Enzo mostly golfs, fishes, does the restaurant. He…putters, really."

Putters? Not exactly how Riley would describe profiting from drugs, vice and extortion, but he kept that to himself. Instead, he said, "The guy hardly needs a driver. Can't he drive himself?"

"It's more of a favor, I think. See, my dad saved Enzo's father's life back in Chicago. He drove a taxi and was waiting for a fare when someone shot at Arturo as he came out of a restaurant. My dad threw him into the cab and drove him to safety, catching a bullet in his thigh for his trouble. That leg still bothers him."

"So, the Sylvestris owe your father."

She stopped working and turned to him. "They're grateful, sure, but it's more about how close our families are."

This was worse than he thought. Chloe couldn't be so naive she didn't realize the Sylvestris were a crime family, could she? Or had she closed her eyes to it? Either way, he was disappointed in her.

Chloe flipped the waffle expertly onto a plate, then swung over to the oven to pull out the egg dish. "Let's eat," she said, smiling at him.

They sat at the table across from each other. The plant blocked his view of her, so he shifted it to the floor.

"This looks great," he said, looking down at his plate.

"Dig in." Chloe waited for him to cut into the waffle and put it in his mouth.

The bite melted on his tongue like cinnamon-flavored butter. "God," was all he could say, going for more.

She grinned. "Now the eggs." She leaned in, waiting.

He sampled the dish. "Incredible. See for yourself."

As she tasted, she analyzed improvements—more oil, less cream, fewer scallions, homemade preserves and a dab of crème fraîche for the waffles.

As she talked, he watched the gleam of butter on her lips, caught glimpses of her tongue until he wanted to take her mouth. He pictured her last night, her hair wild, her body perfect, moving in complete sync with him. *Control yourself.*

Idle's snuffle thankfully distracted him. The dog was nosing into the plant, so he carried it to the living room.

Back at the table, he kept eating. Every time he got the urge to kiss Chloe, he took another bite. Before long he was working on thirds.

"You really like it, huh?" Chloe asked, resting her chin in her palm, watching him as if this were her greatest pleasure.

"Mmm-hmm," he said, swallowing.

"Did you always want to be a cop?"

"I guess," he said, caught off guard by the new topic. "My dad was one." He pushed away from the table, way too full. He'd be in the gym all night working this off.

"Did he retire?"

"Killed in the line of duty when I was twelve."

"Oh. I'm so sorry." She grabbed her heart, like the tragedy had struck someone she loved.

"That was twenty years ago," he said, shrugging.

"What was he like, your father?"

"Strict. Serious. No bullshit. If I even thought about doing anything wrong, he was on me."

"What wrong things did you do?"

"The usual kid nonsense. Fistfights, staying out late, setting off fireworks."

"He must have inspired you, though."

"He didn't talk much about the job, but I knew he was proud." He remembered the crisp uniform and the smell his pop brought in of metal and smoke and upholstery and clean sweat. He'd set down his gun hard, like it was the weight of his job on the shelf, waiting to be picked up the next day.

"Was your mom scared of the danger?"

"She got pissed over his hours. I remember that. When she bitched about a ruined dinner, he'd say, 'What should I tell the folks that got broke into? Cold air coming through the smashed window, their belongings tossed to the floor, scared the guy'll come back on 'em? *Sorry, the wife's got pot roast waiting?*'"

"She probably felt guilty."

"I guess. I was a kid, so I don't know the whole story. After my dad died, she couldn't handle me, so I went to live with my dad's brother, Frank." Who had been distant like his dad, but angrier. Seething and sulky. It took Riley a while to figure out it was because Riley's parents considered his father a hero, while Frank was a mere truck driver.

"Did you get along? You and your uncle?"

Jeez, the woman didn't leave anything alone. "We did

okay." The resentment played out with Frank beating the crap out of him over stupid shit—a broken plate, an unmade bed, coming in at eleven instead of ten-thirty. Finally ashamed, Frank started taking long hauls and staying on for a return job to avoid Riley. "He was a truck driver. I was on my own a lot."

"No aunt on the scene? Or a girlfriend?" She spoke tentatively, as if she'd read something into his silence.

"Frank wasn't much with the ladies. Not that I saw, anyway. He died when I was at the Academy. Heart attack…asleep in his truck. Just how he'd have wanted to go—on the road."

"Sounds like he wasn't much of a parent to you."

"He called once a trip. You can't expect more of people than they have to give. Same with my mother. She did her best."

She was silent for a moment, as if she disagreed, but didn't want to argue with him. "I'm sorry, Riley."

"Nothing to be sorry about. Everybody has troubles, Chloe." You took the blows, got up, dusted off and moved on. That was life.

"You lost both your parents, really. My mom left us when I was ten and my sister was six."

"That's a shame." He didn't know what to say to that. She looked sad. "You see her much now?"

"Mostly she writes. We talk at Christmas and birthdays. She feels guilty about having left us, I know now."

He nodded. "Yeah. Same with my mom."

"So we have a sad thing in common, huh? Moms missing in action." Her blue eyes held his, full of sympathy and sorrow and he got the old ache in his gut. He didn't think about it much, but losing his parents so fast, then trying to live with his belligerent uncle, had been tough. He'd fought to please Frank—cooked him dinner, polished his dress shoes, built bookshelves. The kiss-up bullshit only made the man harder.

As a kid, he couldn't figure it out. He didn't yet know the way people could twist up emotions—turn guilt to fury, jealousy to hatred. "We learned from it, too," he said firmly.

He'd learned to watch out for himself, to respect others' privacy. Not difficult for him, really. He was like his dad—not big on emotion. His squad mates were all the family he needed.

"That's true," she said, but he had the feeling her lessons had been different. He rolled his shoulder, uneasy that he'd said so much about himself. "So you have a sister?"

"Yeah. Clarissa." She sighed.

"What's the big sigh about?"

"Oh, just that it's taken her forever to grow up. She dropped in and out of college, kept running out of money. She's married now, finishing school, I hope. Her husband finally gave up being a rock-band roadie and took a job as a sound engineer. I don't know why Clarissa's so... I guess the only word is flaky. Maybe I babied her to make up for Mom. Maybe I did too much for her all the time."

"You did your best." And spoiled the hell out of her, he'd bet. The woman had a big, soft heart. Hell, she'd adopted a feral cat. He'd never have the patience for an uphill battle like that. "So, where would I get a waffle iron like that?" he asked to change the subject.

She named a gourmet kitchen store and added, "Are you looking to impress the women you bring home?"

"Who says I bring home women?"

"You brought me, remember? You were very smooth."

"That was a special occasion, Chloe." A rare one. When the urge got strong, he hooked up, but only short-term. He didn't want emotional blowback. Couldn't stand hurting anyone. After his encounter last month with Marie Sendrow, a fellow officer, he'd decided to stay clear for a while.

As down-to-earth as Marie was, she'd acted funny after that night—holding his gaze, letting their bodies brush, talking low. He'd decided to keep his head down and focus on work.

Chloe had caught him off guard. She was different from the women he usually chose. Fresh and new and so *awake*.

"What are you thinking about?" she asked him now.

"You," he answered honestly. "And last night."

"Oh." Her eyes warmed with arousal, startled by his admission, he could tell. "I've been thinking about that, too. It's almost all I *can* think about right now." She leaned in.

So did he. When he got close to her, the world went as blurry as a dream, and he couldn't think at all. They breathed the same air, inches apart. His cock fought the confines of his jeans. She tilted her mouth. So did he.

Right before it was too late, Chloe pulled back. "We probably shouldn't do this."

"No. Probably not." Last night was last night. This morning was different. Chloe's father was in trouble with the Sylvestris, who appeared to be Chloe's second family, and Riley had questions to ask. Lots of them.

"I should go," she said, carrying their plates to the sink.

He helped her clean up, then walked her to the door, chewing on the last square of waffle to keep from kissing her.

"Thanks for helping us, Riley," she said. "It means a lot."

"No promises."

"I know," she said, but she didn't. She thought he could work miracles. He watched her walk to her car, her sack of cooking stuff braced on her gracefully swaying hip.

When she drove off, Idle whined as if in pain.

"You're too easy," he said to the dog, who'd fallen in love with Chloe on sight. Idle looked up at him. *Save her, man.*

Great. Now he was putting words in his dog's mouth. Maybe he wasn't so lucky after all.

WHEN CHLOE GOT HOME, her father had left a note, saying he'd gone to an AA meeting. Good. He'd taken the right step. Pepper Spray's tail stuck from beneath the couch, where she must have darted when she heard Chloe come in.

Her message light winked, so she hit Play. "We need you A-S-A-P." Natalie. "Save us from ourselves, Chloe. P.S., you can get oriented to your new job!" Natalie had so much energy. Chloe wasn't surprised the dour Enzo had fallen for her.

Chloe headed over, grateful for something to distract her from her father's troubles and Riley, who crept into her thoughts anyway as she drove. She pictured his dark eyes, square jaw and his smile—slow to arrive and worth it when it came.

She'd felt *close* to him. They shared tough childhoods, but hers had made her hold more tightly to the people she loved, while his seemed to have made him keep his distance.

She'd enjoyed cooking for him. Next time, she'd do eggs Benedict…maybe crepes, since he'd wolfed the waffles.

What next time? New Chloe had had a wild night of freedom and old Chloe had awakened to find her father in deep weeds. There was a lesson there. Never let down your guard.

She was no martyr, of course. You helped loved ones, but you didn't take over their lives or protect them from the consequences of their screwups. But if you could save them unnecessary pain, you had to try.

She reached the Sylvestris' small mansion in an exclusive neighborhood and pressed the buzzer, awed by the lush landscaping, the Doric columns, the statues, the huge fountain. Natalie was enthusiastic about everything she did.

Chloe couldn't wait to hit that cook's dream of a kitchen, with deep sinks, the latest appliances, giant preparation island and every cooking implement there was. Delores, their previous cook, hadn't cracked much more than the microwave, according to Natalie. She'd been hired as a favor to a friend, which was so like the Sylvestris, who were generous to a fault.

In Chicago, Enzo's family was "connected," she knew. Maybe he'd had shady relatives and business associates in the past. Chloe judged people by her experiences with them. People could change, couldn't they? If they couldn't, life would be pretty pointless.

What Chloe knew about Enzo was that he loved his family

and treated his employees like relatives. Many were. Any niece or nephew who needed college money knew they had a job at Enzo's. In the summer, there was practically a busboy or girl for every table. If Enzo had any faults, it was being too kind to people like Sal and his unsavory friends and some nephews' and cousins' kids Chloe found creepy or scary.

"So glad you're here!" came Natalie's cheery voice through the speaker. She gave Chloe the code to let herself in from then on. A few seconds later, Natalie opened the huge front door, wearing a smear of batter across her stylish workout clothes, and releasing a gray mist and the smell of burnt food. "Thank God you're here. My cooking went wrong. Come save us!"

Chloe followed Natalie into the kitchen, where she saw a plate of burnt, doughy-looking pancakes.

"Look what I did!" Natalie said, sounding triumphant. "I was upstairs getting the kids down and *this* happened. I'm hopeless."

"You had the heat too high, and probably not enough oil. Any cook can burn something if they leave it unattended."

"I used to love my mother's pancakes. I wish I'd paid attention when she showed me. Teen girls are *sooo* much smarter than their parents, you know." She sighed.

"God, it stinks in here." Charity, Natalie's sixteen-year-old daughter, loped in for an energy drink from the fridge.

"Not for breakfast," Natalie said.

Charity sipped, then curled her nose. "Get some freshener." She looked over at Chloe. "So you're our cook? I'm doing low-carb. South Beach, but no cheese and I'm going for gluten-free."

"Okay," Chloe said, not impressed by her attitude.

"Like I said, teens know it all," Natalie said. "Low-carb this, South Beach that, gluten-free, mucous-free. What a pain."

"Ma, do some nachos, 'kay?" That was Ronnie, seventeen, hollering from the next room, from which Chloe could hear cars racing and the shouts and groans of guys playing Xbox.

"Say please!" Natalie hollered back.

"Pul-eez. And use good cheese, not that American crap."

"See how much we need you?" she said to Chloe with a sigh. "Not even my nachos are up to par. Let's see if we have good chips." Natalie led her into a pantry as big as a bedroom jammed with pricey gourmet items and piles of junk food. Chloe picked up a jar of truffle oil and a can of caviar, her mind racing with possibilities.

Natalie grabbed a bag of tortilla chips and Chloe followed her to the equally packed refrigerator. "So, he says good cheese…" Natalie lifted a wedge of Havarti. "What do you think?"

"Too sharp," Chloe said. "Perhaps Muenster?" She reached for the container. "It's creamy and melts well. We can add garlic and chili for zing."

"Perfect! I'm thinking you can really shape up the kids' nutrition. Get Charity to eat more—she's a stick and she hates veggies. Maybe add liquid vitamins? I don't know. Ronnie's a disaster. We bought him a weight bench and he uses it to stack gamer mags. Maybe girls will motivate him to get in shape."

She tapped her chin, then looked at Chloe. "Speaking of sex, how did your birthday date go?"

"Oh, that. Uh, okay. It was…nice."

"Look at you. You're all red. You did it. You got laid on your birthday! That's fabulous!"

"Not so loud, okay?" She hoped no one had overheard that.

"Sure, sure." Natalie lowered her voice. "I think it's great. And not a word to Enzo, I swear. In the vault." She brought her hands together like a closing door.

"What's in the vault?" Sal, the man who had ruined her father's life and sobriety, gave Chloe a once-over from the archway. He'd bathed himself in a cloying cologne that made her nose tickle. She sneezed.

"Bless you," Sal said, grinning at her.

"What are you after, Sal?" Natalie asked impatiently.

"A Bud, but I can get it." He leaned between them to get a beer from the fridge, then turned to Chloe. "What brings you to our kitchen, pretty lady?" Another once-over. Ish.

"This is Chloe Baxter, Sal. She's our new cook."

"Baxter? You related to…?"

"Mickey? Yes, he's my father." *Just leave him alone.* She fought to be pleasant.

"And, hey, you work at Enzo's, right? You're a hostess." He pointed a finger at her, then clicked it like a trigger.

"Yes." Sal was a harmless flirt. If a woman actually took him up on his advances, he'd no doubt wilt like celery left out overnight.

"So, you'll be cooking…. I can't wait." He rubbed his stomach and licked his lips, just this side of lascivious.

Chloe managed a curdled smile.

"We have work to do, Sal," Natalie said, making a shooing gesture. "And get Ronnie away from those hellish video games, would you? Every day it's World War III in my house. Boom, crash, rat-tat-tat. Enough. Maybe show him how to fix cars."

"Possible, Aunt Natalie. I'll see what I can do." He looked Chloe over again. "Now if *you'd* like your oil changed, I'm ready anytime." He winked. Gross.

"I think I'll be fine," she said dryly.

"Oh, you're definitely *fine.*" Sal saluted her and Natalie with his beer, then backed away.

"Don't give that guy a thought," Natalie murmured. "Sal is bad news. I don't like Ronnie spending so much time with him, but if I tell Sal not to come over and it gets back to my sister-in-law, major crisis. If I tell Ronnie to stay clear, he'll rebel. Being a mother is so lose-lose."

"I can imagine."

"No one tells you that before, so consider yourself warned." She wagged a finger at Chloe.

"I'll remember," she said, not envying Natalie her kids.

"So, how about we go over your duties, huh? Over cappuccinos? Yes?" She turned to a gleaming metal appliance on the counter. "Can you work this monster? Enzo got it at a closeout from a restaurant supplier. Him and his deals." She rolled her eyes in affectionate annoyance.

"I'll try." The thing looked like it could make bread, create a nuclear bomb and steam shirts all at once.

"The instructions." Natalie presented her with a thick booklet. Luckily, there was a quick-start page and before long Chloe had cappuccinos steaming, nachos bubbling and was mixing V8 with seltzer and Tabasco for a zingy drink with lots of the vitamins Ronnie needed.

When she carried the tray of refreshments into the playroom, she found Ronnie and Sal madly working controllers from the sofa. Slouched on a love seat and recliner were two malevolent-looking guys in black silk shirts. One was clicking out a text message on his phone, the other studied a folded newspaper. Probably figuring the spread on upcoming games, since he didn't look like the crossword type. Maybe that wasn't fair—she tried to give people the benefit of the doubt— but she got a bad vibe from Sal's friends.

Sal noticed Chloe. "Hit Pause, my friend," he said to Ronnie. "Let's see what the pretty lady has for our repast."

"Repast? What the f's that?" the guy with the paper said.

"Chloe, Mr. Ignorant is Carlo and that's Leo over there. Chloe's Mickey Baxter's kid."

"Ah," both men said, then exchanged looks.

Chloe nodded at the two men, then noticed that the game Ronnie was playing was a car race, at least, not death and destruction, except then she watched a character climb out of a car with a machine gun and blast a Hummer to smithereens before Ronnie froze the action.

"What have we here?" Sal said, pretending to look at the food she'd bent to show them while staring at her breasts.

She described the snacks, then waved her hand before his eyes. He grinned, caught, then grabbed nachos.

Ronnie did, too. He chewed and swallowed, then tossed off a "Good," before resuming his game.

"I'd love you to cook up something special for me," Sal said to her.

"I'm the *Sylvestris'* cook."

"Perfect. I'm a Sylvestri."

She just looked at him.

"Give it up, Sal," Carlo said. "She's not interested."

"Never say never, right, babe?"

Please don't wink, she thought, her eyes watering from his cologne.

Sal winked.

"Let Natalie know if there's something you'd like," she said wearily. Being genial with the guy might help her father.

"She's warming up," he said to Carlo, triumphant as a kid. "I can't wait for the next family dinner."

"Me, either," she said, gritting her teeth. As she left, she heard them mutter, then laugh. Something lascivious, no doubt.

Back in the kitchen, she and Natalie sipped cappuccino and Natalie talked through the schedule. "Breakfast is at eight. You can count on me and Enzo. The kids should eat, too, but the crucial thing is them getting to the bus at eight-thirty."

"They have trouble making the bus?"

"Are you kidding? They have trouble waking up, let alone making it to the bus or breakfast. Delores just shouted up the stairs like that would do it." Natalie rolled her eyes.

"So you want me to…?" Drag them downstairs?

"Take any measures necessary," she said. "Whatever it takes. Completely your call."

They talked next about menus. The family mostly ate Italian, but Natalie urged her to be creative. Chloe couldn't wait to try her own riffs on Italian dishes, working in the family's nutritional needs and preferences at the same time.

There was to be a big family dinner on her second day of work. And Enzo's birthday was next week. She would prepare a traditional family meal, followed by a party. She couldn't wait to work up the menus. Soon, she had pages of notes and a partial shopping list.

"Now the housework," Natalie said. "Just the light stuff—laundry, dust and vacuum, clean the bathrooms. We have people for the heavy stuff—the marble floors, the windows and whatever you don't want to do. The kids should pick up their own rooms. Delores despaired and did it herself, but you're so good with people, maybe you can motivate them?"

"I'll talk to them, Natalie, but—"

"I know, I know. We're the parents. Your job is to cook our socks off. The rest is gravy. Get it? Gravy?" She glanced at her watch. "I should walk you through the house, but I've got a tennis game." She smiled, then hugged Chloe hard. "I have such a good feeling about you being here."

"Me, too." Chloe's heart felt like it would burst with happiness. She would do all she could for these dear people, who were paving the way to her dream. All she needed was Riley to come through for her father. One last flare-up to fix, and she'd finally be able to live the life she wanted.

4

ON SATURDAY AFTERNOON, when Riley went to the station to check Michael Baxter's criminal record, he was dismayed to hear his squad mate Max's whistle moving down the row of detective cubicles. Damn. Not wanting to have to explain what he was up to, he'd hoped for the usual weekend quiet.

"What are you doing here?" Max asked. "I thought you were sleeping all weekend."

"Woke up. Got bored." Riley had almost not come, since Idle had seemed under the weather. The dog had a hot nose, no appetite and remained in bed instead of trotting after Riley around the house. It had crossed his mind the dog just missed Chloe. Riley kind of did, too.

"What about you?" he said, to shift focus. "You worked as hard as I did." They paired up on a lot of cases, both feeling the drive to push for the last clue, make one last canvas, one more attempt to reach a missing witness, even when the lieutenant blasted them for too much overtime.

"Just finishing up some DRs and supplementals."

"You're doing reports? On a Saturday? Without the lieutenant ragging on you? Come on."

"Okay, okay. Susan bitched me out for not doing anything around the house. So I told her I had paperwork and left."

"You are purely whipped, man," he said.

"You'll see. Wait'll you get married."

"Like I'll ever do that."

"Sure you will. What about Marie? She's into you."

"That was just sex." He shrugged.

"Sex…yeah, I remember sex. Back when I got some."

"Come on. Susan's good to you." He wanted Max to stay happy—he was one of the few cops Riley knew with a good marriage. Lots were divorced, a few were on shaky ground on the home front, and the single ones were like him: no plans to change status.

"So, who's Michael Baxter?" Max looked over his shoulder at the terminal where Riley was checking records.

"This guy's involved with the Sylvestris and got into some trouble. He wants to come clean, but looks like he's got some beefs back in Chicago. Minor stuff, but stuff." He normally liked the feel of finding somebody had a record. But this was Chloe's father. With his record, jail time was almost a guarantee with this felony burglary. Especially in the law-and-order atmosphere of the state these days. Gloom filled Riley.

"How did you connect with this guy?"

"Through his daughter. Long story."

"Long story, huh? I got time." Max leaned back in his chair, arms behind his head.

But Riley wasn't about to get into it. "I'm going to talk with the lieutenant about pursuing a deal. There's a possible in with the Sylvestris, since the guy works for them." Baxter might make a decent informant. Chloe was their new cook, but Riley didn't want to involve her if he could help it. Already, he was pulling punches on the case. Not a good sign.

Forcing out the thought, he said, "Want some help with those DRs?"

"What'll I owe you?" Max said, suspicious.

"Susan's pot roast some Sunday. And help with my cases if the Sylvestri thing pans out."

"You know I've got your back," he said. "Pot roast it is."

Riley took a stack from Max's in-box. "Go do some yard work. Get on Susan's good side."

"I'd better if I ever hope to get laid again." Max shook his head, but there was a trace of a smile on his face.

Riley saw the appeal of a family, but knew it meant sacrifice and a burden. Max's kids hardly saw him. He'd missed soccer matches and dance recitals, and Susan's family reunion, which had pissed her off big-time.

At least as a detective, Max wasn't in much danger. Not like a vice or street cop. How could those officers put their families through the dread of that call, the officers on the doorstep with the bad news? And, with that on your mind, how could you do the job right?

Riley was glad he was accountable only to himself. Except now he was worried about Chloe and her father. Not good. Emotions snarled good sense, complicated things, muddied life.

On the other hand, the idea of nailing Enzo Sylvestri got Riley's blood moving. Maybe he'd been bored. He'd considered trying for a reassignment as undercover or working narcotics again. He'd wanted to shake things up.

If the lieutenant and the D.A. worked a deal with Mickey Baxter, coordinated with the FBI's Organized Crime Task Force, Riley might get assigned to the case. A lot of dominoes had to fall right first, so he wouldn't get ahead of himself.

He hoped he could help Chloe's father, too. It meant so much to Chloe, which, he realized with a twinge, mattered more to him than it should.

"YOU TOLD A COP!" Chloe's father's eyes went wide with alarm. "What have you done to me, Chloe Marlene?"

"Riley's a good guy, Dad. He'll help us."

"Cops live to clear cases. To them, we're all liars and thieves, believe me. They've got no mercy."

"I trust Riley," she said, though his voice on the phone had been stern. *We need you and your father to come to the station this afternoon to discuss his situation. One this afternoon.*

No *would that be all right?* or *when's a good time?* More like *get your asses down here.* Maybe people were listening, so he'd had to sound terse. When she'd asked if everything would be all right, he'd only said, *We'll talk once you're here.*

She hoped he'd be warmer in person, but when he met them in the lobby, he looked stern, almost angry, and his kind eyes were hard as stone. "Ms. Baxter," he said, nodding at her as if she were a casual acquaintance, not someone he'd held naked in his arms. She felt queasy and disoriented, as if she didn't even know the man, as if her trust had been misplaced.

"Mickey Baxter," her father said, lunging forward to shake Riley's hand.

"My father," she added, emphasizing the personal connection. "We're very nervous about all this."

She tried to catch Riley's eye, draw out a smile, but he opened the security door and said, "If you'll come this way," completely neutral.

He led them to an interview room that looked more like an office meeting room than the grim, prison-green space with a two-way mirror she'd expected. The walls were a soft white. There was a whiteboard and a small laminate table surrounded by three office chairs on rollers. No mirror anywhere.

Two men in suits rose from the table, where a tape recorder rested. "Special Agent Emile London from the FBI and Assistant District Attorney Paul Adams," Riley said, then introduced Chloe and her dad.

Her father sank into a chair, his face pale.

"I had no idea this would involve the FBI," Chloe said, shooting Riley a look. "We were to discuss this with local authorities, weren't we?"

"There are federal statutes involved," Agent London said. "The FBI has an ongoing interest in Mr. Minetti and the Sylvestri family."

"You mean Enzo?" she asked.

"Among others," the agent said.

"Enzo knows nothing about this," Chloe said. "In fact, Sal threatened my father if he said a word to Enzo."

Agent London was clearly irritated by her words, but he focused on her father, who looked utterly beaten down. "The outcome of your case, Mr. Baxter, depends on your cooperation in this matter. If you agree to provide information about all illicit activities engaged in by Sal Minetti, Enzo Sylvestri and any associates of said men, as well as provide a full statement about your crime—"

"My father committed no crime," she interrupted. "Sal Minetti robbed the store. My father merely drove the car as a favor." She put a protective hand on her father's shoulder.

The agent eyed her as if she were an annoying insect he had to bat away. "Your father participated in a burglary. That doesn't go away because he's sorry."

"Sal tricked my father. He threatened him. Is my father being charged? If he is, we'll need an attorney immediately." She was seething with fury. "If he's not, we'll be going." She had no idea what she'd do if they called her bluff.

"Hear the man out first, Chloe," Riley said, a hint of kindness back in his voice. Just to get her cooperation, no doubt. London flashed an annoyed look at Riley. There must have been friction between them.

Chloe fought for calm. Riley was right. Her father's future was at stake. She had to learn their options. "Go on," she said, folding her arms.

"As I was saying—" London paused for effect "—if you provide a complete statement, Mr. Baxter, and agree to keep us apprised of the movements and illegal activities of the aforementioned men—"

"You want him to spy?" Chloe said. "Sal and his creeps have guns. My father's life could be in danger."

Agent London cleared his throat, keeping his attention on her father. "Cooperate with us, Mr. Baxter, and the FBI will refrain from charging you with federal violations. And as to the D.A.—" He nodded at Adams.

"Our office will agree to accessory after the fact, with a year's sentence, possibly suspended."

"*Possibly* suspended?" Chloe said. "That's no deal."

"It depends on what develops," Riley said quickly. He seemed intent on keeping her calm. "If Sal exonerates your father of intent, that would help."

"Until we know more, we can't promise more," Adams said.

"That's not acceptable," she snapped.

"I'll do it, Chloe," her dad said. "I have to."

"No you don't, Dad." These people were using her father as a pawn. Worse, they were after Enzo, too. "Use me!" she said, grasping at straws. "I'll be working at the Sylvestris'. Sal's always at the house. I can find out what he's up to."

For the first time, the agent focused on her. Then he lifted his eyes to the ceiling behind her. What, was he consulting God?

No, a camera, she'd bet. She turned to look and saw a small metal-rimmed lens. Obviously, it took the place of a two-way mirror. Someone outside this room was watching them. How creepy.

"Excuse us a moment." London and Adams backed out of the room to consult with their eavesdropping bosses, no doubt.

"I can't let you do this, Chloe," her father said. "Not with a guy like Sal."

"I'll be careful. It's not dangerous, is it, Detective Connelly?" His look said it all. "So it is. And you were perfectly happy to risk my father's life."

"Your father was involved in a crime, Chlo—Ms. Baxter. The charges concern him. Surely you can understand that." He was talking to her as though she were a child or an imbecile.

"I understand just fine. I happen to disagree. About Enzo, too. If I can prove he's innocent, will my father get his deal?"

Before Riley could respond, London returned without

Adams, wearing a fake smile. "Yes, Ms. Baxter," London said, "your participation will be welcome, along with your father's."

"Along with? No. Leave him out of this." She felt as though she were being dragged into some huge, unstoppable machine, her options limited, her choices nil. She looked at Riley, searching for some shred of hope, but his expression was flat, his mouth grim. The kind, sensitive man she'd slept with had been replaced by a tough cop who wanted to punish her father and arrest Enzo.

"Not possible," London said.

"I'm at fault," her father said. "You stay clear."

Her poor father. Chloe's stomach churned so violently she feared she'd throw up. She wanted to strike out—wipe the smug look off London's face. Smack Riley, too, who instead of throwing them a life raft, had dragged them into deeper water.

"If you're in, I'm in," she said wearily. "I'll be at the house anyway. The sooner we get Sal, the better."

"We're agreed then?" London said.

"I want it in writing," Chloe said.

"While the agreement is drafted, we can take Mr. Baxter's statement." He pushed the recorder closer to her father, fingers poised over the buttons.

"You can leave," Riley told her, "if you'd prefer."

"Oh, no. I'm staying." She wouldn't let her father incriminate himself further. She didn't trust these people as far as she could throw them. And she felt like throwing them through a wall.

With endlessly repetitive questions, Agent London walked her father through what had happened until Chloe wanted to scream in frustration.

"So, you claim, Mr. Baxter, that all you did was drive them to the jewelry store?" London asked again. "You had no idea what they were going to do?"

"He's told you that twice," she said through gritted teeth.

But her father patiently repeated his answer, as he had to all the others London pelted him with. Had Sal discussed any other crimes? Had her father seen any of the stolen items? How had they disposed of the stolen goods? On and on.

Finally, she had to interrupt. "He's told you all he knows," she said. "This is starting to feel like harassment."

London turned to her. "We need these answers, Ms. Baxter. See what you can do about getting them." There was a threat and a challenge in his words, but at least the grilling was over.

The statement signed, the agreement in hand, Chloe and her father followed Riley out of the police station. "Thanks for coming in," Riley said.

"We're so glad we did," she said bitterly. Her father was right. Cops went after bad guys, period. Riley had done his duty by turning them over to the FBI. In the soft-focus of their time together, Chloe had completely misread the man.

"I'll be your liaison," Riley said, ignoring her tone. "I'll be in touch."

"I'm sure you will be," she snapped, turning to go.

"Can I have a minute?" Riley said.

"I'll meet you at the car," her father said, walking on.

She turned to Riley, arms folded, letting her impatience show. "What is it?"

"That was an official meeting, Chloe. It wasn't personal."

"Oh, I got that, all right. That was as impersonal as it gets." She started away, but he grabbed her arm.

"What's with the attitude?"

"I asked for your help and you threw my father to the sharks."

"You don't get it, do you?" A muscle ticked in his jaw.

"I get it fine. You did your job. Cops get their man. End of story. End of us." She whipped around and marched off. Getting Riley angry wouldn't help her father, but she couldn't stop herself. Her head felt wrapped in rubber bands, she was burning with anger and betrayal, and shaking with fear.

She slammed into the car. "A cop is a cop, just like you said. I'm sorry I did this to you."

"You were looking out for me, Chloe," her father said, no anger in his gray eyes. "Trouble is, it's me who should be looking out for you."

How she loved him. "I'll make it right, Dad. Don't worry."

"No, Chloe. *I'll* make it right. It's about damn time." His mouth formed a firm line and she saw determination like she'd never seen in him. "You shouldn't have to take a kitchen job with Enzo to earn your way to cooking school. I'm your father. I should pay."

"I'm excited about the job, Dad. It's practice. Let's get through this and move on—lesson learned."

She'd learned a lesson, too—about Riley. His warm kindness had been an illusion she'd conjured up out of her birthday wish. She'd seen Riley the way she wanted to see him.

He'd gone along, though she could hardly blame him. The sex had been great. *That* had been no illusion. It was also over. *Way* over.

RILEY WATCHED Chloe quick-step across the parking lot. She was *pissed* at him. Thank God. Much better than how she'd looked at him in the interview room—as though he'd betrayed her. That had hit like a punch in the gut.

She didn't get it. His hands were tied. Civilians watched too many cop shows that made them think that if you meant well, you could skirt the law. It didn't work that way and it wasn't always fair, especially when politics played out.

London hadn't helped, acting like a hard-ass, hammering home the worst-case scenario. Riley would explain that to Chloe and Mickey at their first meeting—cast London as the bad cop, establish a rapport. Or maybe he'd been watching too much TV, too.

He'd gotten lucky and been chosen as the department's liaison with the FBI's Organized Crime Task Force on this case. That was big. He'd laid the groundwork hanging out at Enzo's all these months, gathering information he'd shared with the OCTF, but he'd got the job because of Chloe. She'd come to him and he'd brought them her father.

Chloe's misery had been his stroke of luck. He felt bad for that, but he'd do his best to keep her out of harm's way.

It burned him how Mickey Baxter had let her throw herself on the tracks of the train headed for him. He was one of those sad cases—two-bit players, weak and eager to please, who ended up on the shit end of the stick. Wrong place, wrong time, wrong life. Mickey was worse, though, because he let his daughter do cleanup for him.

All the same, Riley had been touched by the unfailing love in her eyes when she defended the guy. It would be nice to have someone to look at him that way. *Get real, Connelly.* The truth was that blind love was Chloe's weakness. She was hopelessly loyal to Enzo Sylvestri, closing her eyes to who he was. When the truth came out, she'd hate Riley for forcing her to see it.

That made it damn good they'd stopped the sex.

There was no point remembering her hands on his cock, her breasts in his palms. Complete waste of time to think about her big eyes, her soft lips, her warm whiskey voice. Better to remember her eyes hot with hatred, her lips thin with fury.

That made him feel hollow inside. Hell, the sad fact was he missed her. This was why he had to keep his head in the game, stay clear of emotional bullshit, do his job.

Back inside, Marie spotted him and came over to bump his arm. "So, what's happening? I saw you in with the Feebie."

"I got assigned liaison to OCTF. We've got informants working on the Sylvestris."

"So all your off-duty surveillance paid off?"

"Yeah." Except it had involved Chloe. It was a drag when you got what you wanted but the price sucked.

"Good deal. And, hey, thanks for covering for me." She moved close to mutter low, "A girl calls in sick and they assume it's some female shit. I threw up so many times I thought my eyes would pop out of my head. Stay clear of the shrimp salad at Alberto's, that's all I'm saying." She stepped back and smiled.

"I'll remember," he said. Trapped at the commode with food poisoning, she'd asked him to take her shift a few days ago, which he'd been happy to do.

"I heard you had to go after my witness," she said.

"The idiot was high on PCP and made me chase him across a couple backyards. Then he decides he's going for the WWE crown." He rubbed his shoulder.

"You get hurt?"

"Just a flare-up from the rotator cuff." He'd injured it training in advanced hand-to-hand combat and it still bothered him.

"I can rub it for you," she said. "I'm good with my hands."

"I just need to stretch more, take it easy for a while."

"Seriously. I'd love to make it up to you." They were in the hall and alone and her voice went intimate.

"Maybe one of these days," he said, wishing he hadn't gotten carried away that night—too many beers on a post-adrenaline buzz.

She studied him. "It's not a deal, if that's what you think. I don't do deals." She meant *relationships*. "It's just physical."

"I get it. I'm just lying low lately."

"Sure. Your loss."

He hoped he hadn't hurt her feelings. She covered her emotions with a gruff style. Police work was still pretty macho and female officers acted bad-ass to keep cred.

"So, how's Idle?" she said. "That is one ugly damn dog."

"Not so good, actually. Lying low himself." He got that rush of worry again. Idle had no energy, hadn't eaten much, though his nose was no longer hot. If he wasn't back to normal after Riley's shift, he'd take him to the vet. If something were to happen to Idle… Well, he wouldn't let it.

"Sorry to hear that," she said. "And if you change your

mind on the other…call me." She squeezed his arm as if to say no harm done. Good.

She seemed to be a loner like him, focused on her career, so he'd figured sex would be safe between them. The women he'd been with who weren't cops got all testy about his hours. He hadn't tried very hard to smooth them, he had to admit. The truth was they wanted more than sex and sex was all he had to give. Better to let it slide.

He wished he hadn't had sex with Chloe in the first place. He'd felt…hell…different. No wonder she'd been furious with him. She probably didn't recognize him.

A few hours later, when he called to arrange a meeting for that evening, she was icy. *I get off at eight, but no later than nine. My father goes to bed early,* she'd said, then hung up before he could agree.

He meant to be early, as a matter of fact, and he was leaving the station at seven when he got a lead on a robbery case he had to follow up on. The last witness lived near his place, so he swung by to check Idle before heading to Chloe's.

To his horror, he found the dog lying on his side, moaning in pain. He'd managed to knock Chloe's plant to the floor. The potting soil in his chin hairs told Riley he'd been at the roots again.

He wrapped the dog in a blanket and picked him up as gently as he could. Idle squealed in agony, looking up at him with pleading eyes. "I'll fix it. I swear." How long had the dog been suffering alone? Riley felt an ache in his chest so big he thought he might need medical help himself.

He called ahead, then took off for the animal hospital. He was waiting in the reception area, a moaning Idle on his lap, when his mobile went off. "Yeah?" he said.

"Where are you? We had an appointment, Detective Connelly." It was Chloe. In his urgency, he'd forgotten to cancel the meeting. "If this is how you stick to your commitments, then I have no hope for any further—"

The vet tech was heading his way, so he cut her off. "Sorry. I can't make it. I'll call you."

"You'll *call* me? That's all you have to say? You have us waiting for hours and you *can't make it?*"

Idle whined piteously.

"Is that Idle?" she asked, concern in her voice.

"Yeah. We're at the vet. He's sick."

"What's wrong?"

"No idea. Look, they're ready for him. I've got to go." He hung up before she could reply.

After the exam, the vet told Riley Idle's symptoms could indicate a number of conditions, including cancer. They'd take blood and X-rays and keep him overnight. For now it was a waiting game.

He's just a dog. He had a good life, Riley told himself as he drove home, his head full, his chest tight.

It was raining again, big fat drops, soft as tears, as if the sky felt sad, too. Stupidly enough, he dreaded his empty, silent house. There would be no cheerful rattle of tags, no friendly nudge of a wet nose.

Approaching his house, he noticed someone sitting on his porch steps. Chloe, he saw, as he got closer, soaking wet and waiting for him. Something in him lifted at the sight of her. He felt an impossible hope.

She stood as he reached her. Her wet hair stuck to her cheeks. Her clothes—a blue shirt with skinny straps and jersey shorts—clung to her skin. "How is he?"

"They're doing tests. They don't know." He focused on her face. "What are you doing here?"

"I felt bad about how nasty I was on the phone. And I wanted to see how Idle was."

"Let's get you out of the rain." He took her by the elbow and let her into his house, unreasonably happy she was here.

Inside, he tried to explain. "I should have called, but with Idle so sick, I wasn't thinking and—"

She threw her arms around him and hugged him hard. "I'm so sorry, Riley. I know how hard this must be for you."

She felt *sorry* for him? Ouch. He never wanted pity.

"I'm fine." He laughed, backing away, showing her it was no big deal. "No need to come all this way in the rain. No need to even apologize."

She swallowed and studied him. "Don't go all macho," she said. "I heard your voice. You're allowed to worry about your dog. You're human."

"Sorry. I just don't do all that…junk." Emotion, weakness, pain. "I'm not like you, Chloe."

"So it's a waste of my time to be here." He'd fumbled the moment, dammit, and hurt her feelings.

"No. I'm glad you came. Seeing you…helps."

"Really?"

"Yeah. You make me feel better." What the hell was he telling her? He let his gaze drop to her breasts, visible clear down to each bump of her nipple, and instantly went hard. "You look good." He forced his eyes up to her face to be civilized.

"No, I don't. I look like a drowned rat." She laughed, grabbing her hair self-consciously, embarrassed by her appearance. Didn't she know how beautiful she was? "I'm not even dressed." She looked down at herself. "This is what I wear to bed."

He let it sink in. She'd rushed to him in her nightclothes, worried about him and Idle. She *cared*. Warmth spread through him, filled him up, made his arms seem too empty without her.

"You look great," he said, the desire to touch her pulsing through him like a heartbeat. "Beautiful."

She went still and her eyes burned at him, huge in the dim light. She wanted him, too, he could see.

Standing here with her, he felt his guard drop, leaving him wide open for any cross, hook or jab she might deliver. He was glad she was here. He pulled her into his arms and just held on. He didn't know what he was doing, only that he wasn't going to stop right away.

5

RILEY'S VOICE ON THE PHONE at the vet's had melted Chloe's heart. The hard-ass cop had been replaced by a bighearted guy broken up over his sick dog. That was the *real* Riley. It had to be. And the real Riley needed her support.

So Chloe had run to him.

She hadn't meant to end up in his arms, but she wasn't sorry. His arms were strong around her, as they had been the other night, and he shook with the same urgency she felt. They both were scared. They needed each other. Maybe she could help Riley connect more with his heart. Maybe she would be good for him.

Come on. She wasn't on a rescue mission here. She wanted him with every cell of her being. She ached with arousal and her skin burned for his touch. It seemed like her birthday all over again. The new Chloe was back—different, open, going for it. She liked feeling this way.

Riley leaned away to look at her. "This is a bad idea," he said. "I'm a cop and you're an informant."

"In the morning," she said, her voice husky with desire. "Tonight, we're Chloe and Riley. Tonight, we need this."

Forget the police station, her father, Enzo and Natalie, even Riley's sick dog. It would all be there in the morning. Tonight there was all this amazing energy between them. Who could resist that? Everything slipped away but this moment with this man.

"Okay," he said with a short nod. He was so far gone, she'd

bet he'd accept any logic, which made her feel all the more aroused and powerful. He held her face in his palms and lowered his mouth to hers, kissing her deeply, drinking her in.

She kissed him back, feeling all she'd felt that first night and then some because she knew what was to come.

"You're all wet," Riley whispered in her ear.

He meant from the rain, but she said, "Everywhere. I'm wet…everywhere."

"I can't wait to touch you," he said, lifting her off her feet. She wrapped her legs around his waist and he carried her to his bed, where he threw back the covers and laid her down.

Joining her, he ran his hand down her body, as if he couldn't believe she was here. He paused for a second, then gave a sad laugh. "I keep listening for Idle."

"You miss him."

His gaze snapped to hers, as if he felt strange admitting it or having her notice.

"If you're too worried. If you'd rather stop—"

"No," he said, coming back to her with fire in his eyes. "I don't want to stop." He was the urgent one now, tugging her damp clothes from her body, removing his jeans and shirt, pressing his body over hers to dry her with his warmth.

He took one of her breasts into his mouth and pressed his tongue over her nipple, sending thrill after thrill across her skin. Her nerves stung with awareness. Arousal surged through her, wave after wave, sensation overlapping sensation—the brush of his stubble, the warmth of his tongue, the cool sheets, their sliding bodies, his murmurs, her cries.

He moved down her belly, kissing and licking and pressing her skin with his lips. Down and down.

He was going to kiss her *there*.

She shivered, not sure she was ready for this intimacy.

But he wasn't asking. He gripped her bottom and lifted her up, serving himself her sex, like a meal he had to taste or die.

"What are you doing to me?" she moaned. Had she dreamed him there, his lips so natural on her most tender place?

"Making you feel good," he murmured, brushing her with his tongue. Fire lapped her nerves the way he lapped her body.

"Ohh, oh, you are… So…good." She didn't know what she was saying or doing. The Riley from her birthday had swept her away again, reminded her how wonderful it felt to just… let…go.

After long, glorious minutes, she wanted to share the pleasure, so she shifted, letting him know he could enter her.

He lifted his face. "Stay right where you are."

"I just thought…if you want…"

"This is what I want." Very deliberately, watching her face, he licked her top to bottom.

She moaned, then struggled up. "I want to do you, too."

"Am I going to have to cuff you?" he said, pretending gruffness. He pinned her wrists to the mattress.

"Mmm," she said, dropping back to the bed. "That's right. You have handcuffs." Sadie had been right about one thing: cops could be damned sexy. "Maybe later," she said, not ready for sex games, but happy to have him keep up what he was doing.

He released her hands to hold her backside so she couldn't move if she'd wanted to, then lowered his head and nuzzled her with his whole mouth. This was the sexiest moment she'd ever experienced. She felt like the hot melted center of a chocolate soufflé, pouring herself out for him to lick away.

His tongue found its way to her opening, making her wiggle and surge, while he nudged her spot with his nose. The combination of his tongue teasing, his nose pushing and the hot wash of his breath threw her into a climax.

Even as the waves of ecstasy poured over and through her, she wanted more. She felt greedy, insatiable.

When the waves faded, she became aware of Riley resting his cheek on her thigh, as if he'd ridden along with her.

"I'm not used to this," she said.

"To what?" He lifted his head, then kissed her skin. "Orgasms? I don't believe that. You're too good at it."

"To letting someone do me. Just me. With nothing for him."

"You give, you don't take? You're a saint in the sack?"

"I want to come, too, but it's usually two-way." She reached down for his penis.

"Two-way is good. Absolutely." He turned her on her side, away from him, so that his penis nudged her bottom. He brought his hands to her front and used both thumbs to stroke her, one after the other while he slid slowly, slowly inside her.

She strained against him, tucked into the curve of his belly, loving how protective he seemed, holding her close, his palms holding her thighs, his thumbs moving on her clit. The front of her body was open to the air, but his hands and penis trapped her, forced her to hold still for him to please her.

"I like how you move," he said. "I like making you come."

"I want to make you come, too," she managed to say.

"Oh, you are." He rocked as he spoke, picking up speed.

She matched him, stroke for stroke. It was like they rowed through water, pulling and pushing, in and out, beautifully together. She reached back for his cheek.

"You're close," he breathed into her ear. "I can tell by how slick you are, by how you breathe."

She could only nod, hoping he was close, too, because she couldn't hold out any longer. She made a sound, then flew free, lifted high by pleasure.

With a deep groan, he released himself, then fell into her, as if he'd given up some terrible weight. They both trembled, shaken by the storm that had passed over them.

She turned toward him and stroked his face. "There you are," she said. "The Riley I remembered from the other night."

He fought a frown, it seemed, ending up looking puzzled. "I'm different with you," he finally said. "I don't act this way…." He stroked her arm.

"Cops get to have personal lives, don't they?"

"Not with informants, they don't." He looked grim.

"We were together before that. We were just two people in bed." She sighed, wishing that hadn't changed.

"It's not that simple now."

"I know. But tonight was unusual. I was upset by today, you were worried about Idle."

"And we won't do it again," he said, as if agreeing with her. The words made her feel suddenly lost. Maybe her feminine pride wanted him to find her irresistible.

"Are you sorry?" she asked.

"I should be," he said quickly, "but I'm not."

"Good. Neither am I." Except now she knew it could be amazing more than once. In fact, it could be amazing again right now. She felt arousal surge through her.

No. Bad idea. Just as the sun would return in the morning, so would Riley the cop, along with what she'd agreed to do. She didn't want to be here when that happened, so she pushed up to go.

Riley caught her arm. "Not yet." He pulled her down and spooned with her, one hand holding her breast, his legs twined with hers. She had to smile at this tough cop wrapping himself around her as though he never wanted to let her go. Pretty intimate for a distant guy.

"For just a minute." She sighed, trying not to sink too deeply into the warm safety of his embrace, his breath steady in her ear, his chest against her back, his arms holding her close.

One day, it would be wonderful to sleep like this with a man she loved. She wanted that, she realized now. She'd dated some, had sex when the guy and the time seemed right, but she always let them slip away. Her life was too complicated for another obligation. But she was freer now, right? So she'd keep her eyes open. Maybe after cooking school…

Tonight, she was Cinderella at the ball, immersed in silk and romance. Tomorrow she'd go back to everyday rags and worry. Tomorrow, Riley would be Detective Connelly out to get the bad guys and she'd start spying on the people she loved.

RILEY WOKE TO THE SOUND of rain and thought instantly of Idle. The vet hadn't called in the night, so Idle had survived. Riley lifted his head to check the time and noticed Chloe asleep on his chest. She'd stayed, after all, which made him smile.

He squinted at the clock. Five-thirty. Early for a call, but he couldn't wait a minute more to check on Idle. He'd have to reach past Chloe for his mobile. She lay almost fully on his body, fingers spread on his belly, her hair brushing his chin, her breath warm against his skin. He liked this, he had to admit. Except it couldn't happen again.

He gently reached for his mobile, hoping not to disturb her, but she stirred and raised her head. "I'm still here. I didn't mean to... What time is it?"

"Five-thirty. Go back to sleep. I'm calling the vet." He searched his call log for the number.

"I should go. I didn't leave word with my father." She rubbed her eyes, clearly struggling to wake up.

"What's he going to do, ground you?" He hit Talk.

"He'll worry, that's all."

The phone was ringing. "Because you're usually responsible and careful and cautious and—"

"Boring as hell. Right." She laughed sheepishly.

"Sunshine Veterinary Hospital, may I help you?" He lifted a finger to let Chloe know he had them on the line.

She nodded, chewing her lip, seeming as worried as he felt.

"I'm checking on Idle Connelly," he said, his heart thudding in his ears. *Let him be all right.*

"Idle, you say? Let me check." The kid sounded way too relaxed. Miserable seconds passed until the tech came back on the line. "He's fine. He was constipated."

"Constipated? With that much pain?"

"Believe it or not, yeah. It causes fever, too. We put him on IV antibiotics, fluids and a laxative. Did he eat anything unusual?"

He remembered the dirt on his chin. "Part of a plant. Could that have caused it?"

"More likely the potting soil. The stuff holds moisture like you wouldn't believe. That's probably what packed his stool. We've seen it before."

"Potting soil, huh? And he'll be all right now?" He nodded at Chloe, who blew out in relief. He wanted to shout, but settled for giving her a high five. "I'll be in to get him right away." He tossed his phone on the bed, grinning like an idiot.

"Where did he get potting soil—" Chloe frowned, then widened her eyes. "Oh, God. It was me. The flowers. I'm so sorry, Riley. This is my fault."

"How could you know he had a jones for sterile dirt?"

"At least he's okay." She hugged him, patting his back as if he needed comfort. He found he didn't mind.

"Want to come with me to get him?" he asked without thinking, but he realized he wanted her company.

"Would you like me to?"

"Sure. You can hold him. He tends to jump around in the car. I don't use a carrier because cages scare him."

"Then I'd love to." She seemed delighted.

"What about your father?" he teased.

"I'll sneak in before he gets up," she said, teasing back.

It all sounded good until they got into his car. Day had returned and with it the case and their daytime roles. The sex-crazed maniacs of the night before were long gone. Riley suddenly didn't know how to behave. Chloe seemed nervous.

"So, today's your first day at the Sylvestris'?" he said to break the awkward silence.

"Yes. I'm starting with breakfast at eight."

Okay, now what? "What are you making?"

"I thought I'd make what I made for you."

"They'll love it."

"I hope so."

Silence.

"This is going to be weird, isn't it?" she said, turning to look at him.

He gripped the steering wheel, wishing they didn't have the case between them. Except without the case, he wouldn't dare see her again. She'd want more than he could ever give.

"I'll do my damnedest to prevent that," he said. "Last night was last night. Today we have jobs to do."

"Right. Saving my father."

He felt her stare drilling into him. "Yeah. That." He wished to hell she didn't think he had that much power. "I still need to go over things with you both. I want to get you both mini-recorders and digital cameras and you a small drive to copy computer files. Have you used a key drive before?"

"I have. Yes. What do you want me to photograph?" She was staring straight ahead now, her posture stiff.

"Important papers, anything unusual. People, if you can do it subtly. Do you have a camera on your mobile?" When she nodded, he added, "The digital offers more clarity in lower light, so use your judgment on which way to go."

She nodded, still not looking at him. They breathed together, the tension tight as wire.

He decided to keep going. "Today, keep your eyes and ears open and tell your father to do the same. Any conversations you pick up, great. Note anything unusual—whispered conversations, private meetings—and track any visitors Enzo gets."

"You mean golf buddies and friends? People from the restaurant? Family? That's who visits Enzo." She sounded angry.

"Everybody, okay? We'll sort it out later." He hesitated, then decided he had to say it. "Don't be surprised if Enzo turns out to be more than a retiree who putters with hobbies."

"I will be very surprised," she said fiercely.

"You have to be honest about what you find, Chloe. For your father's sake."

"What are you telling me? I have to find dirt on Enzo to save my dad?" Her voice broke.

"No. I'm telling you we need to know what's really going on. Good and bad. The truth. All of it."

"Is there anyone you trust, Riley?" Her voice held ice.

"Trust has to be earned."

"That's where I disagree. Most people are trustworthy. Most people mean well. The ones who don't are obvious."

"I guess we run in different circles." There was no point arguing about her naïveté, or explaining the phony sincerity of a sociopath, not when their rapport had gone shaky again.

He returned to the case. "If you can get into their computer, scan e-mails, spreadsheets, docs. When I get you the drive, copy it all. Check papers, get any lists of names, anything with large amounts of cash. Anything suspicious."

Right. Chloe's idea of "suspicious" was a world away from his. If she witnessed a hit, she'd likely see it as an accidental discharge. He wished he could get in her head and rearrange her thinking or somehow take her place in the house. He could cook, but not that well.

"Write it all down. Even once you have the recorder. You'd be surprised how important details slip your memory."

He glanced at her. She was staring ahead, twisting her fingers, her expression stony. He'd scared her, dammit. Sometimes he got so locked on task, he forgot the human element.

He pulled in and parked at the animal hospital, then turned to her. "It's a lot to take in, I know. You have my cell number. If you feel you're in any danger or think they suspect you, get out immediately. No questions asked. Okay?"

She swallowed.

"All right? Chloe?"

She jerked her face to his. "Do you have any idea how hard this will be? Spying on people I love? The Sylvestris gave me this job to help me with cooking school and I'll be using it to sneak around and snoop on them." Her voice cracked.

"Good point." He was so certain Enzo was dirty, he hadn't considered the case through her eyes. He had to smooth this over or he'd lose her. "Maybe they're innocent and you'll prove it. You'll clear them of suspicion once and for all."

That seemed to appease her. She sighed, then lifted her chin. "It doesn't matter. If this is what it takes to save my father, I'll do it. You've given me no choice."

"It's not me. It's the law, the D.A., the FBI…." When her expression didn't change, he felt a spike of frustration. "If you want to be angry at someone, be angry at your father. He did the crime. He dragged you into it."

"Don't talk about my father that way," she snapped.

He'd done it again, tripped over his dick trying to soothe her. "I'm sorry. You love him and want to protect him. I understand that. He made some bad decisions and I hate to see you caught in the middle."

She seemed to fight to calm down. "There's more to it, Riley. More to worry about." She glanced at him, as if deciding whether or not to trust him.

She seemed to decide in his favor because she steadied her green gaze on his face. "My father is an alcoholic. It's a battle every day to stay sober. That's the nature of the condition. He's been sober for ten years and I'm afraid this will break him again. He got drunk the night he told me about Sal. He's back on track again, but I'm afraid the pressure of having to spy will send him down the tubes."

"That's difficult." Terrific. On top of being weak and needy, the guy had a liquor problem.

Chloe let her words spill like a break in a dam, twisting her fingers again. "On top of that, he's hypoglycemic, and if he's not careful to eat, he gets dizzy and passes out. He fainted once and gave himself a concussion. I couldn't stand it if he got hurt."

What the hell could Riley do about that? Give him a bad guy to grab, the fear of God to put into somebody on the brink of trouble, hell, something to hammer or tune or rebuild. Anything but emotional agony like Chloe's over her mess of a father.

"Maybe he's stronger than you think," he finally said.

She raised worried eyes to him, asking for more.

"He loves you. He wants the best for you," he said, wracking his brain for reassuring words. "All we can do is take it one day at a time, like they say in AA." His words earned a faint smile. He felt as if he'd won a marathon and let out the breath he'd been holding.

"You're right, I guess," she said. "Today's the first day so of course it's scary. We'll deal with it as it comes." She squared her shoulders and lifted her chin. She was tough. She took charge. He admired that about her. If she just wouldn't leave her heart out there for anyone to kick to the curb.

"Just be careful," he said. "You don't have as much experience with scumbags as I do. They can be tricky."

"I'm going to assume you're talking about Sal and his creepy friends, so, yes, I'll be careful."

He put his hand on her knee. "I don't want you to get hurt, Chloe."

She lifted her gaze to his and held on. Heat rose again and he felt that tug in his chest. He wanted to take care of her and he wanted to make love to her.

But that was over.

She seemed to realize it, too, scrambling out of the car and practically running to the entrance.

Inside, a tech brought Idle on a leash. When he caught sight of them, the dog's whole body trembled with joy.

"Take it easy, boy." Riley dropped to his knees to accept frantic licks and nose pushes. Idle looked desperately grateful—like he hadn't dare hope for Riley's return. Had he thought he'd been banished again to the caged hell where Riley had found him? Did dogs recover from such scars? Did they blessedly forget? Or were they never the same? The idea made his chest hurt.

I wouldn't leave you, boy. Ever. The promise was as solid as the muscles that moved him through life. The only way to prove it to the dog was day by constant day.

Chloe dropped down to Idle's level and hugged him. "We're so glad you're okay," she said.

Idle whined in ecstasy, pure adoration in his eyes. Chloe had charmed them both.

In the car on the way back, Chloe held Idle on her lap, a gentle hand scratching behind his ears, while she read to Riley the list of bland foods Idle was to eat. "Do you have creamed cereal? Should we swing by the store?"

"I've got canned chicken and rice. We'll be fine." He smiled at her concern.

"Maybe he shouldn't be alone today. I could bring him with me to the Sylvestris' I bet."

"You have a job, Chloe." Two of them, actually. Cook and spy. "I'll swing by and check on him, don't worry. Thanks, though," he added, not used to someone being so helpful.

"If you're sure," she said.

"I'll be over tonight to talk to you and Mickey," he said. "Before nine."

She nodded, then began talking softly to Idle, who stared at her with soulful eyes, tail thumping against Riley's thigh. Riley got a bottomed-out feeling in his gut. It felt good, but also risky and it made his head hurt. Chloe mixed him up, confused him about what counted.

Just being with her made him smile, though, and the smile stayed long after he let her off at her car and she left.

In his house, he put Idle's bed on the sofa, which was off-limits, though the constant wad of black and white fur proved the dog jumped up the minute Riley left. "Just until you get better," he said, setting the dog in place.

He showered and dressed, then headed for the door. He was

due for a strategy meeting with London. At the sofa, he crouched to embrace Idle the way Chloe had done. Idle quivered with pleasure. "I'm here for you, pal," he said and thought he saw understanding in the dog's eyes. The Chloe Effect, no doubt. She had such a big heart. Too big for her own good. To her, Enzo was a saintly family man and when that house of cards hit the dirt, Chloe would be devastated.

She gave her father too much leeway, too. Maybe he meant well, but he was a screwup. You steered clear of screwups. You didn't bail them out all the time.

Wasn't that part of AA? Recovery belongs to the addict, right? His mother had said that to him when she'd called him up to apologize as part of her rehab.

Riley had already forgiven her. She'd done her best. No point dwelling on the past. He wasn't interested in making more of the mother-son thing than there was. He didn't need phony Christmas visits and small talk like Chloe accepted from her lame mother.

She was so different from him. Of course that was part of his attraction to her, he guessed. He couldn't quite figure it out. Last night was foggy in his head, like a dream. He'd flat out lost control. He'd been freaked about Idle, sure, and touched at her gesture, and seeing her body through wet clothes hadn't helped his willpower any, but still…

He hadn't been himself. He would let it go at that, put the wild night behind him and get on with his day. Again.

At the precinct, London was the same arrogant prick he'd been with Chloe. He did, however, know his shit.

The FBI was mostly interested in Enzo. Sal was a small fish, so they were after the sharks above him, assuming there was a multistate fencing ring in place. Minetti wanted Mickey to drive again, suggesting more burglaries were planned. The jewelry store alarm hadn't gone off. Mickey Baxter had mentioned a link with Maximum Security, the company that protected the store. They would look at dirty employees there.

He hoped Chloe and Mickey could come up with tangible leads, without risking too much. Chloe seemed sensible enough—except when it came to wild cats and alcoholic fathers, of course. But she was stubborn, too.

Do I have to cuff you? He'd had to hold her down to make love to her. Lost in her raw response, he'd forgotten his own needs for a while, gotten carried away, and afterward…

"You okay?" London asked, interrupting his thoughts.

"Huh? Oh. Just thinking about the case," he said. Hell, he'd slipped into a daydream.

"Anything worth sharing?" London smirked.

"Not really," he said, his face burning like a kid caught with a *Playboy*. The smartest thing Riley could do was forget about Chloe, except as an informant he needed to support, protect and, yes, use.

CHLOE TIPTOED INTO THE HOUSE, hoping not to wake her father. She'd have to scramble to make it to the Sylvestris' in time to fix breakfast, but she wasn't sorry she'd helped Riley with Idle. She was kind of sorry about last night, mostly because of how painful the transition had been.

The instant they climbed into his car, Birthday Riley and New Chloe disappeared. Maybe that was good. She had to keep the hard-eyed cop in her head because the tender-hearted man devastated by a dog's illness made her ache to be in his arms.

Stepping into the kitchen, she was startled to see her father at the kitchen table, nursing a mug of coffee.

"Dad! You're…um…up early," she stammered. "Are you okay?"

"Your sister woke me up." He tilted his head at her. "She called for you. I told her you were out jogging. Have a good run?" He sipped coffee, not meeting her gaze.

"Uh, yeah. It was good." She blushed. He must know she'd

been with someone. Should she tell him it was Riley? It was too fresh, too mortifying. For now, she'd stick with his face-saving guess. "What did she want?"

"Ryan got laid off, I guess, but she was cheerful. Said she had an idea to talk over with you."

"An idea?" Damn. A business proposal, no doubt. Last time, Clarissa had needed "just a pinch of capital" to start a business making customized baby socks with trinkets in the lace. Not a bad idea, but Clarissa misjudged the market, overspent on inventory and Sweet Feet folded after only six months.

Chloe dreaded the conversation to come. She had hoped her luck would hold and Clarissa and Ryan were finally set. Damn, damn, damn. It was bad enough her father was in trouble, now Clarissa was struggling again. Chloe would have to help.

Or would she? She remembered her birthday cake with its twenty-five fierce little flames reminding her of all the years she'd put her life on hold in favor of family obligations.

It was time to live, to go for what she wanted, wasn't it? She was saving her money for culinary school, not another Clarissa rescue.

"I have to get to work. I'll call her later," she said. When she had more willpower, more determination, more distance.

What if they were in real trouble? Maybe the proposal was a good one. Or at least not too expensive.

Be strong. Stick to your plan. Ryan could find another job and if Clarissa's idea was good, she could get a bank loan.

Chloe poured herself some coffee. "Detective Connelly will be over tonight to discuss our duties. He'll come before nine."

"Okay." Her father sighed.

"Today at work, don't stick your neck out, all right? And if Sal asks you to do another job, say no."

"I'll be fine," he said. "It's you I'm worried about. You've always taken care of me. I've been a terrible father."

"You do your best, Dad," she said, going to hug him.

"I'll fix this. I know you think I'll never change, but I will. I swear." There was fire in his eyes.

"I believe you." She felt the impulse to lean on him, confess her fears, share the worry about spying on Enzo, but she knew that would make him feel guiltier, so she held it in.

Maybe he's stronger than you think, Riley had said. Maybe, but she wasn't willing to risk it yet.

6

EASY TRAFFIC GOT Chloe to the Sylvestris' in record time. She punched in the security code, parked in the curved drive, snatched up the newspaper and used the house key Natalie had given her to open the door.

The house was quiet and dim—everyone must still be asleep—so she put the sports section on top for Enzo, as Natalie had mentioned he liked, then placed it on the kitchen counter, where she found a note from Natalie.

> Dear Chloe! Your cheery smile and fabulous cooking are *soooo* welcome! We talked about a grocery trip today, but please swing by the health-food store for gluten-free something or other for Charity (ask her the name), and Vitamin E and B Complex for me (gotta keep my skin juicy). I've got a day spa appointment at noon, so all questions must be asked before I leave. Next week, come with! You'll need a massage after a week of our craziness.
>
> The kids promise to be nice. Use any means necessary to get them down to breakfast. Is that too harsh? I just mean you're in charge. Okey-dokey?
>
> Love, love, love, Natalie!

Reading the cheerful note, Chloe felt sick. Enzo and Natalie had wrapped their warm arms around her and she would repay them by listening in on conversations and snooping through their computer files.

She set about making coffee with a heavy heart. She'd so looked forward to this job. Now she dreaded it. She could only hope Enzo's innocence would be obvious right away, so the Sylvestris would never have to know of her betrayal. She couldn't live with herself if they thought less of her.

Catching Sal would help Enzo, after all, since Sal's influence on Ronnie had Natalie worried. Enzo's worst mistake might be turning a blind eye to bad relatives. But family was everything to Enzo. She and Enzo had that in common.

Should she tell Enzo what was happening? Enlist his aid in catching Sal? That would make her feel more honest. But she'd promised her father she wouldn't. And she'd promised Riley she'd do her part. For now, she'd stay silent.

She whipped up the waffle batter and was preparing the ham crisps when Enzo appeared in a fuzzy black robe, hair sticking out all over. "How's tricks, Top Chef?" He leaned in to see her face. "Hey, why so glum? You're our morning sunshine. God knows the kids are gray clouds in the soup."

She smiled at the mixed images he'd conjured. "Just thinking," she said, pouring coffee into a handcrafted ceramic mug, which she handed to him. Natalie selected every item in the house with an eye for beauty and quality. "Cream and sugar?"

He patted his belly. "Two-percent and sweetener, or Natalie will bitch. She's worried about my weight. The downside of marrying a younger woman." He sighed. "No mercy on the scale."

"She wants to keep you around, Enzo." Natalie had a reason to worry. A heart attack had made Enzo decide to sell his high-pressured business and move to Arizona with his young family.

"So what smells so good?" He walked over to the waffle iron she'd found in the pantry. "Ah, this fancy deal. Delores never touched it."

"Belgian waffles and ham crisps, though maybe you should skip the waffles if you're watching calories."

"I get the full treatment on your first day. Natalie will approve. It's a celebration—home-cooked food at last." He noticed the paper. "And sports at the ready?" He made a smoochy sound against his fingers. "You could spoil me."

"Everyone spoils you, Enzo." Natalie appeared in a pale blue silk kimono decorated with flying herons, her hair soft against her shoulders. "It's our job."

Chloe handed Natalie coffee with two sugars.

"Mmm, just how I like it." She smiled at Chloe. "Already life is better with you here." She turned to Enzo. "What's on your agenda for today, big man?"

"This and that." He shrugged.

And all perfectly legal, Chloe added in her head. Then Enzo swore, putting a fist down on the newspaper.

"How much?" Natalie said, pinching dead leaves from the African violets on the window ledge.

"Just a couple hundred," he muttered.

"More like a thousand," she said to Chloe. "Sports are big-ticket items in this house."

"I win more than I lose," Enzo said, but he frowned.

"You shouldn't bet if you're going to fume when you lose. Bad for your blood pressure, Enzo."

"I'll tell you what's bad for my blood pressure—Ronnie smarting off. That boy's got a mouth. I tell him not to drive without a license and he tells me to 'chill-ax,' whatever the hell that means."

"He gets the attitude from Sal. Sal swears the air purple and Ronnie practically writes it down to practice."

"I'll talk to Sal about the swearing."

"I don't like him over here so much. He keeps Ronnie out late on school nights."

"What do you want me to do? Sal's my sister's kid. I can't ban him from the house."

"At least make him leave his nasty friends at home. Those two—Leo and Carlo—make me break out in hives."

"I can do that." Enzo nodded, then shoved the sports section into the trash with a disgusted shake of his head.

"Chloe needs money for groceries," she said, kissing him on his bald spot as she passed.

Enzo took his wallet from a basket by the kitchen desk and pulled out three bills, which he handed to Chloe. When she saw they were hundreds, she returned one. "I won't need that much."

"In case you see something extra. Or save it for next time." He patted it into her palm like a tip.

"Enzo, really. This is too much."

"He's right," Natalie said. "Try waking the hellions. You'll earn the extra cash."

"What's wrong with their alarm clocks?" Enzo asked.

"They sleep right through heavy metal music," Natalie said. "They're teenagers, I guess."

Who were staying up too late, Chloe knew from Clarissa's behavior at that age.

"Take up coffee and be persuasive," Natalie urged.

"While you're at it, tell my daughter to stop dressing like she's for sale," Enzo growled.

"Enzo…" Natalie said warningly. "And, besides, Chloe's our cook and housekeeper, not our therapist." She turned to Chloe. "Of course, if you have suggestions, we're open."

"I'll start with coffee," she said, pouring two mugs.

"Ronnie likes half coffee, half cream and three sugars," Natalie said. "Charity wants one Splenda and a strain of milk. Skim."

Chloe tried not to roll her eyes as she added the requested ingredients and headed upstairs.

Ronnie's room smelled of gym socks and incense. "Time for breakfast," she called to him.

He groaned and rolled over.

"I've got coffee here. Mmmm. Plenty of cream and all the sugar you could want." She held it close. "Waffles downstairs."

No reaction.

Any means necessary, Natalie had said. Pour coffee on his head? Not her style. She opted for coaxing. "Make me look good on my first day, huh? Come down and eat with your family. The food's delicious, I swear."

Ronnie's eyes opened and he considered her words, blinking. She held out his coffee.

He sat up and sipped. "This is better than what Delores made," he mused, nodding his head.

"Breakfast will be, too, I hope." She could beat fast-food and frozen stuff with one hand tied behind her back.

Ronnie scratched his head, but he was moving out of bed.

Down the hall, Charity's room was a mix of teen rebellion and childhood treasures. Princess furniture and stuffed animals shared space with posters of metal bands and vampire movies. The girl sprawled, facedown on top of her bedspread in a skimpy silk chemise and a thong.

"Time to get up, Charity," she said, waving the coffee low enough for the aroma to reach her nose. "Skim milk strain and Splenda, just the way you like it."

"Leave it there," she mumbled, and rolled away.

"It's eight. Time for breakfast."

"I don't eat breakfast."

"If you're watching your weight, you should. Protein is crucial. Eggs or lean meat. Maybe skip the Belgian waffles, but do the ham crisps. That'll keep your brain sharp, and your blood sugar and mood steady. It'll help you resist the school doughnuts."

Charity rolled over and blinked up at her. "How'd you know about the crullers?"

"I went to high school, too, you know. Eat three meals a day, avoid sugar, and you'll keep your weight steady. Oh, and avoid alcohol. *Huuuuge* waste of calories."

Charity sat up and took the coffee, considering the advice.

"Energy drinks will mess with blood sugar big-time. I'll watch carbs for you as long as you're on time for meals."

"I have things to do at night."

"You can fit in twenty minutes for dinner. Make your mother happy. Cooperate with your parents on the things they go nuts about and they'll cut you slack on the privileges you want."

She left Charity pondering that and waited on the landing. In a few minutes, both teens emerged in robes, looking mystified and skeptical, but willing to give her a chance.

When they reached the kitchen, Natalie clapped her hands. "You're up! You're here! Bravo!" She squeezed Chloe's arm when she passed and whispered, "It's a miracle."

Once Chloe had set out the plates, Natalie lifted her orange juice in a toast. "To our good cook and the good food she brings. Welcome, Chloe."

The kids didn't respond, but they cleared their plates, which gave Chloe a rush of pleasure. Would they make it to dinner tonight or breakfast the next day? Hard to say. She'd take it one meal at a time.

After breakfast, Natalie suggested they talk about Chloe's cleaning chores. She led her to the laundry room, which backed onto the pantry, which held every cleaning supply on the planet and a vacuum that practically drove itself.

They toured the ground floor, with Natalie giving tips— don't stack Ronnie's game CDs…watch that statue, it's tippy…no abrasive on the granite counters. At the far end of the hall, Natalie opened a door with a sigh. "I saved the worst for last. Enzo's den."

She waved Chloe into the room lined with dark mahogany. It held a huge desk, cracked-leather chairs and a sofa with ornate wooden trim. Giant deep-sea fish had been mounted on two walls and the floor-to-ceiling shelves were loaded with trophies, photos, plaques and sports items—baseballs and cards and uniforms in glass cases, some even with lighting.

"Do what you can in here." Natalie ran her finger over a glass box that held signed baseball cards, coming away with a gray film. "Why do all his hobbies have to collect dust?"

"I'll do what I can," she said.

"He calls this his lair," Natalie said. "Don't move anything, he tells me. Look at this mess. I wouldn't know where to start." She gestured at the antique desk, which held folders, books, catalogs and loose papers, along with a sleek Mac computer in extreme contrast to the hunting-lodge furnishings.

If there's anything to hide, it will be in this room. The realization zinged Chloe's nerves like ice on a sore tooth.

"Skip it if it's too much," Natalie said, misreading Chloe's alarm.

"No, no. I'm happy to clean in here," she said.

Natalie neatened the papers, as if trying to make the job look less daunting, then paused at the deep file drawer, which had papers sticking out. "This should be locked. Enzo's gun's in here. I hope Ronnie hasn't…"

She yanked the papers free, dropped them on the desk and rummaged in the drawer. Chloe noticed the pages held a list of names followed by letters, then dollar amounts in the thousands. Uh-oh. Was this the kind of thing Riley meant? It had been locked in a drawer, after all.

Her heart surged with anxiety. He'd want photos of the pages, she guessed, and she'd need to check the computer, go through all the papers she could find. She'd pretend to be cleaning in case Enzo came in. Her stomach churned.

"There it is." Natalie lifted out a locked box and hefted it. When she heard a thud, she smiled. "The gun's there. Whew. Boys and guns, what a nightmare." She put the box back, then the papers, then reached under his chair, bringing out a small magnetized key box. "Enzo thinks he's so tricky," she said, using the key to lock the drawer, then returning it to its hiding place. Chloe fixed on where it was, knowing she'd need it when she returned.

"So, that's this floor. Should I walk you through the upstairs? You saw the kids' rooms. That's the worst of it."

"I think I have the idea."

"The food is what we hired you for—that's the main thing. Let the housework slide if you need to. We have people we can hire for that."

"I'm happy to do it," she said. "I should hit the store now."

"Sounds good. I'll be upstairs if you need me. Until I head to the spa anyway."

Chloe grabbed her shopping list from the kitchen, gathered her purse and left the house to go to the store. Seeing her father polishing one of the Sylvestris' cars, she headed over to talk to him. Halfway there, her phone buzzed. The display said private number, so she answered it.

"How's it going?" It was Riley.

"Fi-ine, I guess," she said.

"What's wrong?" he asked, picking up her tension.

"Nothing. I fixed breakfast. I, um, looked around..."

"And?"

If she believed in Enzo, then she should have confidence that any secrets he had were legal ones, so she told him. "I found a list of names with money amounts."

"You remember any of the names?"

"It was too quick. I'll...photograph it." The words tasted like dirt in her mouth.

"Great. Anything else?"

"Not so far, no."

"It's a start. Get me a schedule if you can—regular appointments. We can talk this over in more detail tonight. Let's debrief every night for a while. You get off at eight, right?"

"Most nights. Unless I work late. Tomorrow night I can't make it. There's a family dinner."

"Can't make what?" Natalie's voice made Chloe spin around.

"I've got to go," she said to Riley, clicking off, panicked by the sight of Natalie. What had she heard?

"Don't hang up," Natalie said, holding out a piece of paper. "That's the gluten-free stuff Charity likes. Who was it? Your face is bright pink."

"Just a friend. It wasn't important."

"It was that *guy,* wasn't it? Your birthday guy?"

"Yes," she admitted. At least she could tell that much truth.

"And what can't you make tomorrow night? He asked you out?"

"It doesn't matter."

"Oh, yes it does. You can't be turning down dates because of us. That's unacceptable. I know!" Her eyes lit up. "Bring him to dinner. We can meet him, you can show off your cooking, it'll be fabulous." She clapped her hands together.

"But it's your dinner—for family. Plus I'll be working—"

"Friends will be there, Chloe, and you can join us once everything's prepared. Don't forget, Zema will be your assistant. She can serve."

"I don't know, Natalie…."

"Well, I do. I'm your boss and I'm putting my foot down." She stomped a delicate gold sandal on the driveway concrete. "Call him right back and invite him. I'll wait right here."

So she did, hoping her voice didn't sound too fake.

Riley agreed immediately, adding, "Smooth work," at the end.

"Did he say yes?" Natalie asked eagerly.

She nodded.

"Perfect. I can't wait." She swirled away, sandals clacking, clearly happy with her scheme.

Chloe felt ill. Trying to advance Chloe's love life, Natalie had innocently invited a cop after her husband to dinner. And Chloe would have to act like he was her boyfriend. *Awful, awful, awful.*

How could she fake it? She went to her car and sank into the seat, too freaked to drive right away.

She squeezed the steering wheel, hoping the spring heat would ease the chill she felt to her bones, and tried to think this through. It would be weird, for sure, but maybe there was a good side. Riley could see firsthand what good people the Sylvestris were and maybe change his mind about them.

He thought she was really working hard for him, too, so that would help her father. She'd just have to handle it as best she could.

She slid her key in the ignition, then noticed a black SUV pulling up to the gate. Sal Minetti was driving. The gate opened and he headed for the entrance to the garage.

Where her father was.

What was Sal up to? The hairs on her neck bristled.

She watched him step down from the vehicle and stride purposefully toward her father, who stopped working.

She had to know what was up. Slipping out of the car, she dashed toward the side of the garage, careful to stay out of Sal's line of sight. She found a spot between a flowering sage bush and the garage wall, feeling like a spy in a movie.

Unfortunately, unlike in the movies, she could only hear the murmur of voices and an occasional word. Her father was listening with his hands on his hips. She caught "not sure… pretty busy…"

Sal seemed to consider that, then said something else. She caught the words "easy…deal…we've got time."

"I'll think about it." She caught that sentence loud and clear from her father. Sal nodded, then started to back away. "I'll know details tomorrow," he called.

Details? He had to be proposing another drive. She felt weighed down with dread. Then she realized she had to move fast before Sal passed her spot. She scrambled backward and managed to angle herself so she seemed to be heading for her car.

"Hey, pretty lady," Sal called to her.

She turned, pretending surprise. "Sal? Oh, hello."

He met her a few feet from her car. "So, what's cookin'?" He gave her a gentle elbow. *See how funny I am.* Half-sleazy, half-sweet. That was Sal.

"Not much," she said, hoping she didn't sound as if she'd been running. "Heading out for groceries." She moved toward her car. He followed. "How about you? What's up with you?"

"Same old, same old," he said. *Blackmailing your father into more burglary.* She wanted to punch the man for what he'd done to her father—and what he planned to do. "You need any help with your *groceries?*" More ridiculous innuendo.

"I'll manage fine, thank you," she said dryly.

"This your car?" He half sat on the side of her beloved Saturn Ion, patting the hood. "You like it?"

No, it's my horse-drawn carriage. Get off. Don't touch. "Yes. I do like it," she said, then a thought struck her. Here was a chance to cozy up to Sal with something he understood—he owned an auto shop, after all. "Except, now that you mention it, it's, um, making a funny sound. Maybe you could check it out? One of these days?"

"I could do that, sure." He gave her a speculative look. "Providing we go to dinner after. You let me buy you a steak?"

"That sounds—" terrible, horrible, icky as hell, but she didn't dare shut him down "—nice. Let's touch base later, how's that? Will you be at the dinner tomorrow night?"

"Wouldn't miss it for the world. You're cooking, right?"

"Right. Okay, then. See you there." Yeah. She ducked into her car, started it up, wiggling her fingers in farewell as she literally drove out from under the man. He had to catch himself to keep from falling.

Okay, this was good. It was only her first morning and look at all the undercover work she'd managed. She'd snooped a little—though that troubled her. She'd wrangled Riley an invitation to the Sylvestris' where he could see how wrong he was, and she had a plan for buddying up with Sal. Surely that would appease the police and the FBI. If she was lucky, they'd nail Sal before he could drag her father into another evil scheme.

7

THAT NIGHT, on his way to the Baxters' for the first debrief, Riley felt pretty damn good. Chloe was doing her job, despite her misgivings. She'd already reported on a suspicious-sounding spreadsheet and scored him a meet with Enzo and Sal and other possible suspects at a dinner. His lieutenant was pleased to see movement already. That was crucial. Max and his squad would pick up what slack they could on Riley's cases, but if the Sylvestri situation stagnated, Riley would be yanked off fast.

He was proud of Chloe for jumping in with both feet. She was an honorable person. If she could shake free of mobsters and loser relations, she had a chance at a decent life.

Idle woofed, drawing his attention. The dog sat straight up to watch the road, as if he knew where they were headed. Idle seemed fully recovered, but Riley wanted to keep an eye on him. Plus the dog would cheer Chloe, maybe make her feel better about her informant duties.

The sky spit drizzle and he drove too fast for the wet streets. He plain wanted to see her. He liked the grave way she looked him over and the way his name sounded in her husky voice. Maybe she'd even cook for him. Too much? Probably. All he knew was that he was practically wiggling in his seat the way Idle did at the crinkle of the kibble bag.

Like a kid. Like a fool. Maybe both.

Her dad would be there, which was good. A chaperone would keep Riley from getting distracted by how tempting Chloe could be.

She answered his knock wearing something soft and short and pretty, but she looked troubled and pale. "You brought Idle?" she asked faintly, leaning down, absently petting him.

"I thought you'd like to see he was okay."

"We have to talk," she said, backing into the room, inviting him in. "This won't work."

"What won't?" Then he saw Mickey Baxter lying on the sofa, an ice bag on his leg and one on the back of his head.

"My father's hurt. All because of this stupid case."

Mickey sat up. "I'm fine, Chloe. I lost my balance and got a couple bruises, that's all."

"Lie down, Dad," she said, turning on Riley. "I walked in the house to find him groaning on the floor. He got dizzy on a ladder and fell and now he's hurt. He can't possibly go back."

"It's a goose egg on the back of my head and a bruise on my shin. Nothing, like I said."

"It's the leg that got shot. The weak one. Don't minimize."

"What were you doing on a ladder?" Riley asked.

"I was fixing something to eat and noticed the light burned out. I climbed up and got woozy. I can work, Detective."

"He's too worried to eat, so of course he'll get dizzy. His blood sugar is all over the place, no doubt. You passed out. You know you're worried. Sal is after you to drive again."

"He said down the line, Chloe. I made a deal. This has to be. I'll help the case this way."

"I don't care about any deal," she snapped, her expression fierce. "Your fall was a warning. I won't risk your health or your life. I'll tell Enzo you got hurt. He can get someone else like when you had the flu last year."

"Talk to her, would you?" Mickey said to Riley. "She's just scared. She's trying to protect me."

Idle whined piteously from the door. "Looks like he needs a break," Riley said. "How about we take him for a walk?" He looked at Chloe, who was trembling, angry and irrational. A change of scenery, motion and fresh air could only help.

"It won't do any good," she said. But when Idle rushed over to nose her leg, she softened. "All right, I guess."

The drizzle had stopped and the air was clear as they set off down the block, Chloe moving fast, as if to escape him. Idle galloped beside her, looking up at her in worship as he ran.

When the lure of a tree stopped him, Chloe paused and Riley moved in front of her. "You okay?" he asked, taking her by the arms, hoping to soothe her a bit.

She looked up at him, calmer, but determined. "He'll blow the case, you know. The man passed out and fell off a ladder on the first day, for God's sake. He's too worked up to eat. He can't keep a secret and he wants to please everyone. Who knows what he'll say to Sal—"

"We need him," Riley said. "He's our connection to Sal."

"Not necessarily," she said, stepping away from him. "Here's what I figured out. Sal likes me. I talked to him today, asked him to look at my car. He said he'd do it and he wants to take me to dinner after, so I can—"

"Minetti hit on you?" That SOB.

"It's no big deal." She shrugged. "He flirts with anything in a skirt. The point is he likes me and I can use that."

"I'm sure he does, but you're not going anywhere with that guy. Way too dangerous." The creep would be all over her.

"I can handle Sal. Don't worry about that. He's harmless."

The woman was hopelessly naive. "You think you'll bat your eyes at him and he'll confess his crimes?"

"He loves to brag, so why not? It's something. A way in."

"Stay away from Minetti, Chloe."

"I can't. Not if it will help my dad," she said, chin jutted at him, inviting a fight. "My dad is no good to you and you need someone who can bluff and lie and pretend."

"You think that's you? Your face shows every emotion in neon lights, Chloe."

"I'm better than my father. Even you can see that."

She had a point. The man was a wild card. He could foul

things up with Minetti just as she'd said. What was worse was his effect on Chloe, who was so panicked it would show, too.

Riley had to calm her down somehow. Idle had turned toward home so they followed him. Riley thought about Mickey lying on the sofa, leg propped up because of some bruise. What if his leg was worse? What if he were out of commission?

Riley chewed over the risks, options and gains like Idle with a bone as they walked. A block from the house he turned to Chloe. "Here's what I'm thinking. Let's say your dad did more than bruise his shin. Say he broke his leg and can't drive for a while. You said Enzo got a fill-in when Mickey was sick?"

"Yeah. He called a service."

"What if we offer him someone instead?"

"Who?"

"Me. I'm your boyfriend, right, so tell Enzo I lost my job. Say I was driving a truck…yeah…and that I need the money."

"You'd take over for my father? That would be great!"

"That's what I'm thinking. We'll have to work out the details, get the timing down, but it's worth a try, since you're worried about his health."

"Thank you so much, Riley. I knew you'd understand. This is so much better." The relief in her face set off a warm reaction in him. Maybe the plan had flaws, but it made Chloe feel better and that was enough for him right now.

Somehow he'd make it work.

"So tomorrow morning I'll tell Enzo Dad got hurt, right?" Chloe said. He could see her mind was racing with the steps to come. "Then tell him I figured out how to fix it—with you."

"He could say no, you know."

"Not if it's important to me. He loves to help people. Then you can meet him at the dinner that night. This will work."

"We'll see." The situation was more than a little fluid. "Your father might not cooperate. He sounded set on sticking."

"If you tell him it's best for the case, he'll do it, I know. I appreciate this so much." She lunged forward to throw her arms around him. The contact startled him. He wasn't able to brace against his body's response to her closeness.

Her gaze jerked to his, her eyes bright with awareness. In the cool of the spring night, he wanted her with a white-hot burn. He wanted to make love to her, to make the case disappear for a few blessed hours. Impossible, he knew, but deep inside, a primal voice said, *Just hang on. It'll happen.*

Chloe retreated, her eyes darting, afraid to see what he wanted, to acknowledge her matching response. Silently, breathing in sync, they finished the walk.

Chloe was correct about Mickey. Riley laid out the plan and Mickey dropped his objections like a bad hand, mutely agreeing to Riley's stipulations—he would stay home unless he had a ride and maintain the illusion of his injury with a splint and crutches. There was something he wasn't saying, Riley could tell, possibly in deference to Chloe. After they'd finished, Mickey limped to bed.

Riley looked at Chloe beside him on the sofa. She looked drawn and pale with exhaustion. "I'll let you get some sleep," he said, patting her leg. "We've got a big day ahead of us."

"I'm too wound up." She leaned her head back, her face turned to him. "Can I fix you something to eat? Make you coffee?" She wanted him to stay.

"Coffee's the last thing you need if you can't sleep."

"There's no scotch in the house." She sighed. Idle, on the floor by their feet, sighed, too, which made them both smile.

"What's on your mind?" he asked, thinking he could help.

"The details, I guess. What I'll say to Enzo. If my dad will be okay sitting at home. I'll line up rides to AA for him."

"Can't he get his own rides?"

She frowned.

"You said you do too much for him. Maybe if you didn't always jump to his rescue, he'd stand on his own two feet."

Her eyes sparked, her chin lifted and she opened her mouth

to argue with him, then she slumped. "Forget it. I'm too tired to fight about this again."

"I didn't mean to upset you. Hell, I'm no good at this." He was supposed to be making her feel better. "Let's talk about something else. How did your cooking day go?"

"Good." She managed a weary smile at the memory, then told him how she'd coaxed the kids down for breakfast, coached the daughter on her diet and how to manage her parents, and how grateful Natalie was for her help.

As she talked, energy returned to her face. She was so pretty—lively and smart and kind—and she smelled great. "Sounds like you're doing as much counseling as cooking."

"The Sylvestris are good parents, just too indulgent, I guess. Like I was with Clarissa. Sometimes an outsider view helps you see what you've missed."

"You'll be a good mother," he blurted to distract himself from angling for a kiss.

"I hope to be. When I get the rest of my life worked out. What about you? Do you want kids?"

"Me?" The question startled him. "I don't have the patience. I'm a lot like my dad. He wasn't much on affection."

"He loved you, though. You knew that, didn't you?"

"Every father loves his kids. Sure."

Though his father had been different than his friends' dads, who'd wrestled and joked with them, casual and easy. His dad had been reserved, keeping him at arm's length. "He kept a roof over our heads, food in our mouths, clothes on our backs and he came home every night." Until the night he didn't and nothing was right again. "The rest of it wasn't so important."

"Your dad might have been distant, but that doesn't mean you have to be. With me, you've been very warm."

"That's all you," he said. "The Chloe Effect." As if on cue, Idle got to his feet and dropped his chin on Chloe's lap, looking at her with soulful eyes. "Even Idle feels it."

Chloe laughed and her gaze met his, merry at first, then

sparking like an ignition switch. "It's hard to be this close and not touch you," she said.

"Yeah," he said softly, shifting toward her. She turned to him, too, dislodging Idle who dropped to the floor. Riley pushed her hair from her cheek, ran his thumb along her jawline.

"I keep thinking about you inside me," she whispered, her eyes green fire. She kissed his palm, cupping it with her hands. Thunder rumbled outside. "Sounds like a storm. Maybe you shouldn't go out. Lightning might strike."

"I think it already has." He kissed her, unable to resist another moment, forgetting why this was wrong.

She kissed him back, getting into it, shifting her lips from side to side, moving her tongue everywhere at once. She straddled him, her skirt hiked high, pushing her chest against him, wriggling her panties against his cock through his pants. He couldn't stand much more, so he stilled her body and broke off the kiss. "What are we doing?"

"Celebrating my birthday again?" she said, too dazed to come up with a better argument, it seemed.

"Chloe…"

"We're done with the case for tonight. We need this. Don't fight it." She went after his zipper.

He grabbed her hand. "What about your father?"

"Way down the hall and he sleeps through anything." She had him out of his jeans then and he lost all coherent thought except that he wanted inside her and he wanted her skin against his. He tossed off her shirt, then his own. Before he could go after the rest of her clothes, she slid her panties aside, placed him at her entrance and lowered herself. He went deep.

"Oh." Her eyes flared with pleasure. "That feels so good, doesn't it?"

"Good… Yeah." He ground the syllable out, happy to be buried in her, buying every word she was selling.

"I feel so free with you. I never feel like this." She rocked up and down slowly, making little mews and gasps as if each inch held so much pleasure she couldn't bear it.

She was so beautiful above him, her skin pale as milk, her breasts pure art. He ran his hands down her ribs to her hips, guiding her movements, fighting the urge to explode inside her.

On the upstroke, she paused and thrust her breasts at him, so he took a knotted nipple into his mouth.

She shivered like Idle ridding himself of rain, holding herself above him.

Too far away. He grabbed her ass and hauled her down onto him. She gave him a dazed look that steadily cleared to determination as she pushed up, then down again and again, gaining deliberate speed. He was lost in the lushness of her body, in her fresh smell, in the raw urgency of her movements. He let her take the lead.

I never feel like this. Neither did he. He felt alive with her. He felt a secret hope spring open in him—that one day he could find one special someone and stick with her.

Chloe stilled and her eyes widened. "I'm there," she said, her entire body shaking with the force of her climax, which brought on his own. They clung to each other, rocking through the waves. When it was over, she tucked her face into his neck, trembling against his skin.

"You feel so good," he whispered. And right. Too good and too right.

"Don't be sorry," she said as if she'd read his mind. "Why can't we have this at night?"

"We talked about this."

"So what? We *need* this. This *helps.* Why else would it be happening? Is this how you usually act?"

He shook his head. "Never." He was different with her. Open, relaxed, unguarded. Free, as she said. That should scare him, but it didn't. He just held her tight and hoped to hell she was right.

THE NEXT MORNING, Chloe woke to her cell phone's ring, alone, she knew, since Riley had left at midnight, but still wrapped in the glow of lovemaking. *It's him.* He'd promised to check on her in the morning. She smiled and spoke into the phone. "Hello there," she said as sexily as she could.

"'S Riley. Need to touch base before you leave for work." His no-nonsense cop voice made her sit up straight in bed. No tender *did you sleep okay?* Or *wish I could kiss you awake.* Just the facts, ma'am, for Detective Connelly. She felt as if he'd tossed cold water in her face.

"Okay. Yeah." *Get over it.* This was what they'd agreed to—sex at night, the case by day. It had been her idea. She just wished he hadn't made the transition so easily.

"Did I wake you?" he asked as if he'd suddenly realized the possibility.

"No. No. I'm awake." *Completely.*

"Good. I left a camera, a recorder and a jump drive on your bureau." No love note. Just spyware. "Familiarize yourself with the functions. They're easy to use, but be certain."

"Will do."

"Grab shots of that spreadsheet you saw. Cell phone snaps if they're readable, since you can phone them to me. If you have to go with the camera, upload as soon as you can. Getting into their computer would be great. Also, I'd like a guest list for tonight, please, so I can run backgrounds on everyone. You'll alert me once you've offered me as a new driver for Enzo?"

"Sir, yes, sir." She couldn't help the sarcasm.

Riley was silent for a moment. "I don't mean to order you around. The sooner we nail these guys, the sooner this will all be over. We want to optimize our gains."

"Right. I get that. It's just that…last night—"

"We have to forget that." He sounded so flat, so far away.

"I just woke up. I need a minute to shift gears."

"Understandable." Like she needed forgiveness. Oooh, that burned her up. The reminder was good. They were so different. Riley buried his emotions and hers were all too accessible. In neon, he'd pointed out. Even without her father's troubles standing between them, daylight would douse the fire they shared at night every time.

A little more than an hour later, Chloe entered the Sylvestri house, quiet and dim in the early morning, geared up to tell Enzo about her father's injury when he came down for breakfast. Her heart was beating so fast she feared she might faint. Everything depended on how her speech went.

Except Enzo was gone. Natalie had left her a note saying that Enzo's sister Olivia had picked them up to attend a pancake breakfast at their great-aunt's assisted-living center. *The pancakes are wretched, but there's hell to pay when we miss Family Day!*

Damn. She'd have to wait to talk to Enzo. On the other hand, as soon as Ronnie and Charity left for school, she'd have the house to herself for a while.

As soon as she was sure the kids were gone, she slipped her cell phone and the digital camera into her pocket, grabbed a duster and furniture polish and headed for Enzo's office.

Fingers trembling, she unlocked the desk drawer, found the two-page list and snapped photos of the pages with both her cell phone and the digital, worried about what the police might learn about Enzo from this list he'd hid. Why? She trusted him, didn't she? Everyone had secrets. That didn't make them illegal. She hated how Riley made her doubt Enzo.

She looked through the files in the locked drawer first. Nothing suspicious. The labels on the hanging files were faded, the papers inside yellowed with age. Mostly receipts for home repairs, car purchases, invoices from kitchen supply and food distributors. She took lots of snaps all the same, just to prove to the police and FBI she'd done her part.

She flipped on the computer and while it booted, she photographed stuff on the desk, pulling papers from between junk mail and catalogs of fishing gear, boating and sports memorabilia. She wasn't sure how much time she had. Sweat trickled down her sides and her breath rasped in her ears. She stuck to it, knowing that the sooner she found nothing on Enzo, the sooner the police would stop suspecting him.

She was putting back the last stack of papers when she heard the front door open, then voices and footsteps. Adrenaline surged through her and she shoved the camera and phone in her pocket, grabbed her feather duster and ran for it. At the door, she remembered she'd left the computer on, so she dashed back.

Her finger was still on the mouse when Enzo walked through the door. "What are you doing in my lair?" he boomed, clearly joking, which filled her with relief and horrible guilt. The man would never suspect her of something as heinous as what she'd done.

She swiped the monitor with her duster, relieved that the computer had gone black. It had been password protected, so she couldn't be expected to get into it anyway.

"Don't bother to clean in here." He headed closer. "Natalie bitches about the mess, but I know where everything is."

She smiled, hoping her face didn't show the sweat and heat she felt. She glanced at the desk to be sure she'd restored the mess to its original arrangement.

"You get a look at my goodies?" he asked.

Horrified, she jerked her gaze to his face, but he was admiring glassed-in sports junk on a shelf. "V-very nice," she managed to say.

"I know. That one goes next week." He tapped the glass over a framed piece of newspaper with a signature on it. "Babe Ruth, DNA authenticated signature," he said. "Worth over two grand. Can you believe it?"

"That's good," she said.

"Keep this between us, though. We had an incident with a rip-off artist, so I told Nat I'd stay off eBay, but it's too good. Not as fun as gambling, but…" He shrugged.

"I won't say a word," she said. Noticing the feathers were trembling like her hands, she put the duster behind her back.

"So, your pop's not in the garage. What's he up to?"

"Dad? Oh!" She'd almost forgotten her mission for the morning. "I have to tell you. He fell off a ladder changing lightbulbs."

"You're kidding. Is he okay?"

She took a deep breath, calling up the story she'd prepared. "Not exactly. See, he broke his leg."

"Damn. That's a shame."

"It's not too bad. It's a hairline fracture, but the doctor wants him off his feet, so he can't drive for a while."

"Was it his bad leg?"

She nodded.

"Damn. The injury weakened the bone. I'm sorry."

"He hates to let you down, Enzo. He just *hates* it. He wanted to come in, no matter what the doctor said. There was only one way I could convince him. See, the guy I'm seeing— Riley—is between jobs. He's a truck driver, so he can fill in for Dad. What do you think?" She paused. "He needs the money." Too much? She held her breath.

"Riley? That the guy Natalie invited to dinner tonight?"

"Yes, that's him. Riley Connelly."

"You like him a lot?" Enzo tilted his head at her.

"I like him, sure." Birthday Riley, anyway. Detective Riley, not so much.

"He good enough for you? What does Mickey think?"

"He doesn't exactly know…."

Enzo's eyebrows lifted. "He's a secret? That's no good."

"It's just new, that's all."

"Introduce him to Mickey. As a father he should know. He wants to know. Trust me."

She nodded, but she had to get him back to the point. "So what do you think about hiring him?"

"This mean a lot to you?" Enzo studied her.

"It does." It meant her father's life.

"How about I meet him tonight? I'll see that he's a proper guy for you. If I approve, he can drive me around. How's that?"

"That's great. Thank you so much, Enzo." Relief whooshed through her.

"And tell Mickey I'm sorry about the leg. Especially that leg. Damn. He'll always have a job with us, tell him that."

"You've been so good to us," she said, choking up, her eyes stinging.

"Ah, don't do that," Enzo said, blinking. "You're a good daughter, Chloe." He squeezed her shoulder. "Wish you could rub off on my two."

"They're teenagers, Enzo. I'd better get back to work." She had to get away from the man's kindness. She ached with guilt.

"Natalie's upstairs burning treadmill rubber to make up for the two stacks of pancakes she ate—I'd hate to see how much she'd've eaten if they were good." He shook his head, clearly adoring Natalie, for all her inconsistencies.

As soon as Chloe had finished the dishes she'd abandoned in her hurry to snoop, she slipped into the pantry to text Riley that Enzo had okayed the job and to send the cell phone shots.

She was waiting for the photos to send when she heard Enzo's voice through the wall. He was in the laundry room, talking low. Why? For privacy, she guessed. Natalie was upstairs.

From where she stood, his voice was clear as a bell. She stood and listened, her heart banging her ribs.

"So, what are you saying, Mario?" Enzo sounded impatient. "But when? I've been waiting for this shipment for weeks…. It better be…. And no extra charges or any more trouble…. You know what to do, Mario. Do it."

She committed the conversation to memory. Who was Mario? And what was the shipment? Why had Enzo hidden in the laundry room to talk about it? Should she tell Riley?

Wait and see. It was probably something to do with the restaurant. She'd see what came of the papers she'd photographed first. That was enough for now.

AN HOUR BEFORE THE DINNER, Chloe pulled the three-cheese bread from the oven, grateful for the distraction of preparing the family dinner. Starters would be double-tomato bruschetta, sweet figs with savory prosciutto and an exotic cheese tray.

First course was cioppino—seafood stew—and a fresh-herb salad. The main course was osso buco with double-grilled garlic artichokes and mushroom risotto. For dessert, she'd made her special tropical tiramisu. She hoped the loving care she put into the meal would somehow make up for her betrayal.

She moved to the rec room to arrange imported beers in a giant bowl of ice and check the bar supplies. On the couch, Ronnie dozed over a textbook, iPod in his ears, TV blasting.

"Smells good in there," Enzo said, entering the room.

"Thanks," she said, but Enzo had spotted Ronnie and tugged the earphones from his son's ears. "This is how you study?"

"I'm tired, okay?" Ronnie rubbed his eyes.

"In the afternoon?"

"He was out with Sal until two in the morning," Charity said as she breezed in, going for a stack of magazines.

"Is that true?" Enzo demanded. When Ronnie shrugged, he added, "I don't want you partying with Sal on school nights."

"It wasn't that late," Ronnie said.

"And you're not wearing that to the table," he said to Charity, who wore a short white skirt and a nearly nude leotard.

"I'm going out later," she said.

"Not dressed like that, you're not."

Chloe wanted to leave the room, but Natalie stood in the doorway, blocking her escape. "All the girls dress that way," she said to her husband. "It's the latest look."

"Not my daughter."

Ronnie snickered, so Charity slugged him. "He scraped his car, too." She gave her brother a so-there look.

"Not again," Natalie said, lifting her arms in surrender.

"We have insurance," Ronnie muttered.

"The rates go through the roof when we use it," Enzo said.

"And I got an e-mail from your history teacher, Ronnie," Natalie said. "She says you sleep in her class."

"Everyone does when she blabs about her college days."

"You respect your teachers," Enzo said, getting angrier, "and you study. That's your job. If it's not enough work for you, you can bus tables at the restaurant."

"That pays shit."

"You're too good for honest labor? When I was your age I bussed tables, cleaned toilets, whatever I had to do."

"Not that story again."

"Out of my sight, both of you. Charity, dress decent for dinner. Ronnie, do your homework. And no TV or computer."

"I need the computer for my homework."

"Just go!"

The kids stomped off.

"That was too harsh," Natalie said to Enzo.

"How else can I be? You spoil them."

Chloe slipped from behind the bar and into the kitchen to stir the cioppino, but their voices carried. This was the last thing she wanted to eavesdrop on.

"*I* spoil them? You gave Ronnie a car even when his grades reeked. Charity holds out her hand and you put money in it."

"He needs a safe car and Charity needs lunch money. You let her starve herself."

"I talk to her at least. You hide out in your den. You see what you want to see, Enzo. You're inconsistent. You explode."

"You're the mother. You're supposed to know what to do."

"So it's my fault? That's so typical. I give up." Chloe heard footsteps and looked up as Natalie whipped by.

Enzo called after her. "Come on, Natalie. You're too sensitive." He entered the kitchen, stopping when he noticed Chloe. "Can I taste?" he asked.

She lifted a spoonful of the savory stew and he sipped. "Incredible."

"It's coming together."

"You catch all that?" Enzo asked her, nodding toward the rec room. "How could you help it, eh? You think I'm a bull in a bakery?"

"Parenting is tough," she said.

"I'm too old for this. I tell myself not to react, but they push my buttons, those kids."

"That's how you know you're related. Kids act out to test you. My younger sister used to make me furious."

"So how did you handle it?"

"Tried to be patient. The books say to set expectations and consequences and stick to them."

"Don't tell me about books. I'd like one of those experts to try dealing with *my* kids in real time, not from an armchair."

"It's hard, I know."

"But you think Natalie's right…I spoil them?" His brown eyes connected with hers, demanded the truth.

"It's not for me to say."

"You must know something—you got them down for breakfast."

"It was the food, not me."

"Be that as it may, I'm glad you're here with us, Chloe. You're a good influence."

"I'm glad, too," she said, hating how every lovely moment was tainted by her secret.

"You don't sound glad, cupcake." He patted her shoulder. "You're doing fine. Hell, if I use your advice and it works, I'll have to pay you like a shrink."

"You pay me too much already."

"Do me this favor—next time I put my foot in my mouth

with the kids, give me a sign, would you?" He pretended to cut his throat.

"If you really want that."

"I do. For now, I better go make nice with Nat. Got any marriage advice?"

"Me? Are you kidding?"

"You're wiser than your years." He gave her a hug, which made the camera stab her hip. The man loved her like a daughter and she'd treated him like a crook. She couldn't bear it. When the truth came out, she hoped no one she loved would get caught in the cross fire.

8

RILEY WAS EARLY for the dinner party so he could track every arrival and eavesdrop on them all. He also needed time to impress Enzo. He'd recognized a couple of made guys from the guest list, along with three Sylvestris who'd been involved in drug cases in the past. There were also wives and children.

The Sylvestri property looked like something from the Vegas strip with its oversize fountains, too many columns, statues and overdone landscaping. He recognized the black Escalade registered to Minetti parked by the garage. He could meet the guy before the rest of the guests arrived.

He pushed the buzzer at the security gate.

"Yes?" Even the tinny speaker couldn't mask Chloe's voice.

"It's me," he said.

"But you're early."

"I wanted to see my girl," he said, playing his role in case anyone was listening in.

"Come in," she said on a weary sigh, and released the gate.

He pulled in and parked. Heading for the front door, he checked the tape recorder he'd slid into his blazer pocket to be sure it was set on voice activation.

Chloe opened the door to him, pale as death, wearing a cook's hat and apron over a black dress.

He leaned in to kiss her—he was her boyfriend, after all—and she went stiff. "We're a couple, remember? We should act pretty friendly."

She backed up, letting him in, trying to smile, but chewing

her lip. He hated how the assignment had affected her. Her worry hung in the air, ominous as smoke, and her eyes showed tension.

It couldn't be helped. They both had jobs to do—tonight his was to convince Sylvestri to hire him as a driver. His lieutenant had okayed the undercover job, as long as he didn't let his other cases slide. *Sure. No problem.*

Damn. He wished like hell Mickey had stuck it out, but there was no helping it now. At least Chloe felt better—on that front anyway. When they'd discussed him being at the dinner, she'd told him what Enzo had said. *He wants to know if you're good enough for me.* She'd paused, as if she wondered the same thing. Why? Was she interested beyond the case? He had no business caring.

Chloe led him through a huge room crammed with expensive furniture in pale leather. Lots of flowers, thick Persian carpets, more statues, a white baby grand and massive paintings with fancy gold frames, then down a marble hall to the kitchen, where the great cooking smells he'd picked up on entering intensified.

"Smells great in here."

"Thanks."

He lifted the lid off a pot on the stove and got a blast of buttery seafood, garlic, onions and other spices he couldn't name. "What is this?"

"It's cioppino. Shrimp, scallops, clams, mussels and crab. Here." She lifted a spoon for him to taste.

It was as good as it smelled. "Damn, I'm glad I'll be sitting down to a bowl of this."

She smiled, her anxiety fading into pleasure.

"How about a piece of this?" He reached for a loaf of golden-brown bread.

She slapped away his hand. "Wait for dinner." He'd relaxed her, at least, and she described the rest of the meal in mouthwatering detail. Standing in the kitchen, warm with the food she'd lovingly prepared, he wanted to tug her close and kiss her, tell her it would be all right, even though it might not be. He settled for brushing a fleck of flour from her hair and coaxing a smile onto her pretty face.

"So, who's this?" Enzo Sylvestri stood in the archway, wearing a big phony grin.

"Enzo!" Chloe turned pink. "This is, um, Riley. Riley Connelly. Enzo Sylvestri."

Sylvestri took his hand for a hard shake, holding his gaze just as aggressively. "You taking good care of our girl?"

"I'm doing my best, sir," Riley said, deferential even as the guy's proprietary tone burned him.

"We think the world of her. She's a terrific cook, too. As you'll see tonight."

"Thanks, Enzo," Chloe said, blushing like a kid with his praise. Riley felt a pang of sadness for her.

Enzo turned to Riley, his expression abruptly serious. "Chloe tells me you're interested in filling in for Mickey."

"Yeah. I'm between jobs, so if I can help you out…"

Enzo assessed him, his expression hard. Abruptly it softened. "Hell, if our Chloe vouches for you, that's good enough for me. Start tomorrow? Show up at seven. Tee time's eight. Some errands after that. Be generally available. Natalie might need a ride. The kids mostly drive their own cars, but offer anyway. Keep all the cars clean, waxed and serviced—"

"Whatever you need me to do," he said. If it was crooked, so much the better.

"How are you with schmoozing tight-ass accountants?"

"I'd give it a try," he said.

"You haven't met my accountant. He's a penny-pincher, that one, and he keeps me on a budget." Again, he took Riley's measure. "The Ferrari, you'll be glad to know, needs to be driven every week." He winked. "No tickets, though. That's the deal."

"No problem." He grinned a real grin. He wouldn't mind taking a Ferrari around the block.

"I'd better finish dressing for dinner," Enzo said, looking

down at his god-awful shirt—purple with a huge flamingo—
and pinstriped slacks. "Natalie says these don't go." He shook
his head, as if he were whipped but didn't care, then left them.

"Score," Riley whispered when they were alone.

Chloe frowned and moved away.

"What? We got what we wanted."

"You're way too happy about tricking him. Enzo trusts
you because of me."

"You're doing the right thing, Chloe." If only she hadn't
fallen for the guy's phony charm. Guys like Enzo knew how
to work people to get what they wanted.

"Go introduce yourself to Sal. He's in the rec room. I've
got work to do." She jutted her chin toward the hall.

"See you at dinner." He kissed her neck.

She kept watching the stew, but a smile teased her lips.

The first thing he noticed in the rumpus room was the larg-
est plasma he'd ever seen and every game system there was. A
teenager on the sofa thumbed a controller taking the onscreen
car through a racing course. Two guys wearing flashy silk shirts
and too much jewelry looked on, drinking imported beer. Carlo
Santos and Leo Monte, he knew. Same two guys Mickey had
reported at the burglary. Both had records—B and E, bad
checks, transporting stolen goods…not much time served.

The wet bar was loaded with pricey hard liquor and held a
silver bowl of ice with a bunch of beer, imported and domestic.

Sal Minetti emerged from an alcove, adjusting his belt.
He'd been in the john, no doubt. When he looked Riley's
way, Riley held out a hand. "Riley Connelly," he said. "I'm a
friend of Chloe's."

"Oh yeah?" Sal seemed to size him up, as if deciding
whether or not he was a rival. "I've seen you somewhere…."

"Maybe at Enzo's? I live in the neighborhood."

"I guess so. You're here for dinner?"

"Yeah. I was talking to Enzo about a job, too." He reached
for a beer, acting casual.

"Yeah? What job?" He cocked his head, curious.

"I'll be filling in for Mickey Baxter as a driver."

"What's with Mickey?" His head went straight, signaling more interest.

"He fell and broke his leg. Has to be off his feet."

Sal shot a look at his two pals, then shook his head in disgust. "Guy's a screwup."

"Maybe he just has bad luck," Riley said. He figured this was a good chance to let Sal know he was no model citizen himself. "I had a bad break at my last job."

"What happened?" Sal said, giving himself a healthy pour of Glenlivet over ice.

"I was driving a truck and a few laser printers came up missing. They blamed me." He shrugged.

"You knew nothing about it, right?"

"That was my story." He smirked.

They all laughed. "So Enzo hired you, huh?" Sal looked him over again, nodding slowly, as if considering what that meant to him. So he'd registered on the guy's radar.

"I start tomorrow, yeah."

"Leo and Carlo," Sal said, nodding at his friends, who tilted their beers in Riley's direction.

"And that kid hogging the controller is my cousin Ronnie. Hey, Ronster, you ever gonna give us a crack at those ganstahs?"

"When I bust this level," Ronnie said, not looking up.

"You get a girlfriend and you'll be bangin' something besides your thumbs. Heh, heh." Leo and Carlo hooted.

Red crept up Ronnie's neck.

"So…" Sal said. Silence swelled and he and his buddies exchanged looks that told Riley they had something to discuss, but wouldn't with him in the room.

"John this way?" He nodded toward the hall. Sal nodded, so Riley went there, stopping just out of sight to listen.

"So, we all set on that business?" Sal asked levelly.

Someone clunked ice on the counter and Riley missed the

reply. Then Carlo or Leo said, "Around fifty," then argued about whether it should be the same as last time, then more numbers. They could be discussing drugs or bets or, hell, stocks and bonds. Riley realized the game sounds had stopped, so Ronnie was either part of the talk or had left the room.

The doorbell rang and he heard Enzo speak, so he eased into the bathroom to flush the toilet, then came out, nodding at Sal and his friends on his way to see who'd arrived. Ronnie was still in the room. Interesting…

Besides the Sylvestris, Riley recognized Nico Roman and Sammy Sargeant, connected high up. Even if he hadn't known who they were, their importance was obvious in how everyone deferred to them, even in casual conversation.

The group moved to the game room. Riley stayed close and quiet, pretending to be watching the basketball game on the screen. They talked sports, discussed betting losses, complained about their kids, the price of college, the relative gas mileage on Hummers and Escalades. Nothing he could use.

The hard liquor flowed, along with the beer, and a maid carried appetizers around. Figs and proscuitto, the bread he'd sampled and a plate of fancy cheeses and sausages.

By the time Natalie called everyone to the table for soup, the men were cheerfully loaded and laughing too hard.

Chloe emerged from the kitchen without her apron.

"Here she is," Enzo said. "Our future famous chef. *Salute!*" He held up his wineglass in a toast everyone joined.

"Thank you." Chloe gave a slight bow, then took her place between Riley and Sal. She was pink with pride, so obviously happy to be here and proud to cook for the Sylvestris.

Maybe they were genuinely fond of her, but if Chloe failed to deliver what they expected, she'd be out on her ear, Riley knew. To the Sylvestris, people were tools to be used. If only she would hold back a little instead of laying her whole soul out like that.

She craved the feeling of family, of course. He understood.

The Harlequin Reader Service — Here's how it works:

Accepting your 2 free books and 2 free mystery gifts places you under no obligation to buy anything. You may keep the books and gifts and return the shipping statement marked "cancel." If you do not cancel, about a month later we'll send you 6 additional books and bill you just $4.24 each in the U.S. or $4.71 each in Canada. That is a savings of at least 15% off the cover price. It's quite a bargain! Shipping and handling is just 25¢ per book, along with any applicable taxes.* You may cancel at any time, but if you choose to continue, every month we'll send you 6 more books, which you may either purchase at the discount price or return to us and cancel your subscription.

*Terms and prices subject to change without notice. Sales tax applicable in N.Y. Canadian residents will be charged applicable provincial taxes and GST. Offer not valid in Quebec. All orders subject to approval. Credit or debit balances in a customer's account(s) may be offset by any other outstanding balance owed by or to the customer. Please allow 4 to 6 weeks for delivery. Offer available while quantities last.

NO POSTAGE
NECESSARY
IF MAILED
IN THE
UNITED STATES

BUSINESS REPLY MAIL
FIRST-CLASS MAIL   PERMIT NO. 717   BUFFALO, NY

POSTAGE WILL BE PAID BY ADDRESSEE

HARLEQUIN READER SERVICE
3010 WALDEN AVE
PO BOX 1867
BUFFALO NY 14240-9952

If offer card is missing write to: The Harlequin Reader Service, 3010 Walden Ave., P.O. Box 1867, Buffalo, NY 14240-1867

He was close to his squad mates. Hell, he was godfather to Max's son. But he was on the fringes of their lives, and he was fine with that. Poor Chloe was a burnt dish away from heartache.

The maid served the soup and bread and soon the guests exclaimed over how good it tasted.

Chloe passed the bread basket to Sal.

"Very nice," he said, looking down her dress. Riley wanted to deck him. He wanted to protect her every minute.

"You mean the bread, I assume," she said, putting him in his place with her sarcasm. Good for her.

She was a smart, capable adult. She didn't need him to guard her, but the urge to do so was like a pulse in his head. Because he'd pulled her into the case? Or just because he cared?

No conversation of consequence went on during the meal and before long they were eating what Chloe announced as a tropical tiramisu with coconut, macadamia nuts, pineapple and God knows what else. He'd never tasted a dessert quite so delicious.

"You can cook for me anytime, babe," Sal said with a wink. Male eyes moved to Riley, expecting him to put Sal in his place, but before he could speak, Chloe squeezed his hand above the table, where everyone could see. "I'm pretty booked, Sal."

Perfect. She'd neutralized the moment, without jeopardizing whatever rapport Riley had established with Sal. She was good. And he liked holding her hand.

The women were talking about day spas and some charity event they were working on and the men headed for brandy and cigars in the game room.

Charity, Enzo's daughter, bounded across the room, her purse over her shoulder, wearing a very short skirt.

"Where are you going, young lady?" Enzo growled.

"Out with my friends."

"We've got family here. And you have school tomorrow."

"You let Ronnie go out with Sal all the time."

"Not anymore," Enzo said. "He's staying close to home, too." He shot a look at Sal. "No more late nights, right, Sal?"

"Sure," Sal said, catching on. "You gotta get the grades, *paesano,* if you want to run with the big dogs."

Ronnie kept his head down, shoulders hunched, but he sneaked a look at Sal—they'd worked a routine for Enzo's benefit. Very interesting…

Charity opened her mouth to smart off, but Chloe cleared her throat and Charity looked at her, seemed to pick up some cue, then said, "If I don't go out tonight, can I go to Tucson on Saturday with Rochelle?"

"Rochelle? She the girl with the chains and the boyfriend with the Harley?"

She clearly wanted to say something snotty, but she looked over at Chloe, as if for encouragement. Chloe gave her a slight nod. "There'll be a bunch of us," she said. "And just girls, so don't worry about any funny business."

Her father considered this. "See what your mother says."

"I will. Thanks." Charity kissed him, then grinned at Chloe. This must be part of the coaching she'd done. Chloe was something else. A cook and a counselor and an incredible lover.

He hoped she was a good informant, too.

9

WHEN HER DOORBELL RANG at midnight, Chloe knew it would be Riley and dreaded letting him in. At least her father was in bed, though she knew Riley would want to discuss the people at the dinner with him at some point.

The dinner should have been a triumph, but it was such a sham, she'd cringed when Enzo raved about her afterward. If he had any idea what she and Riley were up to... It made her sick at heart and she wasn't up for facing Riley, who had been entirely too delighted about the scam they'd perpetrated.

Through the peephole she saw he hadn't brought Idle. Too bad. At the moment she liked Riley's dog better than him. She sighed and opened the door.

"Hey there," he said softly.

"Come in," she said, turning away to avoid his gaze.

"Hang on." He caught her arm. "You're upset."

"I'm just tired."

"It's more than that. You wanted me to put Sal in his place? I thought you handled it well, so I didn't jump in."

"That's not it," she snapped. "I hate that we tricked Enzo, that he and Natalie welcomed you to their table and you're trying to ruin them. I hate that I have to lie to them."

He sighed. "I know it's not easy, but, look at it this way. Enzo may be retired, but the others sure as hell aren't. The names of every male adult at the table show up in investigations."

"Innocent people get investigated, too. Enzo's a good man.

He loves his family and he looks out for me and my father, too. Surely you saw that at dinner. You're not that blind."

"I wish you weren't so invested in these people." His eyes held pity, which infuriated her. "Sure, they're kind to you, but their loyalty only goes so far."

"Why are you always negative?" she said sharply. "Why is it always about protecting yourself and worst-case scenarios?"

"Because the worst happens, Chloe. I see it all the time."

She hated the hard planes of his face and the way his eyes flashed dark fire. This was *Detective* Connelly and she realized with a sad jolt that he was far more comfortable in this role than as Birthday Riley. "Not with Enzo and Natalie," she insisted. "You saw how they care about their kids. Enzo wants to keep Ronnie away from Sal."

"Ronnie's lying through his teeth to his father, running an obvious game with Sal." He hesitated, as if there were more.

"What is it? What's going on? If Ronnie's in trouble, Enzo should be told."

"Don't say a word," he snapped. "We watch, we wait, we see what develops."

"Ronnie could get hurt—"

Riley shrugged. "That's not your affair. You are not to interfere or blow our cover in any way."

"How can you be so heartless? You'd sacrifice anyone, wouldn't you? No matter who gets hurt."

Anger sparked in his eyes. "My job is to protect innocent people from bad guys. If we can keep Ronnie out of trouble, we will, but you can't speak to Enzo about any of this."

"Wouldn't want to do anything to keep you from getting your *collar,* would we?" Fury made her pulse race. "Things aren't always clear-cut, Riley. People do the right thing for the wrong reason or the wrong thing for the right reason. You act like everyone is either a perp or about to become one."

"And you shut your eyes to obvious troubles. Take your father—" He stopped, clearly realizing how that would hurt her.

"My father's not perfect, but he got into trouble trying to help me. He wanted to pay for my schooling." Her voice wobbled.

"Can we start over, Chloe? I don't want to upset you."

"No, you just want me to distrust people I love. How do you even get up in the morning with your attitude?"

"Sometimes it ain't easy." He gave a mocking smile, trying to smooth over the tension, she could tell. He brushed her hair away from her face. "Maybe I'll be proven wrong, okay? I just don't want you to get hurt."

"I know you don't." She softened. He was trying to be kind. That might be the best she'd get from Detective Connelly.

"Truce?" he asked.

"I guess," she said, sad that they'd quarreled, sad that they saw the world so differently.

"I should go. It's late for a debrief. I passed the digital photos you took on to London. He's having them analyzed. Keep doing what you're doing. I'll see you tomorrow over there."

"You'll be driving Enzo, right." Listening in on his conversations, too. Meanwhile something was up with Ronnie and Sal. No matter what Riley said, she would talk to Sal about working on her car as soon as she could.

Riley left and she felt suddenly lonely. It was Birthday Riley she missed, not the man who'd just walked out of her house. She missed the way he looked at her, how right she felt in his arms. She should be past that, but she was too much of a realist to pretend she was. At least they had that in common.

ON HIS WAY to his first day as Enzo's driver, Riley spotted Chloe in her red Ion tearing up the street like a NASCAR driver. She'd no doubt collected a few speeding tickets in her day. Still, he smiled watching her zoom ahead.

Things would be awkward between them after their quarrel. He hated seeing her take scraps from the Sylvestris' table. At least he'd be around to watch over her, even though he'd be AWOL from the new cases his squad had racked up.

The pressure was on to break the case fast. London had put a forensic accountant onto the docs Chloe had photographed, but God knew how long that would take. Riley would eyeball them himself when he had some time.

Chloe pulled through the security gate and Riley parked behind her, then went to open her car door. "Hey," he said.

She smiled, then seemed to remember how things stood and her grin disappeared. "You're all dressed up," she said, climbing out of the car.

He'd thrown on his funeral blazer over a white dress shirt. "Want to make a good first impression." He patted his jacket, noticed a lump, then pulled out a pair of cuffs he'd forgotten were there. "Whoops." He gave Chloe a sheepish look, then shoved them into his inner pocket where they wouldn't show.

"I hope you're not too disappointed you won't need those," she said, turning to march toward the house, her gait angry.

He caught up with her at the massive front door. "So, I'll see you later?"

"If you come into the house, I suppose, but we both have jobs to do." She sounded distant and weary.

"Just be careful, Chloe."

"Unlike you, I don't see danger where there isn't any." She unlocked the door and pulled it open, then turned to him, her eyes softer. "Good luck, I guess. The sooner you get evidence on the real crooks, the sooner this will be over."

"Exactly." And when it was over, she'd never want to see him again. That truth sank in him like a stone in a dark pond.

Enzo met him at the garage right on time. "Good man," he said to Riley, as he loaded clubs into the Mercedes' trunk. By the time Riley got into the driver's seat, Enzo was on his cell phone in a conversation about acid reflux, cholesterol and what was good for constipation. His conversation sounded retired, at least.

At the club, Riley offered to caddy, hoping to eavesdrop, but Enzo laughed. "Relax, kid. You'll earn your keep. And let me warn you. Be careful when you offer to help my wife or she'll have you making calls for charity donations."

While Enzo played golf, Riley called in a records check on the supposedly retired businessmen who made up Enzo's foursome, then made a few calls on his cases so as not to waste time.

Once the golfers hit the clubhouse for breakfast, Riley positioned himself at the bar for coffee so he could listen, but the talk was social and he got a callback telling him that if the three men had committed crimes, they'd never been caught.

Back home, after Enzo showered, Riley drove him to a chichi restaurant for an endless lunch with Enzo's sister Olivia, who talked about a foundation she ran that seemed to offer grants to people with unlikely ideas.

All very innocent. The top guys insulated themselves from the actual crimes, so Riley wasn't surprised. He'd track the tip of the iceberg, catching odd trips, furtive meetings, mysterious conversations and hope they'd lead to more.

Riley was polishing the Ferrari in the late afternoon when Minetti pulled into the garage driveway. Just the man he wanted to get to know.

Sal came over and ran his hand along the hood of the race car. "I love this beast. I service it, you know."

"Care to listen to the pistons?" He held out the keys.

"Sounds good." Sal climbed into the driver's seat and Riley sat beside him. "This baby is a waste of horsepower. Enzo never drives it."

Sal drove way too fast, showing off, so Riley was relieved they returned in one piece. Sal jerked to a stop in the driveway. "So, Chloe, huh? You're a lucky man." Sal gave him a suggestive wink.

Riley fought the urge to level the guy, who seemed to be picking a fight. "She's great, yeah." He bit the words out.

"I'll just bet she is." Riley was about to tell him where he could shove it when Sal laughed. "Chill, man. I'm jerking your chain. I'm not her type, I guess."

She's not into pompous sleazebags? He managed a smile.

"Her loss. I get no complaints from the ladies." Minetti ran his hands along the sides of his hair in a parody of a womanizer. At least the guy could laugh at himself. Maybe he was as harmless as Chloe seemed to think.

It occurred to Riley that this was a way to let the guy know he was open to side jobs. "It's tough to keep a girl like her happy," he said, rubbing his fingers together to indicate the need for cash.

"Chicks'll cost you, all right."

"No shit." He nodded, then added in a confidential tone, "If you need a driver or an extra set of hands, I'm available."

Sal seemed wary. "I hear of anything, I'll let you know."

"Mickey can vouch for me." In fact, he intended to ask Mickey to suggest Riley to Minetti for the "special" duties.

"Good to know," Sal said, dismissing him as he got out of the car.

Riley wasn't sure the heists were tied with whatever Sal had been discussing with his crew at the dinner last night or whether Enzo was involved in any way, but he'd pursue every lead he could until the pieces of the puzzle clicked into place.

Two new hires at the security firm had been "persons of interest" in a couple of robberies, so they would look hard at them. Maybe Riley would tail Sal, get a warrant to check out his auto shop and his house. He'd prefer not tipping the guy that they suspected him, though.

The rest of the day was uneventful. He managed to see Chloe when he went inside to use the john, but she was busy with housework and the smile she tossed his way didn't reach her eyes.

At eight that night, he drove Enzo to his restaurant, his last duty of the night. Enzo wore a spotless tuxedo and whistled all the way there, strolling in with a grin like a comic expecting to kill. Riley had seen Enzo in the restaurant before, working the room, but he hadn't noticed how in love with the place the man was.

From a bar stool, Riley watched Enzo greet a table full of made guys, then circulate to other diners before he headed back to the office to talk with the manager. Riley stood near the door, as if waiting for his next assignment, but Enzo sent him home, saying he'd catch a ride.

Riley couldn't figure out a way to stick around and eavesdrop, so he left, stopping at his house to grab Idle before the debrief with Chloe and her father. The dog was again eager to get to Chloe's. "I wore out our welcome, pal," Riley said, but Idle didn't seem to care.

Riley had been a fool to think they could keep their days and nights separate. He wished the world were a kinder place for Chloe's sake, but she was better off facing reality.

All the same, when she opened the door, his heart lifted and he felt the peace he'd known as a kid before his dad died, when his life had been solid and safe and good.

She tossed a "hi" in his direction, then bent to pet Idle. "Hey, boy, you feeling better?" She stepped back but just enough to let him into the entryway. "Anything happen today?"

"Not much. I let Sal know I needed extra work, but he didn't nibble. I need Mickey to call him about me."

"He's out at the moment. His sponsor took him to an AA meeting across town. I guess he has to take rides when he can get them." She shrugged. "You find out about the papers I photographed?"

"Not yet, no. Mind if I come in and sit down?" He felt like a salesman she was trying to shoo out the door.

"Okay," she said, not that happy about it, he could tell.

He removed his blazer, flopping it over the back of the sofa. There was a clunk.

She reached over and felt around in the jacket, then pulled

out the cuffs. "So you didn't need these after all?" She wiggled them in his face.

"No," he said, taking them from her to place them on the table. He sat on the sofa and patted for her to sit. "How did your day go?" He hoped an ordinary conversation and Idle's presence would ease the tension a little.

"Good, I guess." She sank onto the sofa with a sad smile. "Dinner went well. I made swordfish Milanese, shrimp salad on endive. Managed a low-carb version for Charity and a low-fat one for Enzo. The low-carb bread was a hit. Charity even said it didn't taste like dirt."

"That's a compliment?"

"From her, yeah. She seems to be taking my advice about her parents, at least. She even scaled down the slut factor in her wardrobe."

"That's good," he said.

"But you're not interested in the family or my cooking, are you, Riley? You're interested in crime. I'm afraid I don't have any illegal activities to report. Looks like Ronnie's pirated some CDs and Charity wore a dress twice before exchanging it and, no doubt, Natalie's cut the tags off the pillows—"

"Cut it out, Chloe. The sarcasm doesn't help."

"It helps me, Riley. I have to do something to get through this nightmare."

"We have to work together, Chloe. Why make it worse?"

"How could it be worse?"

Idle whined miserably.

"What's wrong?" Chloe reached down to pet the dog. "Is he in pain?" She lifted her gaze to his.

"That's not a pain cry. That's an anxious cry."

"What's he anxious about?"

"The tension between us, I'm sure." He was stroking Idle's side, while Chloe scratched his muzzle.

"So he doesn't like us to fight?" She smiled a little.

"No. And neither do I. I know this isn't easy for you and I'm sorry I was harsh last night."

"You said what you believed, I guess. I just hate this."

"I know."

They were rubbing both sides of the dog, not looking at each other.

"I guess we'll have to agree to disagree about the Sylvestris," she said. "And human nature." Their fingers met in the dog's fur and their gazes snapped to attention, the tension between them instantly sexual.

Chloe tightened her fingers around his. "I missed you."

"I missed you, too." He leaned forward and kissed her, long and slow until he was lost again.

Idle flopped to the floor with a giant sigh and they broke apart for a quiet laugh.

"Guess he approves," Riley said. This time her smile went all the way to her eyes. "That's how you smiled at me that night."

"I felt like smiling that night," she said. "And you're looking at me the way you did then. Your eyes are softer. Can we stay this way for now? Forget what happens during the day?"

"I sure as hell hope so," he said, all the reasons not to fading to black.

They were just getting into it when Chloe's phone rang, making them both jump. She reached past him to the side table for a handset. She read the display. "My father." She sat up and answered. "Dad? Are you okay?" She listened, glancing at Riley, then said, "Okay, sure... Thanks for letting me know." She clicked off thoughtfully. Riley returned the phone to its place.

"He says he's going for coffee with people from the meeting.... He said not to wait up." She spoke slowly.

"Something wrong?"

"Probably nothing. He used to stay late to talk with his sponsor some nights, so it's no big deal, I guess."

"Is he avoiding me?"

"That's possible."

"Tomorrow, have him call Sal about me, okay?"

"If Sal doesn't take you on, then what?" She started to look worried again and he wanted her smile back.

"We'll punt. Don't worry. The FBI is working on surveillance on Sal, but it takes jumping through hoops to authorize. They can take their time building their case. I don't have that luxury. I'd trail the guy myself if I had time. I'd love to search his shop."

She blinked and colored. "I know how you can," she said eagerly. "Remember I asked Sal to look over my car? He wants us to go out to dinner, too? While I'm with him, you can search his shop, his house, hell, his underwear drawer."

"No way, Chloe. You can't be alone with that sociopath. He'd attack you as soon as look at you."

"He's harmless. Even if he wasn't, he knows if he tried anything, he'd have to answer to Enzo. Besides, I can defend myself. I took a self-defense class."

"You took a class? That's cute."

"Don't patronize me, Riley," she said, pushing to her feet, pulling his hand. "Come on. Try to assault me."

"What?" He stood reluctantly beside her, not liking where this conversation had led them.

"I'm serious. Do it."

"Chloe…" But he grabbed her wrist and yanked her against him, pinning her arm behind her back, wanting to end the debate.

Reacting fast, she raised a knee to his groin and he barely shifted away in time. "Watch the equipment there. You'll need it later."

"You get the point, right? Now try grabbing me from behind." She turned away from him.

He sighed. She wasn't going to let this go, so he made a halfhearted grab.

She jerked her head back, stopping before she slammed the crown of her head into his face.

"Not bad," he said.

"The skull is the hardest bone in the body. Makes a great weapon. Or I could do this." She shot her arm at his face, heel of her hand extended, stopping just short of his nose, a potential kill shot.

"I'm impressed." He reached to hold her, to end this, but she grabbed his arm, turned to aim a sidekick to his knee—which would have been a crippling blow. "You have skills. I get it."

"The point is I can handle myself with Sal." She sank onto the sofa and he joined her.

"A self-defense class won't do shit if he slips you Rohypnol," he said. "He's too lazy to work for it. I appreciate your offer, but I can't allow it. It's too dangerous."

She studied him, considering options. She wasn't giving up, he realized with an inner moan. "Okay, so I won't go to dinner with him. We'll work at the Sylvestri garage and I'll make sure Enzo's there. That make you happy?"

"Not very."

"You'll need more time to search, right…." She tapped her lip. "I know. I'll ask him to explain how a car works, or show me how to change my oil. He loves to show off."

"Chloe…" He started to shake his head, but she was so stubborn he knew it was pointless to argue. He could work with her compromise. "He can work on your car, but only if you stay three feet away from him at all times and always out in the open. Keep one hand on your phone with 9-1-1 coded in, the other on the trigger of the pepper spray I'll give you. If he gets strange in any way, shoot him blind and call for help."

"Deal," she said, beaming with triumph. "I can't wait. Finally I can do something useful."

She thought that through a few seconds, then leveled her gaze at him. "You realize we've got time alone now. My dad's gone for a while. Now where were we?" She pushed him down on the sofa again, her eyes full of fire and confidence.

"That's about right," he said, glad to go along with this particular move.

She reached past him to the lamp.

"Don't turn off the light," he said. He wanted to see every detail of her face and body.

"If you insist," she said, grinning mischievously. She slid her body over him, then ran her hands down to weave her fingers with his, then pull his arms overhead. What was she up to?

She rose to her knees, jabbing his groin.

"Ow," he said, then he felt metal on his wrist and heard a click. His cuffs. He'd left them on the table.

"What are you doing, Chloe?"

She grabbed his other wrist. He could resist, but decided to let this play out and let her close the other cuff around his wrist. "There!" she said.

He looked back and saw she'd cuffed him around the pole of the lamp. He rattled the chain. One yank and he'd pull it over. He wasn't thrilled about being restrained, but he'd play along for her sake.

"Now I can do whatever I want to you," she said. He watched as the implications of her own words dawned on her. Her expression went from playful to knowing to aroused. He realized he was seeing the new Chloe again—the girl who went after what she wanted, no holds barred.

"What did you have in mind?" he asked. He was in trouble now. The good kind.

"First, I want you to see I'm no helpless girl." She ran a fingernail down the buttons of his shirt, giving him a charge.

"You? Helpless? Never." He captured her hips with his legs. "Give me back my hands. I promise you won't be sorry."

"Not yet." She unbuttoned his shirt, then ran her tongue down the middle of his chest. He was hard as stone and had trouble breathing. "How was that?" She leaned back.

"I'm about to yank down this lamp and show you."

"And damage property? That doesn't sound like a good cop, Detective Connelly."

"Then get the key." He raised his hip to indicate where.

"You want me to check your pockets?" she asked in pretend innocence, then pressed her palm on his cock. "You've got something there, all right." She widened her eyes. "Something hard and long."

"You made it that way," he said, pleased when a shiver passed through her. "Let me free and we can use it."

"Not yet." She surveyed him. "I like you in cuffs." Keeping her eyes on him, she took off her shirt. Her breasts swelled from her bra cups. He couldn't help trying to reach them and the lamp shook and rattled.

"Let's take our time, huh?" She slid her breasts up from his chest to his face. "Doesn't this feel good?"

He grabbed the bra clasp with his teeth and jerked, opening the bra, then managing to get a breast in his mouth.

Chloe writhed and gasped, then pushed away from him. "Not so fast, Riley." She was breathing hard, her playfulness overcome by arousal. She unzipped his pants and he raised his hips so she could get them and his briefs off.

She widened her gaze at the sight of his erection and took it into one tightened fist. He had to groan.

"Give me my hands. I want to touch you."

"Soon," she said, continuing to rub him, getting into it, her eyes glazing, her breath coming in pants. She wouldn't be able to play much longer, he could tell.

"I give. You win. What do you want? Whatever it is, I'll do." He felt just that desperate.

10

CHLOE COULDN'T BELIEVE how sexy she felt. She'd put Riley in handcuffs, for heaven's sake. The new Chloe had come out to play. In spades. Showing off her self-defense skills and convincing Riley she could handle Sal had made her feel strong and sexual. And now she was acting the part. She was so proud of herself. And so aroused.

Seeing how much Riley wanted her, knowing all that male strength wanted nothing more than to get at her body…well, she could almost come just thinking about it.

"What do you want?" Riley asked in a sex-rough voice.

She knew instantly what to say. "Your mouth on me."

The words thrilled through her. She meant to tease her panties off, but she wanted this too much, so she yanked them off, straddled Riley and aimed herself at his mouth.

He looked up at her, gold flames in his brown eyes.

"Do me," she said, loving the sound of the raw command.

Still watching her, he extended his tongue to touch her.

She melted against him and he closed his lips around her clit, sending a charge through her that woke up every nerve in her body. When he slid his tongue downward, she sprouted some new ones and every single one burned and ached on overload.

With a moan, she pushed away from his mouth.

"Where you going?" he said, grabbing her hips with his knees.

"Catching my breath," she said, pleased that with Riley in

cuffs, she had control of the experience. She could back away when it became too much or mash herself against him for more.

When she'd recovered a bit, she leaned in and he obliged her with a firm stroke that spiked her lust. She would come any instant.

"Not…so…soon," she said, unable to move away, hardly able to speak. "I don't…want…to…come…yet."

Riley held her with his legs, his tongue working her over, leading her forward, urging her to fly.

"Don't. Oh. Don't." Her words were a quiet squeal. She'd shackled Riley, but he'd pinned her in place all the same. It took more than handcuffs to diminish his power over her. He nuzzled her, sucked her. His tongue swirled and pressed and tugged.

"Yes…yes… Don't stop."

Then he did. His mouth went away. His tongue disappeared. She looked down. "What are you doing?"

He looked up at her. He knew his power over her, she could tell, and he intended to tease her. Then something he saw in her face, maybe how desperate she felt, changed his expression. His eyes went from gold flames to a white-hot spark and she knew he couldn't stop, either, not even to prolong the thrill.

He went at her, fast and firm, and she shot into space, gasping, shaking all over, her body burning to ash.

Riley kindly propped her trembling body with his bent legs and when the climax passed, she fell against him. "That was amazing." She'd been in charge, but in his power, too, and both ways she felt safe with him.

"Now give me my hands. I want to touch you," he said. The heat in his gaze almost scared her.

"Soon," she said, wanting one more experience with Riley in chains. She rose to her knees, led him to her swollen opening and sat on him.

He groaned and closed his eyes. Instantly, the hungry burn began again, as if she hadn't just come, as if she would never get enough. They held each other's eyes as she moved up and down, lost in a fever dream of lust.

Riley leaned forward to capture her mouth and they drank each other dry while her hips lifted and lowered, seeking her own pleasure and his.

She felt close to climax again. Seeming to sense it, Riley shifted to go deeper, to angle the base of his shaft against her clitoris, offering a new intensity to the approaching release. He said her name as if it contained an emotion he couldn't hold in any longer.

She said his with such a yearning she didn't recognize her own voice. Three quick movements and they both exploded. She fell forward, holding on to him, her fingers around his up-stretched wrists, fingers slipping under the metal of the cuffs.

Their hearts pounded and sweat slid between their bare chests. She felt as though they'd been through something death-defying and now clung to each other, glad to be alive.

Wanting his arms around her, she found his key chain in his pants pocket and freed his hands.

The cuffs clunked to the floor and Riley pulled her onto his lap. She felt so *good,* so satisfied, so startled by the power of what had happened. Riley looked equally freaked.

What if this was more than short-term need? What if it could be something deeper? Like love?

Foolish and impossible. Too much stood in the way—her father's troubles, Riley's cop attitude, his emotional distance.

They should stop this now, she knew, but as she tucked her face into his neck, she only wanted more. "How about dessert?"

"It could kill me," he said on a groan, stroking her back.

She chuckled, then lifted her head. "I mean actual dessert. I feel like cooking."

He laughed. "Stick a fork in me, I'm done." Then his face went serious. "That was…something else."

"I know. I've never felt like this before…."

"Me, either."

"You don't sound happy about it."

"It's okay," he said slowly. "Because it was you." His cheeks went pink. She grinned. She'd made this tough guy blush.

"Maybe it was the cuffs," she said, not sure why she wanted to explain it away.

"It was more than the cuffs, Chloe," he said, low and sure.

She didn't know what to do with the heat and triumph that rushed through her, so she changed the subject to something she did know how to handle. "Come on. Let me feed you."

"You already did." He let his tongue flick his lips. She blushed, then bent to pick up her blouse.

"Do you have to do that?" he said, running his hands across her bare breasts.

"I can hardly cook naked. My father will be back."

"At least skip the panties," he said, gripping her hips, "so I can slip inside you."

"Oh." A thrill shot through her. She wanted him *again*. It was as if all this desire and need had been locked away, saved for later and Riley had busted down the door and she wanted to drown in the flood that followed.

He helped her dress, hooking her bra, buttoning her blouse, closing her skirt zipper. She liked him taking care of her. "What's your favorite dessert, Riley?" she asked.

"You," he said, straightening her collar with a pat.

"Seriously. What is it?"

"I don't know…. My mom used to make a bread pudding at Christmas. Raisins and cinnamon and a caramel sauce. I got to melt the caramels and throw in the raisins."

"Bread pudding it is. I think I have all I need."

ME, TOO. The words came into his head as natural as his next breath. Stupid and sentimental, but he managed to not say them out loud. Bad enough he'd admitted never feeling this way before. He hoped he wouldn't pay for that confession.

He felt so damn close to her. Easy, comfortable. Like she was in his head and he was in hers. It almost hurt.

He pushed away the thought and walked her into the kitchen to make his favorite dessert. Too good to be true.

In the middle of setting out all the ingredients, she suddenly turned to him. "Sex can't possibly keep being that good, can it?"

"Hard to say." What a question.

"I'd never get out of bed." Neither would he. She chewed her lip, worrying over the idea. "Maybe you take it for granted. Like people who work in bakeries get sick of the smell."

"Maybe." How could any man not value every minute spent with her? She looked so pretty, her hair tossed, her color high, her eyes shining.

She seemed content with that option, as if she'd wanted to explain this away. He understood the impulse. He was pretty flipped out himself.

"Oh, my God." She was looking beyond him into the living room, so he turned to see a black cat curled against Idle, who'd made himself at home on one of Chloe's overstuffed chairs.

"I've never even seen my cat in the living room, let alone cuddling. And with a *dog?* Unbelievable."

"Connellys are irresistible, I guess."

She grinned and kissed him. She looked so happy he wanted to do everything in his power to keep her that way.

He set the table and watched her cook, letting them be two people enjoying food after great sex. It occurred to him that some people had this every day. Not every day. She was right. Nothing this good could last. Reality waited just outside—the case, the crime, the danger, their different worlds.

Shut up, he told himself. *Be happy with now.* Cinnamon and caramel filled his nose like delicious smoke and he grinned and let it all go.

Soon they'd carried bowls of piping hot pudding to her bedroom—a comfortable place, not too girlie—and they climbed into her soft bed to feed each other the first bite.

"Mmm," he said.

"Good as your mom's?"

"Better." Sauce dripped onto his chest, since he'd left his shirt open.

Quick as a cat after cream, Chloe licked it off. Her wriggling tongue made him instantly hard. "Take off your jeans," she said with a wicked grin. "I have an idea…."

He did so and soon she was dribbling sauce on his cock. She scooted down to distribute it everywhere with her busy tongue. He groaned with pleasurable agony and closed his eyes.

The next thing he knew, she'd sucked him into her mouth. He opened his eyes to watch her labor over his body, enjoying the warm wetness, her tongue, the occasional brush of her teeth, all of it making him shake and surge.

Seconds later, he was ready, so he signaled her.

She stayed in place, sucking even harder. He erupted into her mouth and she swallowed his fluid like it was more dessert.

He pulled her to his chest and held her, something inside him melting like that caramel sauce. He felt so good he couldn't speak, so he chose action, rolling her over to spoon a streak of caramel down her stomach and below.

"Mmm," she said, rocking into the mattress, ready for his mouth. He smiled at her eagerness, like a kid in a candy store with too much money to spend.

He licked her and sucked gently, loving how she rocked against his mouth. The sweet smell of dessert, the heat of her need, her moans, filled him up and spilled over, flowed out, carrying them both away.

After she came, he lifted her in his arms and took her to her shower, where he washed every part of her, then made love to her against the shower wall, slow and careful, remembering everything, not sure they would be able to keep this up, not sure what he'd do when they had to stop.

When they were dry, naked and warm in bed, Chloe

cozied onto his chest with a sigh. "This is so nice. I like how I am with you."

"That's good."

"And I like how you are, too." She rose to look at his face. "You seem more yourself to me."

"Yeah?" She may have a point, but he felt uneasy about where she was going.

"I think you're afraid of your emotions maybe. It had to have affected you, losing your dad so young."

"I guess." But that wasn't the worst of it. "It was more when my mom disappeared in a fog of tranks. For a while, I hated my dad for what his death did to her. I guess I hated her, too, for being weak. That was stupid. She was hurting. I knew that but I was still angry."

"Of course you were. Kids are supposed to be able to count on their parents. When my mom left, I felt like it was our fault—my sister and me. Our love wasn't enough for her. *I* wasn't enough."

"It was between your parents." He hated thinking of her hurt so badly. He was lucky to be built like his dad—not much heart in him, so he hadn't suffered much.

"I know that now. She had her own troubles. Like your mother. She loved me. I know that. And your mother loved you. They both still do. That's what counts."

For her maybe. He wasn't so sure himself. Mostly he didn't like to think about it. He was better off staying clear.

He didn't speak, simply held her, smelling her skin and the caramel they'd gotten on the sheets, feeling her breath on his neck, her ribs expanding and contracting against his own. Gradually her breathing slowed, her body relaxed, and he knew she was asleep.

He liked holding her this way, taking care of her. The Sal encounter she'd planned worried him. If anything happened to her... His mind stalled.

Part of him wanted to drop the case altogether, let Enzo

Sylvestri slide, just to keep Chloe out of the line of fire. Sex with her only made things worse. Yet he'd gone for it again. He knew himself too well to pretend he'd stop now.

IN THE MORNING, Chloe smelled caramel and smiled, remembering what she and Riley had done with dessert. Before she even turned to look, she knew he was gone. He'd had to leave before her father woke up, of course, but she was actually relieved not to have to see which Riley would look at her across the pillow.

Maybe she could help him get in touch with his emotions, show him how warm he truly was. She wanted to fix him, she realized in disgust. Riley didn't want her to fix him. He didn't think he needed fixing.

She dragged herself out of bed, woozy from lack of sleep and achy from all the sex. She felt good, too, she had to admit, and calmer than she'd felt in a long time.

In the kitchen, she was surprised to see her father up and at the table, his knees bobbing as they did whenever he had something on his mind.

"What time did you get in?" she asked him.

"This isn't like you, Chloe," he said, honing in, ignoring her question.

"What isn't like me?"

"I saw the dog. Riley's dog."

"Oh." She felt hot with blush. He knew Riley had been in her bedroom.

"If you're doing it to help me…"

"Doing what?" Then it dawned on her. Her embarrassment turned to anger. "You think I'm trying to…make points…that way?"

"I didn't think so," he said, sounding relieved. "But I know you'd do anything to save me." He reached out to grasp one hand, his own trembling, his eyes red-rimmed with distress. "I hate that I've done this to you."

"We're fixing it now. We all have a part to play. Which reminds me—Riley needs you to talk to Sal about giving Riley your special duties. Vouch for him, okay?"

"Sal won't want to hear that from me." He looked away.

"It's the fastest way to catch Sal and that's what we have to do to get your deal."

"I'll try." Her father studied the tablecloth, running his fingers over the blue checks.

"Dad?"

He looked up. "Is it serious? You and the cop?" She had the fleeting impression he'd asked the question to change the subject.

"His name's Riley, Dad. And no." How could it be serious?

"Chloe?" Her face must have contradicted her words.

"We enjoy each other." She liked how she was with him. Instead of bracing for what might happen next, she could ease back, let go, be herself, breathe. But it was only for now and only at night. There'd been that moment when Riley held her so tight, and the way he'd said her name…

"It's easy to get hurt." Her father looked suddenly sad.

Could Riley hurt her? Not if she kept this in perspective. And how could she hurt him? He was so insulated, so guarded.

"It was tough with your mother. See, she was the best thing that ever happened to me and I was the worst thing that ever happened to her." Her father shook his head. "In a way, I was relieved she left. I knew she would find a way to be happy."

Her heart squeezed at his words, at the sorrow on his face, and the memory of that awful first year—lying awake listening for the distinctive ping of her mother's engine, even though the postcards were clues that her mother was far away.

"You're a smart girl, Chloe, but the heart is tricky."

"Don't worry about me, Dad."

"That's a father's job," he said. "I'm always thinking of you, whatever I do. Remember that. I want to help you get what you want." What was he trying to tell her?

She didn't want one more thing to worry about, so she rose

from the table. She noticed his cast lying by the garage door, as if tossed there. She picked it up to bring it to him, then noticed an impression on the bottom, as if from a car pedal.

"You're not driving, are you? What if someone sees you?"

"We ran out of milk." He shrugged, not meeting her gaze. "I hate sitting around every day, helpless."

"You have to do it. It's your part of the plan. If you need something, call me and I'll get it."

"Okay," he said, but he wouldn't meet her gaze. She decided to trust him. She'd told Riley she had faith in people. How could she doubt her own father? Had Riley done this to her?

He had her doubting Enzo, too. She realized she'd held back the mysterious phone call to Mario about a shipment out of fear that it meant something bad. She liked herself with Riley at night. But the daytime was another matter altogether.

11

"I'LL BE FINE, Riley. Really," Chloe said, watching Riley return from parking the third of Enzo's fancy cars in the driveway. She'd just parked her Ion inside the garage. It looked so puny in the huge space, which smelled of the car polish her father was always applying.

Riley was leaving work for the day and Sal was due in an hour to check out the nonexistent noise in her sturdy car, then show her the steps of basic maintenance. She would keep him busy while Riley checked out Sal's auto shop.

Riley came to stand behind her, his arms tight around her. Together they looked out at the moon. For a lovely moment, she rested against him, feeling protected and safe. Then she noticed something very hard against her bottom. "That for me?" she teased, rubbing against it.

"Actually, yeah." She felt him reach into his pants, then he held something in front of her—a small black canister. "Pepper spray."

She laughed. "I thought that was…you know."

"That's for you, too—for later." He grinned, grinding against her backside. "You know how to use it?"

"Oh yeah," she purred. "I know *exactly* how to use it."

"I mean the pepper spray." He chuckled, low and sexy.

"Point and shoot, right? Go for the eyes. I doubt I'll need it. Enzo's in the house. I can run if I need to." She lifted one running-shoe-clad foot. "And we'll keep the door open so I won't choke on Sal's fumes."

"You mean that god-awful cologne he wears?"

"It makes my eyes water."

"All the same, keep the spray handy. I know you're smart and careful and you've had self-defense, but cops wear vests, even in a Phoenix July."

"I will, worrywart."

"Give me your phone."

She handed it over and he began keying in numbers. "My mobile is seven on your speed dial," he said.

"That's pretty nervy."

"You can ditch it when this is over…if you want to." He gave her a quick smile. Then he studied her phone and frowned. "This needs a charge, Chloe."

"I know. I think my battery is going."

"You have a car charger?"

She shook her head, then looked at the phone. "That's enough for tonight. As soon as you're finished looking around, you'll call me so I can wrap it up with Sal."

"Shouldn't take long. I had patrol officers check out the place. They couldn't see much from the windows. There's a dog, but he's friendly. I'll slip through a gap in the fence and break in with as little damage as possible."

"I'll find out what I can from Sal," she said.

"I'm not happy about you being alone with the guy."

"I feel better being useful."

"If you weren't so stubborn…" He gave her a quick kiss. "Just be—"

"Careful. I know. I will be."

With a last look, he took off. Watching his broad shoulders and confident stride, she couldn't help thinking about later, being alone with him, celebrating whatever they learned tonight. For the first time, she felt part of a team that really could fix things for her father.

In an hour, Sal drove up, and she braced herself for the encounter. He climbed out of the black SUV, wearing a silk shirt and dress pants instead of work clothes. She wore an old T-shirt and jeans.

"Is that how you dress to work on cars?" she asked.

"Jumpsuit's in there." He jabbed his thumb in the direction of his SUV. "This is in case you change your mind about dinner." He gestured at his outfit.

"I can't, Sal. I have plans with Riley later."

"The guy keeps you on a tight leash. Not that I blame him." He winked, which was supposed to flatter her, she guessed.

"My car's in here," she said, walking back into the garage, reminding herself to take this slowly to buy Riley maximum time.

"So this is, what, three years old?" he asked, walking around it.

"Yes. I bought it new. I liked the bare-bones pricing."

"Saturn makes a decent car. I've worked on a few."

"It's been very dependable. I hope you can find what's wrong. It's only now and then that it rattles."

"Let's take her for a spin. Since this looks like the only action I'll be getting tonight." He winked again, then reached for the key she held out. Ish.

She climbed in beside him, immediately gagging on a superstrong dose of Sal's scent. He'd poured it on to impress her, no doubt. She sneezed.

"Got a cold?" he asked, roaring into Reverse.

She grabbed the handrest as he spun around only to slam on the brakes to allow the gate to slowly open. "It must be something in the air," she said, fighting whiplash. Her eyes smarted and began to water.

"Allergies, right? My sister has 'em. You're not allergic to me, are you?" He turned to her.

"Maybe your soap…or…" being honest might excuse her from a clinch should he try for one later "…your cologne?"

"Can't be," he said, shaking his head as he roared down the

street. "I spent a fortune on this special blend tuned to my own smell. Supposed to make me irresistible to the ladies."

The perfumer should be shot, she thought as her sinuses tightened and her head throbbed, though that could be nerves.

"What kind of noise is it?" he asked.

"Kind of a click, rattle…a ping, I guess. Intermittent." She added that because she knew her engine was just fine.

They reached a stoplight and he revved the engine, head cocked, listening. "I don't hear anything."

"It's usually when I'm going slow." Hint, hint.

"Okay," he said, starting off at a reasonable speed as they traveled a few blocks. "Hmm," he said. "Nothing so far."

"Give it time," she said, thinking the delay would help Riley.

"I'm not going to get my nuts kicked by your boyfriend for doing this for you, right? You're hot, but not enough to risk my matching set."

"You're just checking my car and showing me how to take care of it, right? Where's the harm in that?"

"Not even a drink after? Oil changes are thirsty work."

"Riley's the jealous type."

He sighed. "Fair enough." They drove farther. "So, a click or ping, huh? Could be the gas mix. You use regular or premium?"

"Regular."

"Is it worse when you first fill 'er up?"

"Uh, maybe. Yeah."

"Or it could just need a tune-up. We'll check her out." He patted the dash, as if to comfort the car. He went back to driving fast then, changing lanes, whipping through yellow lights, heading for the freeway, she guessed, since they were in the center of town.

She decided to steer the conversation toward him hiring Riley. "I appreciate you showing me how to service my car, Sal. Money is tight for me and Riley's always short of cash."

"Yeah, he mentioned that." Sal seemed to think that over, maybe putting it with what her father had said about Riley.

"If you hear of anything he could do...?"

"Yeah, yeah. I'll let him know."

She didn't dare push anymore or he'd get suspicious. She'd move on to finding out more about what he was doing with Ronnie. "So are you showing Ronnie how to work on cars?"

"When he wants to learn, I guess."

"I know Natalie's hoping you'll help him make better choices. He looks up to you, you know."

He laughed. "Don't be turnin' all Doctor Phil on me, okay? He's a kid. He's got more on his mind than picking up a trade."

"Enzo worries about him," she said, then took a deep breath. "Kind of how I worry about my father."

"Mickey? He does all right." But he twisted his hands on the steering wheel.

"Not so much lately. Could I ask you a favor, Sal?"

He shot her a cagey look. "Maybe. What is it?"

"Would you keep an eye out for him? Make sure he doesn't gamble? Or do anything...dangerous? I know you see him a lot." She stared at the side of his face, demanding he look at her.

He kept his eyes ahead, but he squirmed. "I can't wipe his butt for him. He's a grown man."

"See, if he got in trouble with the law, Sal, it might kill him. His heart's not strong." Not exactly true, but something Sal would understand.

"Jeez, enough with the heavy talk," Sal said, sounding annoyed. "Your dad makes his own bed. It's not on you."

She didn't speak, but she could tell she'd pricked his conscience. At least he had one.

She noticed they were in an industrial part of town. She'd been so intent on the conversation she hadn't noticed they hadn't turned back toward Enzo's. She had a sudden jolt of alarm. "Where are we going?"

"To my shop to put the car up on the lift."

"Oh. No. We're working at Enzo's, I thought. This was just to listen to the engine." They were headed straight for Riley!

She had to fix this. "Won't it be better to show me there? I won't have a lift when I do it myself." She fought panic.

"What's the prob?" he asked, looking at her strangely.

They whipped past grim warehouses, then across abandoned railroad tracks. "This is a scary part of town," she said. They were about to arrive at the worst possible place they could be.

"Relax. You're safe with Sal." He chuckled.

She had to let Riley know. "Oh. That's my phone," she said, pretending her phone had rung. She flipped it open and pressed speed dial seven.

He answered immediately. "You okay?"

"Hi, Dad," she said loudly. "What's up? I'm fine, Dad. Sal's taking me *to his garage. This very minute.* To show me how to change my oil. We're almost *there.*"

"I get it. I'll get out. Thanks for the heads-up."

Her heart raced. For the first time, she realized how risky this could be. Sal had a gun, no doubt. If he saw Riley, figured out their plot, not only would the case be completely blown, but they could both be in danger.

Sal stopped the car at the gate to a chain-link fence. Behind it was a corrugated metal building that held a sign with Minetti's Auto Haven in faded letters.

Sal got out of the car, taking keys out of his pocket, and headed for the gate. She jumped out to go with him, her heart in her throat, desperate to distract him in case Riley was still on the premises. She looked through the fence. There were four white trucks parked outside the shop. She saw no movement.

"I'm just unlocking the gate," he said.

"I know. I just wanted to see. So this is your place?" She sounded like an idiot, but she had to stall him.

"Yep. This is it. I'll give you a tour."

"Nice sign," she said. It was horrid and bleached out, but she had to say something.

"No need to get sarcastic. Not like we get walk-ins."

"No. I like it. The typeface is…good."

Sal looked at the sign, then her, as if she were a kook.

She squinted into the darkness beyond the orange glow of the security lights. Was Riley hiding? Was he trapped? Her eyes darted everywhere.

As Sal undid the padlock, she saw a shape at the edge of the building. Riley. He was pointing deliberately a few feet away at a dog chewing on something—a bone?

Riley waved something floppy—a piece of meat?—at the dog, then tossed it near the fence. The dog galloped after it just as Sal pulled the gate open.

"A dog!" she shrieked, sounding stupid and girlie, but she had to distract the man. Riley had said the dog was friendly.

"That's just Thrasher," Sal said.

"I'm afraid of dogs." She grabbed his arm and hid behind him, as if for protection.

"Relax. He's just for show. He's got a big bark and he slobbers like a motherfu— Anyway, he's a baby, aren't you, boy?" He bent down to scrub the dog's neck, talking baby talk. Sal was a funny mix of tough guy and kid.

Beyond him, she saw Riley slip through a loose section of chain link, then drop into the weeds on the ditch beside the fence. The only sound was a whispery rattle of chain link.

Whew. Riley had escaped. Her heart hammering in her chest, she knelt to pet the dog. "He *is* a nice dog," she said.

"Let's get working on your car," Sal said. He returned to drive the car through the gate. Her cell phone rang.

"Hello?" she said, keeping her voice light.

"You okay?" Riley whispered.

"I'm fine. He's pulling my car in."

"I didn't see much. Look around while you're there. Hang tight to the pepper spray. I'm a block away watching."

"I'll be fine."

"Thanks for saving my ass," Riley said.

Sal got out of the car, so she smiled at him. "My pleasure," she said into the phone in a falsely light voice. "See you later." She ended the call. "That was Riley checking on me. Your nuts are safe, Sal."

He laughed. "You're a funny lady. Pull your car in for me, would you? Right over the lift?" He unlocked the door to the office and in a few seconds, the shop door ground upward, revealing another white truck—this one with its hood up.

She drove where he'd indicated and got out. Meanwhile, Sal had pulled on a jumpsuit. "So, we'll do an oil change, check your fluid levels, your filters and your spark plugs. First thing, get me your owner's manual. That's your bible."

She leaned into the passenger side to get it from the glove compartment, aware he watched her butt the entire time.

He flipped through the pages, showing her the maintenance schedule and droning on about oil weight and the proper tools for the proper task, while she stole glances at the garage, trying to memorize what she saw.

"Chloe? Are you following me here?" he asked impatiently.

"Sure. It's just that your shop is so clean." It wasn't dusty or even very greasy. It smelled of paint and plastic and she noticed welding gear and spray-paint stains on the floor. Did that mean something?

"We like it that way," he said. "Come over here and I'll show you how to check your oil."

Sidestepping his attempt to put his arms around her while they worked, she put on a damn good ditz act so he ended up changing the oil for her, while she looked around more.

The truck looked brand-new, the engine clean. The ones outside seemed new, too. The bench held tools, some she didn't recognize, and there were rolls of duct tape and a stack of white plastic tarps. A crate caught her eye. Inside she saw what must be air bags, but in several shapes and sizes.

"You want to make sure you get this bolt tight afterward," he said and she hurried closer.

"Absolutely. I can see that."

He brought her car back down. "Let's check those spark plugs, okay?"

"Sure. Sounds good," she said. Glancing to the left, she noticed his office. A good place to snoop. There was a soda machine there. "I'm going to get a Coke. Want one?"

"Are you interested in this at all?" he said, annoyed.

"I'll be right back." She managed to half watch Sal and snoop in every corner. The effort exhausted her, so she was relieved when Sal gave up and declared them done.

"Thanks so much," she said, climbing into the car. "I learned a lot."

"Could have fooled me," he fumed.

She gushed about his skills and how well he'd taught her and declared the engine noise completely gone until he was so puffed up with pride he'd forgotten her bizarre behavior by the time they reached the Sylvestris' place.

The minute Sal drove off, Riley pulled in. He jumped out of the car and nearly ran to her. "You okay?" he said, taking her by the arms and watching her face.

"I'm fine," she said. "I'm sorry I blew it for you."

"You're safe. That's all that matters." He wrapped her in his arms. Only then did she let herself realize how frightened she'd been, how knotted with tension. She was damp with sweat and shaking all over.

Riley held her, giving her the warmth of his arms, the comfort of his strength.

After a while, she pulled back to talk. "That was awful. If he'd seen you, the whole case would have been blown."

"I never should have allowed you to take such a risk."

"I had pepper spray and you on speed dial." She tried to smile, but her throat was too tight.

"I knew better." His eyes were full of fire.

"I had to do something, Riley. I can't stand being on the sidelines. It's over now. We're both safe. And now I can change my own oil." She tried to get him to smile, but he wasn't nibbling. "Let me tell you what I saw and see if it helps."

"Go ahead," he said, still holding on to her.

"There were several new white trucks. Did you see them?"

"Yeah. F-150s. Maybe they service a fleet."

"The place was really clean inside." She described the work bench, the spray paint, the air bags, the tools she'd recognized.

"All signs of a chop shop," he said. "Air bags are big for resale. Not sure about the duct tape. Maybe for mufflers, maybe to pack chopped parts for shipping. You said there were cardboard cartons around?"

"Yeah, broken flat, though. And in the office the filing cabinet was locked. I didn't dare turn on the computer, but I did notice a stack of license plates tucked behind the desk. In this jar there were metal strips with numbers."

"VIN numbers. Yeah. Perfect. License plate and VINs. They're absolutely trading in stolen vehicles. Great work, Chloe. That's enough to score a surveillance team to see what goes on out there."

"I'm glad. Oh, and I also mentioned to Sal that you need more money, but he didn't say any more. Maybe that will help."

"Possible."

"Should we try it again? I could tell Sal the noise came back."

"No way. You're not risking another minute with Sal."

"He's no more dangerous than his guard dog."

"Trust me. If you got in Sal's way, you would be handled." She decided not to argue about this with him.

Her body had begun to respond to being in Riley's arms. The leftover adrenaline was shifting to desire. "I would be handled, huh? Let's go to my house and we can handle each other."

His eyes caught and flared with heat. "You okay to drive?"

"Absolutely," she said.

By the time she got to the house, she was on fire for him. Maybe it was the adrenaline, the excitement of making head-way on stopping Sal, or just Riley and the anticipation of getting naked with him again. She didn't care why. As soon as she made certain her father was safely in bed, she threw herself into Riley's arms.

He cupped her cheek and she noticed blood streaks on his sleeve. "You're hurt."

"Just a scrape getting through the fence." He went in for a kiss.

"Let me fix you up." She tugged him to the bathroom, the femininity of its pale blue walls, silk calla lilies and tea lights contrasting with Riley's vivid maleness.

In the small room, she pulled off his shirt, exposing his muscular chest and belly. She ran water, then gently washed the abraded part of his forearm and elbow. "This is like in a thriller where the girl patches up the cop she doesn't trust and they get over their hostility and make wild love," she said.

"Oh yeah?" He lifted her by the hips and set her on the edge of the sink. "Kind of like this?" He pressed himself between her legs and held her breasts through her blouse.

"Exactly," she breathed. They seemed trapped in the small room, prisoners of their lust. If only she had those handcuffs.

He undid her blouse and bra and shoved them off her body. She was busy with his belt and zipper, which buzzed deliciously in the silence. She took him into her hand, making him groan.

Pulling her skirt up, his fingers dug into her flesh, holding back, she could tell, so as not to bruise her. In the medicine cabinet mirror, they looked so sexy—light glancing off her breasts and his muscular arms. She spread her thighs and arched her back, lifting her hips to show him where she wanted him.

"Chloe," he said, sliding into her body, taking her hard. She banged her heels into his tight backside.

"You make me forget everything but this." He buried his face into her neck, bit in with his teeth.

"Mmm," she said, wanting him to make a mark on her.

She rocked on him so that the base of his cock pressed her clit, which throbbed with its own urgent pulse. "I'm going to come too soon," she said in despair.

"It's never too soon." He put a thumb on her spot, making her cry out with sharp delight. "I love how you come."

She tossed her head back, thudding into the mirror, aware of his low chuckle of pleasure, of his smooth skin and dark hair, of the smell of outdoors still on him. Digging her heels into his ass, she felt supremely sexual.

Riley's butt muscles tightened and released as he thrust into her. The pressure built until they climaxed together, shuddering and shaking, holding each other as they flew away.

When it was over, she turned her head to look in the mirror. "Look at us," she said.

"I don't need a mirror when I have you here." He ran his hands along her arms, then cupped her breasts. "I can't stop thinking about you." He was still breathing hard and she licked a dot of sweat from his neck. "Having you…what you do to me…"

That was a big speech from such a quiet man. She took in the words, memorized them. She and he, they were different like this—she was wilder, he was more in touch with his heart.

Making sure her father was nowhere in sight, Riley carried her into her bedroom. Through her curtains, she saw it had begun to rain. "Another storm," she said, nodding in that direction.

Riley carried her to the window and she cranked open the glass. "I love that smell." He took a deep breath.

So did she. Wet desert. "We need the water," she said, resting her cheek on his shoulder, loving how nature and sex and comfort combined to make her feel vividly alive. Thunder rolled overhead. Raindrops glistened in the light from the street and wind whipped the mesquite trees into a gray froth.

Riley carried her to the bed, then lay down beside her. As she turned to him, she was startled to notice Pepper Spray in the doorway. "Look," she whispered. They watched as the cat stepped gingerly forward. Riley slowly extended his hand and she sniffed very carefully, then delicately rubbed her cheek against his fingers.

"She never does that," Chloe whispered.

"She just smells Idle."

"She likes you, Riley. And so do I." She rolled closer to him and looked into his eyes. "This will be hard to give up."

"I know."

"It feels like more than we meant when we started."

He was silent. "Yeah," he finally admitted. "It does."

"Maybe we could spend some time together?"

"Some time?" He looked wary.

"We could spend the morning together, maybe. I go in late because of the party. You're due at the Sylvestris' at noon, right?"

"True." He seemed to hesitate. "What about your dad?"

"He knows we're seeing each other. What do you say?"

"I'd like to wake up with you in my arms."

"We can just…see how it goes."

"Yeah. We can." He kissed her and she kissed him back, hoping they weren't making a bigger mistake than they'd already made.

12

HE WASN'T POSITIVE, but Riley was pretty sure he'd just agreed to get involved with Chloe. Not just at night. Regular hours. After the case. He might even have been the one to suggest it. It was kind of muddy in his mind.

He had work he should do in the morning—check with London on the docs, touch base with his lieutenant, work on some cases. He'd be at Enzo's late, since he was bartending for Enzo's birthday party. But he'd said he'd stay. He *wanted* to stay.

He waited to panic, but nothing happened inside. He felt normal, like any guy with someone he cared about.

All because of Chloe. Would it wear off? He didn't want to think about that. Not when he had her in his arms.

She'd been so brave. Without hesitation, she'd led Sal around by his dick to buy Riley time to escape and done a decent job of surveillance while she was at it. She was tough and smart and brave. He liked that. A lot.

They'd left the window cracked to let in the wet desert smell, and he watched the sheer curtains billow, then looked at her lying naked beside him, the moon shining on her curves. She looked so vulnerable. He wanted to cover her with his body, protect her. Somehow that would make him safe, too.

Bizarre.

It might just be the sex, of course. He looked at her soft mouth, those lips that gave and took. Buried to the hilt in her body had been heaven.

It would be nice to come home to a dinner with her. He'd help her cook. They'd be a team in the kitchen, the way they'd been at Minetti's shop. Idle sure loved her and her wild cat seemed okay with him. Animals had instincts, didn't they?

In the morning, he slipped away quietly to head home to let Idle out to pee, then bring him back. He left her a note.

When he returned, Chloe was in the kitchen wearing a tank top and very short shorts. The air was filled with scents of sugar and garlic and fruit and he buried his nose in her tender neck and breathed it all in. Yeah, heaven.

She turned to smile at him, then bent to pet Idle.

"What are you making us?" He held her while she poured batter into a large pan.

"Blueberry crepes and shrimp-and-feta omelets."

"Yum." If his entire body could salivate, it would be doing so right now.

"After we eat, what will we do?" she asked.

"Go back to bed," he muttered into her neck.

She laughed. "Something with our clothes on. Read the paper? Take Idle for a walk? Then—"

"Go back to bed?" he asked hopefully.

"The idea is to do something ordinary."

"That's not sex. Not with you anyway." He couldn't stop wanting more. "We could talk, I guess." Talk? Was he crazy? He hated chitchat. "Go for a drive? Shoot some hoops?" No. Something *she* liked. "Shopping?" God, he'd lost it completely. "Whatever you feel like doing, Chloe." *Please, God, don't make it shopping.*

"That sounds so lovely," she said leaning back, letting him rock her. Hell, maybe she could make shopping fun. She turned to look at him. "This doesn't feel quite real, does it?"

"No." And he wasn't himself. He'd offered to *chat* and *shop.*

"Let's just see how it goes," she said again, more faintly. They pondered that in silence while Chloe finished cooking.

The food was delicious and he tucked into it, enjoying

every bite until he noticed she was watching him, resting her chin in her palm.

He stopped midbite. "What?"

"I was just wondering…"

"About what?" He doubted he'd like her answer.

"Do you ever see your mother?"

He cringed. She was about to do more poking around in his past. He'd keep it brief. "I visited once before she got straight. We didn't know what to say to each other." She'd acted angry, as if she was sorry he'd reminded her he existed. Except when he went to the bathroom, he noticed an open box of photos on her bureau—tattered family shots covered with finger marks. She cared about her memories, at least.

"And after she got straight? Did you try again?"

"Is this how it's going to be? Twenty questions all the time?" He tried to make a joke out of his discomfort.

"I want to get to know you, Riley."

"Okay. Sure." He sighed. Get it over with. "When I graduated from the Academy, I went to see her, yeah."

"She must have been proud of you—taking after your dad."

"She didn't seem that glad about it." She'd said more that he'd found troubling. *I don't know why I fell apart when your dad died. It was the idea of a husband I missed. He was never there for me.* He didn't dare tell Chloe that. She'd never let up on him.

"Did she ever talk about her addiction?"

"She apologized. She said Dad's death was just her excuse. Addicts can always find excuses, she told me."

"Did you ever worry about addiction for yourself?"

"Not really. I don't even like to take aspirin. How about you?"

"I tested myself in high school. I got so sick on lemon schnapps I still can't stand the smell of lemonade."

"You gave yourself a test? That sounds like you—head down, push forward, get it done."

"I hope that's a compliment."

"It is. You're remarkable. Brave…and smart…and stubborn. And nosy as hell."

She laughed and something warm shifted inside him. Then she ruined it. "Is your mother in town? So you can talk to her?"

"She's here, yeah. She knows how to reach me."

"Are you angry with her?"

"No. Who knows? It doesn't matter." She was getting on his nerves now.

"Sure it does. You should talk to her. Work it out."

"Why drag her over the coals again?" The thought made his gut churn. "It's over and done. Why make a big deal of it?"

"So you can replace the bad feelings with good ones. To give you both a fresh start at a relationship."

Like a little chat would change either of them. Chloe's phone rang before he had to point that out.

"It's my sister," she said, looking at the readout. "I should take this. I owe her a call." She rose from the table.

"No problem. I'll keep eating." He was relieved to escape interrogation.

She left the room and he served himself seconds, then looked up to see Mickey standing in the doorway. "Detective Connelly," he said. "Over for breakfast?"

"Uh, yeah." At least he had gone home and come back. Riley stood, scraping his chair. "Call me Riley. Please." He motioned at a chair. "Can I get you some breakfast?" He was going to serve the man in his own house?

"I'm fine," Mickey said, pouring himself coffee, then sitting. He gave Riley the hard look of a father not happy with his daughter's date.

"I should update you on the case," he said. Anything to avoid declaring his intentions—not that he was certain about them yet. "We have reason to believe Sal's running stolen cars through his shop. Did he ever indicate as much to you?"

"No," he said. "Sal didn't talk much to me."

"But you did call him and suggest he ask me to drive the special jobs?"

"I called him." The man shrugged. "You don't push Sal."

"Do as much as you can, that's all we're asking."

"I am." There was an edge to his voice. Mickey held his gaze. "You're looking out for her over there, aren't you? Because I don't want her in harm's way."

"Of course. Yes."

"Good." He relaxed a little. "I would do anything for Chloe. She wants cooking school, she'll get cooking school."

"That's admirable."

The man caught the hesitation in his tone and his expression went hard. "You think I'm an asshole and a bad father, but life's not so simple. When you're young, you think life works a certain way, but it doesn't. Not for some of us."

"I know that," he said, but he didn't buy the excuse. The guy had had a wife and kids counting on him.

"Chloe's been there for me, thick or thin," Mickey said. "She's a good person."

"I know that." And she was way too forgiving.

"She gives you the benefit of the doubt even when you don't deserve it." Riley was startled to realize the man meant Riley, not himself. "She'll put up with a hell of a lot. Don't put her through any of it." His eyes were fierce, his tone hoarse with emotion. The guy loved his daughter, even if he'd leaned on her instead of supporting her.

"I don't intend to hurt her, Mickey." But a voice in his head spoke the truth. *You will anyway. Just being who you are.*

"I want you to know that what I do, I do for her, to get her dream for her," Mickey said.

"What are you saying?"

"Just remember that."

What the hell did he mean? Before Riley could probe, his phone rang. Private number, so he answered it. Mickey left the table and the room.

It was Special Agent London. "I've got the report on the docs Ms. Baxter sent us," he said, sounding angry. "It's garbage. Nothing. Bills, receipts, meaningless paper. That spreadsheet with the names and amounts? It's sports memorabilia sales. Looks like Enzo Sylvestri's selling baseball cards online. He's got a goddamn store on eBay."

"Shit. That's it?" *That's what he'd locked away?* "What took so long to get it analyzed?" he said to put London on defense.

"We've got a logjam, Connelly. And she swamped us with paper. I think she's covering for the guy, playing a little shell game to keep us away from what's really going on."

"No," he said, automatically defending her. "She's doing everything she can. She risked her life for the case last night." He explained the details of what had happened at Sal's, then urged London to put a rush on the surveillance request, but his mind raced the entire time with what he hadn't pointed out.

Chloe would do all she could to get Sal arrested, but she thought Enzo was pure as snow. Would she pull her punches, hide things from him? He didn't want to believe that of her, but his judgment was completely colored by their time together.

He'd just hung up from his lieutenant when Chloe returned to the kitchen. "My sister's husband lost his job and she's worried," she explained to him. "I want to help, but—" She stopped, having read his face. "What's wrong, Riley?"

"I just talked to London. That printout you found in Enzo's office? Names and dollars? Turns out Enzo's selling sports crap online. Baseball cards and whatnot."

"You're kidding!" She laughed. "That's so funny. I should have figured it out. He showed me this glass case he was selling for two thousand dollars and told me to not tell Natalie. That's why he'd locked it in the drawer." She laughed again.

He watched her. She seemed honestly relieved, which meant she'd been worried they might find something among the papers she sent. That was a good sign.

"There wasn't anything else, right?" she asked.

"Nothing from what you sent, no," he said slowly, but she was too excited to notice his hesitation.

"Of course not. We're proving Enzo innocent and that's good. I have to admit that with all your suspicions, you made me doubt Enzo a tiny bit. In fact…" She took a breath, then winced. "There is one conversation I overheard I should tell you about. Enzo took a call in the laundry room and I heard it through the pantry wall."

"The laundry room?"

"It was someone named Mario. A shipment was supposed to come, but it's late. He seemed upset, but I was sure it was just the restaurant and—"

"Tell me exactly what he said, Chloe," he said levelly.

His tone caught her short, he could tell. She repeated the conversation she'd heard and Riley's suspicions spiked higher.

"He didn't say when the shipment would arrive?"

"No, but I'm sure it's just—"

"You didn't get Mario's last name?"

"No."

"It could be Mario Canzo, though I think he's still in prison…." He leveled his gaze at her. "When exactly did this conversation take place?"

"The first day, I guess."

"And you're telling me now? I told you I needed important information as soon as possible."

"I didn't think it was a big deal." But she was avoiding his eyes. She'd had doubts, all right.

"We need all the facts, Chloe, not just the ones you like."

"I'm sorry, okay? This is a lot to handle. I'm doing my best." She was getting ready to bristle and he needed to keep her calm.

"I realize that," he said. "I know this is difficult for you. You did great with Sal. You saved my ass. But you're reporting on Enzo, too."

"I know. I gave you a lot already. I'll go through the office again if you want."

And provide more worthless receipts and meaningless invoices? He hated doubting her. "Do that. And if you hear anything more about this shipment, let me know instantly."

"Like I said—"

"Even if you think it's nothing. Let us decide that." He tried to smile, to act like it was no big deal, but he felt punched in the gut by the truth.

Chloe had withheld information to protect Enzo. Maybe unconsciously. She'd been a reluctant informant from the beginning and he knew that. She would protect the people she loved. That put her at war with her integrity. How had he let himself forget? The nights with her had clouded his judgment.

"I should get to the station. I need to write up my report." What he needed was time away from her to think straight.

"Sure." She sighed. "So much for our ordinary morning."

"That wasn't realistic." How could things between them ever be ordinary? They were together because of the case, and being together had compromised his performance. This had to stop.

AT FOUR THAT AFTERNOON, Chloe unwrapped the perfect pork loin she would cook for Enzo's dinner, grateful to occupy her mind with preparations for his birthday.

After her morning with Riley went sour, she'd gone early to the Sylvestris', seizing the chance to search Enzo's office while Natalie had him out shopping for his birthday gift.

His computer was on, so she'd copied his e-mail and document folders onto the key drive, telling herself it was for the greater good. For extra measure, she photographed all the papers on the topmost layers of the mess on the desk.

The truth was Riley didn't trust her. Maybe he was right. She should have reported the conversation the first day, but she'd hesitated, doubting Enzo, which made her ill. She just wanted to be done with this.

After she'd finished that nasty duty, she'd busied herself with the party. Making the pasta for the gnocchi, mixing up the spicy tomato sauce—Enzo's nonna's recipe—and assembling dessert—her twist on Enzo's beloved canolis: chocolate-filled towers made of a delicate vanilla-bean crust.

She was stuffing the loin when Enzo walked in with the mail just as Charity took a protein drink from the fridge.

"Dammit, Charity," Enzo said, waving a piece of paper at her. "On my birthday you get a C in physics?"

"It's just a midterm," she said defensively. "The teacher's a jerk—only one test and half of it he didn't cover."

"How can you shrug? A C is a disgrace for a girl so smart."

Chloe cleared her throat.

Enzo glanced over and she made a neck-cutting gesture, hoping her intervention wouldn't make things worse.

"What?" he snapped, then caught himself and took a deep breath before he turned to his daughter. "You're *acting* like it don't matter, but it really does, right? You feel…bad?"

Charity looked startled by her father's insight. "I dunno. Maybe." She seemed to fear this was a trick.

Chloe watched Enzo wrestle with his impulse to bark, to accuse, to vent.

"Do you have a plan for fixing this?" Chloe asked Charity, nodding at her, urging her to resist the snotty remark that was no doubt bubbling in her brain.

Charity nodded slowly, getting it. "Yeah." She turned to her father. "I'll fix it by the end of the semester. You happy?"

Enzo opened his mouth to snap, then spoke through gritted teeth. "I'll pretend you meant that and say, yes, I'm happy."

"Good." Charity waltzed out of the room as if she'd won.

Enzo banged his fist on the table. "Now how did that help?"

"She has pride, so she can't fold completely. She feels bad, you can see that. You showed her you can hold your temper."

"I don't know, Chloe. I need a drink."

"Miracles don't happen overnight. Trust takes time." She couldn't believe she was quoting Riley.

"She has until the end of the semester," he groused.

"I just talked to Charity!" Natalie beamed from the doorway. "So we *can* teach an old dog new tricks, huh, Enzo?"

"I'm not that old," he protested as she came close to him.

"And you still have tricks." She put her arm around him and rocked him toward her. He smiled grumpily.

It was a start, Chloe thought, glad she could help, but doubting her coaching would make up for her betrayal with the Sylvestris. Maybe when the material she'd sent and the late shipment turned out to be nothing, they would stop pestering Enzo. Maybe Chloe's role would never come out.

She longed to simply enjoy her work here, designing meals that matched the mood and dietary needs of each family member, but still had her flair.

Getting ready for the party had been fun. She'd decorated the rec room and dining room with Mylar balloons and flowers and set up the traditional family fishing game in the alcove. Everyone would dangle a toy fishing pole over a cardboard barrier where Natalie would clip on a gift—toys for the kids, gag gifts for adults.

Chloe had set the meat under the broiler to give it a nice crust when she remembered she hadn't separated the kid gifts from the adult gags to make it easy for Natalie. She swept into the rec room and ducked behind the barrier in the alcove to complete the quick task.

She was about to rush back to rescue the pork, when she heard Enzo and Sal enter the room, talking intently.

Instinctively, she ducked down. She'd promised Riley she'd report everything. She held still, her heart beating so loud she feared they could hear it.

"So how are things at the shop?" Enzo asked.

"We're doing okay. Busy." *With stolen cars,* though he'd never admit that to Enzo.

"You keeping better books? The IRS watches us like hawks. We have to be above reproach." Her heart lifted. Enzo was obviously a solid citizen.

"Sure. Sure."

"You *say* sure, but you don't *do* sure."

"What does that mean?"

"You watching over my Ronnie?"

"When I can. He's a teenager."

"What's he up to?" His voice was serious. "I need to know."

"He waves money around, shows off for his friends, the usual."

"What kind of money? And where'd he get it?"

"I fronted him some. Maybe a couple grand."

"A couple grand? For what?"

"He's hosting a party at a hotel for some dance. Renting a suite, buying booze."

"Booze. God. He tell you all this?"

"Some of it, yeah."

"You're supposed to be watching out for him, Sal."

"I'm doing what I can, okay? Don't get neurotic. You're the bow, not the arrow, Enzo."

"What the hell does that mean?"

"It means you send him off, but it's his life to live."

"That's some wise shit you're shoveling. You get lessons from Chloe?" Enzo's tone had lightened. He'd set aside his worry, but too soon, Chloe thought. Natalie was right about her husband—he tended to see what he wanted to see.

"She's pretty hot," Sal said in that creepy tone he thought was sexy. "I'd like some lessons, all right."

"Watch it. She's taken."

"Yeah. And what's with that guy? Riley. I don't like him."

"He drives me where I need to go. Shows up on time. Chloe likes him."

"Something about him ain't right."

Enzo didn't respond. She imagined he'd shrugged. When he spoke again, his voice was low. "I've been meaning to ask you. You know that merchandise you brought out? From your guy in L.A.? I got a golf buddy could use any spare you have."

Chloe's heart stopped. What was Enzo asking for on behalf of his friend? Please let it be legitimate, not drugs.

"I can fix you up, sure. I mean your *buddy*. Tonight."

"That's good. How much I owe you?"

"Forget it. It's a gift. Happy birthday, Enzo."

"Thanks, Sal. I appreciate that." She heard Enzo leave the room, then Sal's phone rang. Damn. *Please leave, please leave.* The meat had to get pulled or it would dry to leather and here she was, trapped in the alcove on her hands and knees.

"Yeah?" Sal said to his caller. "What do you mean you need more? You haven't paid me for the last batch. I just told your pop I'd keep you out of trouble." He listened. "No more up front... It's none of your business how much I've got... Yeah, yeah, okay. I'll see if I can rotate some inventory, but that's it."

She felt sick at what she'd heard. Sal was talking to Ronnie about a batch of something she doubted was cookies. And had Enzo asked for drugs? Her heart sank and sank.

The sour smell coming from the kitchen told her she might be too late for the pork already. The leather sofa gave a squeaky whoosh. Sal must have sat down. If she crawled behind the couch without a sound, she could escape.

She made it around the corner, only to run into a pair of legs. Riley, she saw when she looked up. He helped her to her feet. She saw he'd pulled out the pork loin, which was ruined completely. "I smelled smoke," he explained.

"I was eavesdropping and got trapped," she whispered.

"Hear anything good?"

She explained the conversation Sal had had with Ronnie and decided at the last minute not to mention the request Enzo had made. It was for a friend, anyway, she hoped. At the party, she'd keep an eye out, just the same.

"And no clue when this will go down?"

"Not that I heard." She looked down at the spoiled meat. "What am I going to do? This is Enzo's favorite dish." She'd ruined Enzo's birthday dinner by spying on him.

"What meat you got?" Riley opened the freezer, then pulled out a butcher-wrapped pack of beef ribs.

"They're frozen." She couldn't think past her screwup.

"So we boil them. I have a great recipe from this Kansas City joint where my uncle ate on his cross-country trips."

"Barbecue? How would we…?" She fought to focus, locking onto Riley's warm eyes. He was offering her a way out. "Okay. We grill the ribs, but they have to taste Italian. I can rescue some sauce from the pork. We add your barbecue ingredients for zing and sweetness." Natalie expected her to add her own touches, right?

"Sounds like a plan," Riley said.

"Thanks," she breathed, back on her feet again, ready to make this work. Before long, the ribs were boiled and she walked Riley out to the huge outdoor grill, complete with tile counters and a row of cupboards. "You handle the grill and I'll finish up the side dishes."

"So you're both cooking?" Natalie asked, walking over with a happy smile. "And what's going on the grill?"

Chloe took a deep breath. "Listen, Natalie, I spoiled the pork loin. I'm so sorry. I lost track of time. But we're substituting ribs with a terrific sauce I think you'll like. Italian flavors with a Kansas City zing from Riley."

"Ribs, huh? Let's see what you got." She stuck a finger in the sauce. "Mmm. Wow. This is too good *not* to be Italian."

"I'll pay for the meat I ruined," Chloe said.

"Forget that. What did you tell me? Anyone can burn something if they leave it on too long. You're human." She looked over at Riley. "I know just what you need."

She leaned down to open a cupboard and lifted out a "Kiss the Cook" barbecue apron and a chef's hat, which she plopped onto Riley's head. "Enzo never uses these."

"Thanks," Riley said, tying on the apron.

"Looks good," Natalie said. "The family that cooks together stays together. Enzo says you're doing a good job. He says you're on time and you stick like glue."

"I do my best."

She leaned in. "He goes to a doctor, let me know, okay? He thinks he has to be Iron Man, keeping it all inside. His blood pressure's through the roof." Her gaze veered to where Enzo was playing croquet with his niece's children on his putting green.

"I love that man," Natalie said on a sigh. "Those kids are tearing the hell out of that putting green—it cost a fortune. Special soil, special grass, insane—but does he care? Not one bit. It's for family."

"That's just Enzo," Chloe said, shooting Riley a look.

Natalie went off to talk to people and Chloe headed back to the kitchen to finish the food. Between turns of the ribs, Riley helped. He was the perfect sous chef, plating the courses as fast and beautifully as a professional. When everyone had been served, Natalie insisted they both appear in the dining room.

Everyone cheered.

"How did you know ribs are my favorite?" Enzo asked.

"Hey," Natalie said, "you always say it's Nonna's pork."

"If I said different, Nonna would have plucked out my eyes with her scallop knife." Enzo paused for the laugh, then stood and lifted his wineglass. "A toast. To the chefs! For a perfect birthday meal with my favorite dish. Pure genius!"

Everyone lifted glasses and drank to them. Chloe couldn't help smiling at Riley. They'd been a great team. In the kitchen anyway.

Back in the kitchen, she poured them both glasses of water. They'd been sweating madly. "You saved me, Riley," she said, handing him a glass.

"I just found the ribs. You worked the magic."

"We did it together," she said. "To us." She lifted her glass in a playful toast.

"To closing the case," Riley replied soberly, clicking her glass. Things had changed between them, and she felt a stab of pain. They would never get past the case to each other's arms.

Maybe that was for the best, but *still...*

13

WITH THE MEAL FINISHED and more guests having arrived, the party was in full swing when Riley noticed Enzo disappearing from the room with an unknown man. He followed until he saw they were headed to the laundry room where Chloe had reported that earlier secret talk.

He slipped into the pantry to listen in, grateful the kitchen was empty, since Chloe and her assistants were passing hors d'oeuvres. He held his breath, listening hard.

"The delivery's on," the other man said. Was this Mario?

"When?" Enzo replied.

"Tuesday night. After midnight."

"Finally. After all this bullshit," Enzo said. "This deal makes me nervous."

"We knew this distributor might be trouble."

"You need me there?"

"Randy can let us in. I've got it, Enzo. Here on out, we work only with regulars. You get what you pay for."

Enzo growled in agreement.

It was bold to take delivery of contraband at Enzo's restaurant, though the place had plenty of storage, Riley knew, and it would be late at night.

Electricity blew through him. This was it. Time to move on Enzo and Sal. They had a date, place and time. It was all coming together, just as he'd suspected earlier that day.

First, he'd learned of two more "silent" burglaries—

another jewelry store and an electronics place—and both used Maximum Security as their alarm company.

Second, he'd figured Enzo was involved, based on what had happened that afternoon. He'd asked Riley to drop him off outside a downtown office building and pick him up two hours later instead of waiting for him.

Riley had idled down the block to see what Enzo was up to. Sure enough, the guy walked to the next corner, crossed the street and ducked into a building—Franklin Medical Plaza.

Riley had double-parked and reached the lobby in time to see the elevator door close on Enzo and one other man. The lights showed stops at levels four and six. According to the directory, the fourth floor held mostly medical offices with a few businesses. Level six was the jackpot. Maximum Security had an office on that floor.

There were no coincidences, Riley knew, and for all his retired-guy style, Enzo did nothing by accident.

Now, shuffling feet told Riley the men were leaving the laundry room, so he backed from the pantry, grabbing a paring knife from a kitchen wood-block to pretend that was what he'd been after.

At his next break, he slipped out to call in a request for warrants and a tactical team for Tuesday night's delivery. He caught his lieutenant at home, pleased by the response he got. Riley was to be available for a briefing as soon as the team had been arranged.

Adrenaline poured through him. They were closing in on Sylvestri. Minetti, too, he hoped. It was tough to calmly fill highball glasses with pricey booze for Enzo's guests when his mind was racing with next steps.

Chloe's light laugh made him look up. There she was, dancing from group to group, smiling as each person selected something from her tray. She had assistants to pass the food, but he knew she loved watching people enjoy what she'd made.

She reached the group where Enzo's wife stood. Natalie put her arm around Chloe's waist and said something to the group that made Chloe blush. He felt a stab of pity for both women. Natalie seemed sincere enough, but just like Chloe she'd closed her eyes, accepted the false front Enzo put up to hide his crimes. No way had the man retired and Riley was days away from proving it.

Chloe moved on and held out her tray to more people, her eyes bright, a happy smile on her face.

Damn, his hand hurt. What the—? He looked down and saw he'd gripped a glass so tight he could shatter it.

He put it down. He'd have to tell her tonight about the bust. She'd need to brace herself and tune in to any details about the delivery that Enzo might discuss around her.

She caught him watching her. He motioned her over.

"Hey, Riley," she said softly.

"How about we touch base after we're done here? My place?"

"Your place?" She steadied her gaze on his face.

"Yeah. You'll finish before me, so take my key." He took it from his key chain and held it out.

She ignored the key, her eyes glued to his. "What are you saying?" She wanted to know if this meant something about them being together. Did she sound hopeful?

"It's about the case," he said flatly.

"Oh," she said, getting it, her expression dimming. "It can't wait for tomorrow? I'm beat."

"No. It can't."

"All right," she said with a sigh and took his key.

"I'll see you," he said, wishing he had some way to cheer her. Maybe when this was over… What a fool he was. Chloe got to him. She made him want to be part of something bigger than just him and his dog. Despite all evidence to the contrary, he hoped that whatever was between them wasn't over.

Hell, he *had* been watching too much TV.

THE PARTY WAS WINDING DOWN and Chloe was in the pantry grabbing a trash bag when she heard Enzo's voice through the wall and stopped dead. He was in the laundry room again, like the day of the secret phone call. She froze, listening hard.

"You got it?" Enzo asked.

"Right here." The other man was Sal and her heart sank. This was the exchange they'd discussed earlier. "I'd be glad to deal direct with your friends," Sal said. "Save you time."

"They'd rather stay anonymous."

"They're embarrassed? Why? Young guys go for the blue, too. More bang for your bang. I could go all night and hammer nails in the morning. Try it yourself, you'll see."

"With my blood pressure, my doc says no. I mean he *would* say no, if I needed it, which I don't." He laughed awkwardly and she heard plastic rattle as he must have accepted the package.

"You change your mind, let me know," Sal said.

Chloe wanted to laugh with relief. *The blue* had to be Viagra. Enzo's doctor must have nixed a prescription, so he'd gone to Sal. That was hardly major crime. Thank God. A spurt of shame burned through her that she'd doubted Enzo again.

She would be so glad when the suspicions and doubts were out of her life. She couldn't wait to tell Riley I told you so. This was just like the innocent sports memorabilia list. What was so urgent he had to talk to her tonight?

When he'd asked her to his house, she'd thought it was to try again. She felt like an idiot thinking that. Worse, for wanting it. She only hoped he hadn't noticed.

When she'd finished up the kitchen, she left her assistants to manage the last of the trash and headed out. Riley seemed to be waiting for the last drinkers to empty their glasses.

At Riley's place, Idle greeted her wildly and she bent to hug him. She loved this dog. If only things were different, she could see him and Riley every day. She'd love that. She'd make big lovely meals and they'd make big, lovely love….

Stop. She was overtired. She rested her head on the arm of the sofa and let her lids fall closed. Much better.

She woke with a start to someone banging on the door. She'd fallen asleep. She staggered up, struggling to think through the fog, and opened the door to Riley.

"You okay?" Riley asked.

"I fell asleep." She ran her fingers through her hair, backing up to the sofa, where she sat.

"Sorry it's so late," he said, sitting beside her. "Natalie finally called a cab for the last two clowns."

"It was a good party," she said with a yawn.

"Your food was sure a hit."

"Yeah." She wished that was all she had to think about—how happy everyone had been, how she could make each dish slightly better next time. But that wasn't possible and that irritated her. She decided to start with her news. "I've got a hot tip for you on Enzo," she said, leaning in conspiratorially.

"Yeah?" he said, taking the bait.

"He sneaked into the laundry room to make a big drug buy from Sal." She widened her eyes to build suspense.

"Yeah?"

"And the drug was…Viagra! Yes. It's true." She filled him in on what had happened. "The only trouble Enzo's in is with his organ. Poor guy. I hope he's not risking his heart. Natalie wouldn't want that."

But Riley wasn't smiling and he was way too quiet. Her stomach flipped. "What's the matter?"

"Enzo's in real trouble, Chloe."

"What are you talking about?"

"The delivery's Tuesday night at midnight at the restaurant. We're bringing in a tactical team to search the truck and make arrests."

"No. You can't be. The shipment could be anything. Lobster or Kobe beef or, hell, new furniture. Enzo wants to redecorate."

"At midnight? Hardly. We have other evidence."

"Like what? Something from the computer?"

"Enzo visited the security company we suspect is involved with the burglaries. There have been two similar heists."

"So maybe Enzo wants a new alarm system."

"This is it, Chloe. We're moving on this."

"You're just dying to ruin that family, aren't you?" she said, furious at his evident excitement. "The best you can scrape up is he has a late-night delivery and he visited a security company?"

"I wanted to prepare you." He seemed to think he was telling her the truth for her own good. "We need you to keep your eyes and ears open until Tuesday. You'll be working at the restaurant this weekend, right? If anything related to this comes up, let me know."

"How can you prepare me for this travesty? You've seen the family. You know how much Enzo cares. This is insane." She spoke too loudly.

"Calm down, Chloe."

"Don't tell me how to feel."

"Enzo won't be there, if that makes you feel better. We'll handle his arrest quietly, to avoid upsetting his family any more than is necessary."

"You think that makes me feel better?"

"I'm sorry that people you care about are up to no good, but there's nothing I can do about that."

"There's plenty you can do. Call off this sting or bust or whatever it is. Investigate more. Let *me* investigate more."

"It's happening, Chloe." He was so stubborn. And so wrong. *And she was going to prove it.* The idea burst open in her mind, warm and true. She had four days and two shifts at Enzo's to find out what was in that shipment. She'd be careful not to blow her cover or alert Sal, but somehow she'd prove Enzo innocent once and for all.

"Consider me prepared then. If we're done, I'll be going." She stood, eager to get away from this man and his black views.

He stood, too. "I wish I were wrong. For your sake."

"No, you don't. You're dying to be right. Why do I keep forgetting that about you?"

Still. Even as she slammed Riley's door and marched down his walk, she felt a tiny flame of hope, fierce as her birthday candles, that if she proved Enzo innocent, Riley would see that people deserved his trust. It wouldn't happen overnight, of course. Change took time and patience. But she had plenty of both. Maybe that was all she needed.

MONDAY MORNING, the tactical team briefing made Riley late to the Sylvestris'. He wasn't needed until ten, so he hoped Enzo wouldn't notice his tardiness.

Part of him couldn't wait to nail the guy. The rest dreaded what it would do to Chloe. He hated being torn. It made his head hurt. His life had been simple before he met her.

He was polishing the car when he heard Chloe call his name. He looked up and saw her running toward him from the patio, grinning. Something good had happened. He loved her smile.

When she reached him, she checked to be certain they were unobserved, then thrust a piece of paper at him like a weapon. "It's liquor. Here's the shipping invoice. Completely, utterly legal. No drugs, no jewels, just alcohol."

He looked down. It was a copy of an invoice from Quality Distributors that listed liquor brands, quantities and prices. The delivery date had been stamped for Tuesday. "How did you get this?" he asked, as the implications filtered through him.

"Last night at Enzo's, I noticed the bartender opening up a case of liquor from Costco and I asked him why they'd bought from there. He said they'd run low because of some deal Enzo was after. 'Him and his closeout bargains.' That's what he said."

"Okay. Go on."

"So I asked him what he meant and he said Enzo arranged

for a truckload from a warehouse liquidation and when it didn't come, they thought it was a scam. They did fill-in orders from Costco and discount liquor stores because of that, except it's finally coming *tomorrow night late*. Randy's pissed because he has to wait for the truck."

"So, how'd you get this?" He waved the paper.

"I knew you wouldn't take my word for anything, so I pretended I needed my time card and searched the office. I found the invoice and made a copy."

He looked it over again. "We'll have to check this out," he said grimly. "Make sure the shipping numbers are legit." Disappointment burned through him.

"You were wrong about Enzo!" she said, her eyes hot. "You were sending a SWAT team to break up a legal business deal."

"The liquor could be stolen, the numbers fake. It happens."

"Come on. The only thing Enzo is guilty of is trying to save money on booze. He's always looking for deals. This makes complete sense. Admit you're wrong."

"If this pans out, if the company verifies it, we'll call off the bust." Damn. "It's good you looked into it, Chloe," he said, knowing it was true, though he hated hitting another dead end. "If you're right, you've saved police resources and preserved our cover so we can keep up the investigation."

"Give up on Enzo, Riley. Sal's the criminal. Accept that."

"Maybe I jumped too soon. We'll see."

"You'll see? The proof's here." She slapped the paper.

"Like I said, we'll check it out."

"You *still* suspect him?" She looked so hurt and so angry, he wanted fix it, but she was right. He did still suspect Sylvestri. "I don't believe it. You are so… I give up." With a disgusted noise, she spun and stomped back to the house.

He reported what he'd learned and his lieutenant called off the operation, but agreed to put two officers in unmarked cars to observe the delivery, just in case. Since the FBI still hadn't okayed surveillance, the patrol from Sal's shop was assigned the duty. Not enough budget to run two patrols. Riley hoped to hell Tuesday wasn't Chop Shop Night at Minetti's Auto Haven because the place would be wide open and unprotected.

TUESDAY NIGHT AFTER WORK, Chloe headed home, still angry at Riley. She'd been right about the delivery, but he *still* suspected Enzo. She'd never forgive him. Since she'd showed him the shipping notice, they'd barely spoken and every word they did exchange bore thorns.

The evening stretched long before her. She wasn't up for questions from her father, so she stopped at the pet store—she'd called earlier in the day and he'd mentioned they were running low on cat food. She wanted to nab some tempting cat toys. Only Idle and Riley seemed able to entice Pepper Spray into the open.

She lingered in the store, giving her father time to go to bed, checking out every toy, finally settling on a felt snake and a tiny fishing pole with a feather for bait. By the time she pulled onto her street, it was nearly nine.

She was startled to see her father climb into his car, which he always parked on the street, no air cast, no crutches. Where was he going this late? And driving, no less. His usual AA meeting was at seven. The cross-town meeting with his sponsor maybe? Surely he wasn't drinking. No.

Something was wrong; she knew by the prickling of her skin. She'd sensed it before, but ignored it. The way her father avoided her gaze. The driving marks on his cast. That strange late-night AA meeting. She'd been so caught up with Riley, she'd pushed it out of her mind. Had there been another robbery that night? Was her father driving again for Sal?

She found herself following him, her heart in her throat, her palms sliding on the wheel from nervous sweat. This was sneaky. Didn't she trust him? She was assuming the worst like Riley did. She hated that. She had to know where her dad was going. And if it was something bad, she had to stop him.

In case she needed help, she felt for her cell phone, which she kept in her pants pocket during work. Her right pocket held the minirecorder, so she fished her phone out of the left one. Flipping it open, she saw two bars of charge. Enough for a few calls anyway.

Maybe she was wrong. She'd follow her father to a meeting across town and feel like a fool. So what? She'd rather waste gas than lose her father to crime. She kept her eyes on the tail-lights of her father's ancient Cadillac and hoped for the best.

As her father reached central Phoenix, then headed south, Chloe's spirits began to sink. He was going to Sal's shop.

She could make him pull over, stop him now….

We watch, we wait, we see what develops. That's what Riley had said. She would watch and wait, and maybe find exactly the evidence she needed against Sal. For all she knew, her father might be doing exactly that.

At the shop, Carlo opened the gate for her father. Chloe parked a block away and scampered in the dark to the gap in the fence Riley had slipped through. A wire caught her arm and she felt a stab and a scrape. Riley had suffered the same injury. Looking down at the oozing blood, reality hit her. She could be in big trouble. If she were caught, she could be killed.

Sal was a flirt, but when it came to business, she had no doubt he would be ruthless. Her earlier bravado was nowhere now.

Her heart pounding, she crouched down, suddenly afraid of where her impulse had led her. This was no game. Things could go very, very wrong. Her body shook and she felt icy cold, though the air was warm with spring.

She looked around. The streets were deserted except for her car and a parked pickup. No people, no lights. Just beat-up warehouses, rusty tracks and a vacant lot filled with trash, abandoned tires, shopping carts and weeds.

Weren't there supposed to be cops watching this place? Probably too busy tailing Enzo. Dammit, Riley. His precious bust had been called off. He should be watching the real bad guy.

She would just do his job for him. She had to know what her father was up to before she called for help. She was here. She had to act.

Determined now, she slid forward as soundlessly as she could, navigating the dips and mounds and clumps of weeds in the uneven ground in the dark.

She knew she had to get close—listening to her father and Sal at the Sylvestri garage had taught her that. She aimed for three steel drums right outside the shop door, angled so she could see inside, but not be seen. The garage door was up, the lights on, so anyone inside would have trouble seeing her.

After agonizing seconds, she crouched in the oily grass between the rusty barrels and watched her father, hunched as if against cold or misery, walk beside Carlo toward the garage, where Sal used a wrench on something under the hood of that white truck, Thrasher gnawing a bone at his feet. Leo sat at the bench, his back to her, and seemed to be ripping off tape.

Why was Sal working on a car this late?

Then he pulled up a piece of metal from the engine revealing a space from which he lifted a duct-taped plastic bundle, which he carried out to meet her father and Carlo.

"Right on time," Sal said to her father, holding out the bundle. "Party's waiting."

She should record this, she realized. From this distance, the sound might be faint, but it was worth a try. She felt for the buttons in her pocket, then pushed, just as Thrasher barked and ran to sniff at her father, tail wagging.

Her father stared at Sal. "I won't do it," he said firmly. "Not this time. Not with kids."

The package held drugs, she just knew. Illegal drugs. A chill ran from her neck to her nearly numb toes. Worse, her father must have been driving for Sal all along.

"You made a deal with me, Mickey," Sal said, hefting the parcel. "I keep you out of the thefts, pay you, and you drive whatever I need delivered. No questions asked."

"Not this, Sal. Plus, it's Ronnie. I won't do that to Enzo."

"Enzo will never know, Mickey. Ronnie's the supplier, not the user. He's old enough to make his own decisions. Take this to the party and be happy. No victims. Everyone gets what they want. We all win. Even you."

Her father shook his head. "I don't care what you do to me. Enough is enough." He turned for his car, walking stiff-legged, scared, she'd bet, but determined. She felt a surge of pride beneath her shock and horror, watching as he drove off, kicking dust as he went.

He wanted the money for her schooling, she was sure. He'd been so wrong. Would his quitting count with the FBI or the D.A.? Could she argue he was seeking proof against Sal?

"What are we gonna do about him?" Carlo asked Sal.

"Got any ideas?" Sal asked wearily.

"I could go after him. Take care of him."

Sal made a disgusted sound, then looked skyward, holding out his hands. "Why am I surrounded by wing nuts and retards?"

He looked back at Carlo. "On the street? What about witnesses? You gotta use this." He poked at his own temple. "Think. Work out details. Cover your ass."

Carlo hung his head.

"Deliver the goods," Sal snapped, thrusting the plastic bag at Carlo. "Grand Avenue near the tracks. That boarded-up bar. The Velvet Glove. Three taps on the service door, then whistle. Count the cash. Ronnie's a sneak. He'll try to short you because he's family, but cut no slack. No cash, no carry. They expect you in forty-five. Be careful. I've got places to be."

Seconds later, Sal roared away in his Escalade. Thrasher watched him go, whining at Carlo and Leo's feet.

Her legs were cramping, so she shifted silently, fighting a groan. What now? She'd slip away and call Riley so he could catch Carlo with the drugs.

She stepped back a step, silent, silent. CLICK. The noise nearly stopped her heart. The recorder had reached the end of the reel. She looked toward Carlo and Leo, but they hadn't noticed. Whew.

Then she saw Thrasher at attention, ears pointed her way. He'd heard, all right. He gave a joyful bark and galloped toward her, the men watching him go.

Oh, God. If she ran, they'd spot her for sure, so she froze, hoping she could wave the dog away. No luck. Thrasher jumped on her, knocking her to the ground, barking cheerfully.

Terror burned through her. She was in real danger now. She had to talk her way out of this somehow.

"What the hell?" Leo said, standing above her. "You're Enzo's cook. What are you doing here?"

She pushed Thrasher off her and got to her feet. The truth was her only weapon. "I followed my father. I was worried about him." She took a backward step. "But I saw that he's fine, that he's working with Sal, so I'll let you get back to it." She took another step backward, but Carlo grabbed her by the arm, his grip like a vice.

"I'll call Sal." Leo lifted his cell phone to his ear.

"Not yet," Carlo snapped. "Get the tape. We'll put her in the trunk. Sal thinks I can't think. I'm gonna think."

Leo returned with the duct tape. Chloe struggled until she got elbowed in the temple and her vision went black. Before long, she found herself in the trunk, hands and feet taped, mouth covered, her skin burning from the struggle.

When the lid came down, she was terrified she'd run out of air, but once her eyes adjusted to the dark, she saw light through holes here and there—the key, the taillights. She would at least be able to breathe.

"Now what?" Leo asked from somewhere near the trunk. "We can't drive all over with the bitch in there."

"I know, *ese*," Carlo said. "I'm thinking, like I said."

She held her breath, praying Carlo wouldn't drag her out and shoot her dead. What would Sal do? Would he believe she wouldn't say a word? To protect her father? That was a lot of trust for a limited man. If Sal was as evil as Riley believed, he'd kill her without hesitation.

She shuddered, tears filling her eyes.

She felt the car sink as one of them sat on the trunk. Soon she smelled cigarettes. With her fate in their hands, they'd taken a smoke break?

"Think faster," Leo said. "We gotta go. Just call Sal."

"He won't want anywhere near this. Never near the dirty work, not Sal."

She felt helpless. She groaned behind the tape on her mouth. Why hadn't she called Riley? He'd told her to be careful with Sal. *Good cops wore vests even in a Phoenix July.* She'd been stupid, stupid, stupid. So intent on helping her father she'd risked her own life. She felt herself slip into panic.

Save yourself. Or at least try. She could do something, couldn't she? Under her hip was a lump. A jack maybe? And she still had her cell phone. If she could get her hands in front, she could free her mouth and call for help.

She curled into a ball, hoping to pull her arms beneath her butt, but the space was too cramped. Clanking around might draw their attention. One of them still sat on the trunk, though they were quiet. Letting Carlo think, no doubt.

She decided to get the phone, at least, though she'd still have to get the tape off to talk. Shifting to the side, cramping her shoulders, she could just…barely…reach into her pocket. There, smooth metal… No. It was the damned minirecorder—the very device that had gotten her in this mess.

Leaving it out, she rolled for her other pocket and slid the phone into a slippery palm. Got it. Step one accomplished.

Now to free her mouth. How? What about the tool beneath her? She scooted deeper into the trunk until she could see the jack. Rubbing the tape against it, all she got was a scraped cheek. The tape didn't budge.

Then she noticed a bolt in the side of the trunk. Bending

at an impossible angle, she managed to hook the edge of metal under the tape and rip one side of the tape free. Whew. Step two achieved.

Now to call. With a jolt, she remembered how low the battery was. Whatever call she managed had to count.

"Okay, I got it." Carlo spoke and the trunk lifted. He'd stood up. She held her breath and fought to hear over her thudding heart. "We got her and her father to deal with, right?"

"Yeah. So?"

"So I figured how to do them and cover our asses. After we drop the package, we take her to her place. Mickey's there, right, so we help Mickey shoot her, then kill himself."

"Why would he kill his own kid? The cops won't buy it."

"Easy. They fight. She bitches him out. He's drunk. We pour booze down him so it looks good. And blam—gun goes off by accident. He freaks. How could he do it, kill his kid, blah, blah. Blam, he ends it all. Happens all the time on TV."

"Not bad," Leo said.

"Let's hit the buy," Carlo said. "I'll drive her car."

"Why are you…? Ah, *sí,* you *are* thinkin', hombre. We can't leave her car here. She drives it home. Sure."

She heard the rattle of keys. "Drive nice and easy," Carlo said. "Stop at all the lights. No speeding. We've got a body in the trunk."

She heard the two men high-five each other, then walk away, ready to implement their plan. Terror rolled through her in cold waves, chilling her to the bone. She had to get help before they reached her house. She had time while they dropped off the drugs. Trembling, she flipped open the phone and craned to see the numbers. She could barely make out the top, which showed one bar of signal and one bar of battery.

Could she figure the number by feel? Risky. Pressing Talk twice would ring the last person she'd talked to—her father. She'd called about the cat food. Good enough. He'd be home by now, she hoped. She'd warn him to get out of the house and send help. After that, she'd try for an operator. She wasn't sure she could manage 9-1-1. Maybe Riley's speed dial. Wasn't seven at the bottom of a column? But which one? Icy sweat sprang out all over her body. Do not panic. Be careful. Be right.

She found the top, odd-shaped button. Had to be Talk. She pressed it twice. Faintly, she heard ringing. She dropped the phone and rolled over so her mouth was close to the mouthpiece.

Please be there, Daddy. Please.

But she got voice mail. Her recorded voice cheerfully promised to call back as soon as possible. But would it be soon enough to save her?

She felt the driver-side door open and close and the engine start. Leo was driving her away. She left a message. "I'm leaving Sal's auto shop tied up in Carlo's trunk. It's a black Monte Carlo. I didn't see the license. They're driving to Velvet Gloves, a shut-down bar on Grand Avenue to deliver drugs, then they're taking me home. They want to shoot us. Get out, Daddy. Get help. Call 9-1-1, call Riley. Do it fast." She clicked End as the car sped up, having hit the street.

One more call. One more hope. Her life depended on the fragile bit of electrical power that remained. She hit the bottom number—zero for the operator. A mechanical voice told her the number was incorrect. She'd forgotten her pay-as-you-go cell didn't include operator assistance.

Riley next? What if she couldn't find the seven? What if he didn't answer? Nine-one-one would be certain. It was so hard to move her fingers and they were slippery with sweat. She pushed three numbers, then Talk, but she got the "incorrect number" recording. She tried again. Same thing.

She closed her eyes and tried to picture her keypad. Wait, was the pound sign by itself on a button? *Below* the nine. Yeah. She'd been hitting Pound instead of nine.

At last, she had it. A dispatcher answered immediately. "Nine-one-one, what is your emergency?"

"I'm in a trunk, being driven to—" She'd only gotten out the house number when the signal died. She pressed Talk twice, praying she had enough juice. Yes. When the dispatcher picked up, she shouted her address. Again it cut off, this time for good. The screen was black. Damn. She wasn't sure "Avenue" had gotten through. If the dispatcher guessed "Street," the police would be many blocks away. Even if the address had come through, she hadn't had time to explain about the drug delivery. What if the police were early and the house was empty? They'd figure it for a false alarm.

All she could do was hope her father caught her message in time and the police got it right. But lying there hoping wasn't enough. She had to do *something,* anything, to occupy her mind.

For a while, she tried to bang the jack against the trunk latch, or to knock out a taillight, but she couldn't get leverage. The last try knocked the recorder against her cheek.

She could record what she knew. That way, if something *happened,* the police might find it…*on her body.* Assuming Carlo and Leo stayed too stupid to check her pockets.

She swallowed hard, sick with fear and dread, but determined to make her last words count.

Her slippery fingers fumbled the buttons, but eventually she managed to turn over the tape, turn it on and position her mouth near the microphone. She explained the drugs in the engine compartment of the truck, about Ronnie and the bar, about Carlo's plan for her and her father. She stressed that her father had gone along with Sal to help the investigation, but had refused this last assignment, incurring Sal's death threat.

After that, she left a message of love for her father, in case he survived, urging him not to blame himself. She told her sister how much she loved her and how much confidence she had in her ability to make her own life. Then she left words for Riley— telling him how she felt about him and what she hoped for him.

Her voice broke twice. She was proud she'd mostly sounded calm and together. She'd showed grace under pressure. Of course, she didn't yet have a gun pointed at her head. She might yet melt into crazy hysterics. She hoped she'd be strong and dignified to the end.

She slid the phone and recorder back into her pockets, hoping the idiots wouldn't notice them. The tape would help bring Sal and his crew to justice. She knew Riley wouldn't let this alone until it was right. This was one place where his stubborn ways would serve her well. Or serve her memory anyway.

That done, she gripped the jack and waited. Once Carlo and Leo left to deliver the drugs, she would scream and bang on the trunk. Maybe Riley would be waiting at the bar. Maybe the police were at her house. Maybe every time a star fell an angel got her wings.

14

I'VE GOT YOU THIS TIME, Enzo. Through binoculars, Riley watched Enzo park in the dirt next to three vehicles outside a big barn—a perfect place for a drug stash.

Late that afternoon, he'd heard Enzo tell someone on the phone he'd meet him at *the ranch,* then lie to Natalie about his plans. It was Tuesday, the night of the mystery liquor delivery and Riley didn't believe in coincidences.

Careful to stay far enough away not to be seen, he'd followed Enzo to this spread in the desert west of the Valley. When the man turned onto a dirt road leading to the barn, Riley parked under a tree on the lookout for a chance to get closer unseen. He'd wait all night if that's what it took to find out what the guy was up to. Even if he had to miss the midnight liquor delivery. Not that he didn't trust the patrol assigned to check it out. He wanted to see for himself.

He sighed. Even when it panned out, night surveillance meant hours of boredom and fighting sleep. A partner helped, but after the false alarm, he didn't dare ask anyone to join him.

Once Enzo disappeared into the barn, Riley made sure his phone was on Vibrate, then loped down the road, hoping whoever was in the barn would stay put until he was hidden.

He saw no livestock, but he smelled manure and hay, so this had been a working barn at one time. As he reached the side of the barn, he heard country music. Huh? He climbed a parked tractor and looked through a dirt-caked window.

Five men sat at a wooden table playing cards. The chip stacks were high, so big money was at stake. Two of the men wore cowboy hats and he watched one spit tobacco into a beer can.

Incongruously, there was a wet bar and an entertainment center against one wall. Hence the music. What the hell?

Maybe they were killing time before a drug drop. The conversation was relaxed—trash talk and jokes from what he could hear—and they didn't seem to be waiting for anything except the next shuffle. If they were armed at all, it had to be with concealed handguns.

Was this just a card game with cronies? Riley got that heavy drag on his insides that told him he had to face bad news. Enzo must have lied to Natalie because she didn't want him gambling. He'd heard the man swear over big sports losses.

Goddammit. He could practically hear Chloe's jeer that he'd gone on another wild-goose chase after *poor, innocent Enzo*.

Dammit. He retreated to his car, thinking he'd hang awhile in case something happened. The minute he sat, his phone vibrated in his pocket. The readout said Chloe's number, but it was Mickey on the phone, his voice raw with panic. "You have to save my girl."

Adrenaline flooded Riley and his heart felt like a fist punching his ribs. "What happened? Where is she?"

"She's trapped. Carlo has her in his trunk. She must have followed me to Sal's and—"

"Did you call 9-1-1?" he interrupted, starting his car, spinning around, sending stones flying as he roared away.

"Police are on their way."

"How long ago did she call?"

"Almost an hour. I tried to call her back, but it went straight to voice mail. Her battery must be dead. She forgets to charge her phone some—"

"Play me her message," he snapped.

He listened to Chloe's frightened whisper, his hands tight on the wheel. In his head, he did the math on travel time for himself and Carlo. He told Mickey to stay by the phone and called dispatch for backup and to arrange a patch to the patrol officers driving to the house.

He called Mickey back. "They've made the drop by now. They're heading to your house. Get out of there. Somewhere safe. The police are close and I'm on my way." If only they were in time. "What were you doing at Sal's shop anyway?"

The guy hesitated.

"You're driving for him."

"Not for robberies. Deliveries. But I quit tonight."

"Not soon enough." Chloe had followed him with some crazy idea she could help, no doubt. Fury flared at Chloe's foolishness and her father's idiocy, but there was no time for recriminations now. "Just get out of the house."

"I need to watch for Chloe. I've got my rifle."

"For God's sake, no weapons. Go. Get out."

"I'll try to talk to them, delay them maybe."

"Don't be stupid, Mickey."

"I'm not leaving. It's my daughter," he said firmly.

"You should have thought of that before you dragged her into this. Leave. That's the only way to help her now." Riley hung up, surprised by the guy's sudden backbone.

He was pushing the engine for all it was worth, but he was too far away. He'd chased Enzo to a card game in the desert while Chloe was putting her life on the line. If those creeps manhandled her, hurt her in any way… The prospect filled him with raw rage.

She'd sounded so scared. If he didn't get there in time, he was afraid no code of conduct in the world would keep him from killing the bastards.

When the patrol officers alerted him via the tactical channel that they'd found Mickey alone in the house with his rifle, Riley relaxed a little. He was close, too. The creeps must have been delayed at the drug drop. He had to hope they hadn't detoured to get rid of Chloe early.

Riley and the patrol officers planned their operation over

the radio as he drove. Riley would get Chloe from the trunk, with backup from one officer, while the other waited inside to take down the thugs once Chloe was safe.

More cops would also arrive to boost their defenses.

Riley was two houses away when he spotted Chloe's car coming down her street. For a second, he thought it might be her, returning safe and sound. Then he recognized Carlo at the wheel. Sure. They had to get Chloe's car in place. Leo trailed Carlo in the Monte Carlo that held Chloe in its trunk.

Mickey's Cadillac was parked out front, so Carlo opened the garage door with Chloe's remote and both cars eased into the garage. The garage door slowly closed. Riley was out of his car and running for the backyard in seconds. On his way, he signaled the officer at the side of the house, then plastered himself beside the back door to the garage, unlocked already. His job was to free Chloe as soon as he could, depending on how the two creeps handled Mickey.

His blood burned in his veins. He fought to be smart, cool, assess before action, when all he could think was *Let her be alive. Let her be safe.*

He raised himself high enough to peek into the window in time to see both men enter the house. He entered the garage and raced to the trunk, where muffled thuds and movement told him Chloe was alive. *Thank God.*

A crowbar made short work of the lock and the lid lifted to reveal Chloe, duct tape hanging from one side of her mouth, her face red and damp with sweat or tears, a scrape and streak of blood on her cheek, more blood on her arm.

"My father? Is he safe?"

"Are you hurt seriously? More than scrapes?"

"I'm okay. What about my father?"

"There's an officer inside with him." He freed her arms and legs and helped her out. She was shaking badly. "Can you walk?"

She nodded and he watched her gather her strength. She was brave and tough and smart. "Take off. Go to a neighbor's. We'll handle it from here." The officers were awaiting his signal.

She just stood there. "Dad's inside?"

"Go," he said again, pulling her toward the back door and out into the yard, where she stood, shaky and uncertain and worried.

"Go," he whispered. "Mickey will be fine. Trust me." He couldn't stay to be sure she left. They'd be coming for her any second and he had to surprise them from the garage.

As the door to the house opened, Riley ducked behind it, then grabbed Carlo, hand over his mouth. "Keep quiet or you're dead." Carlo went limp. Riley cuffed him, then handed him out to the officer from the side yard.

Next, Riley sneaked inside, weapon at the ready, and found Leo holding a gun on Mickey in the middle of the front room.

"Leo!" he said sharply. The man turned, allowing the other officer to emerge, gun out, and tell Leo to put down his weapon.

Leo dropped it like it had burned his fingers and was soon being led out the front door, whining about how Carlo had the dumb idea and had forced him to help at gunpoint.

"Chloe?" Mickey asked.

"She's fine," he said. "She's safe. I sent her to a neighbor's." They all were fine and Leo and Carlo were being tucked into patrol cars. Murder averted. Two creeps who would surely roll over on their boss. This was all to the good.

"Riley!" Chloe's frightened voice from the kitchen had him running there, gun ready, Mickey at his heels. Just inside the door, he saw Sal holding Chloe against him, a 9 mm at her temple.

"Take it easy, Sal," Riley said, holding up his hands, his Glock still in one hand.

"Let her go!"

Mickey started forward, but Riley stopped him. "Calm down. We'll work this out. Won't we, Sal?"

Mickey backed off and Riley focused on Sal. "No need to

make this worse on yourself, Sal. Kidnapping is much worse than a little misunderstanding over a business deal, right?" He kept his voice calm, confident and friendly, as he'd been trained, despite what was going on inside him at the thought of Chloe in danger. "That's all that happened here, right? A business deal."

"So you're a cop." Sal sneered. "I knew there was something wrong about you. Enzo's a blind fool."

"What do you want, Sal? How can we help you?"

"That's what I like to hear," he said, relaxing as Riley wanted him to do. "I want the keys to her car and three hours to make Mexico—four just to be sure. I'll let her off just over the border."

"We can do that," he said, moving closer. "But let Chloe go first. Show us goodwill."

"Stay back!" He extended the weapon in Riley's direction. The guy was so damn predictable. "Put down your gun."

Riley stopped and slowly lowered his gun.

"I don't know what happened to my pepper spray, Riley," Chloe said, her voice shaky but strident. "I guess I'll have to *use my head*." What was she saying? In a flash, he got it. She was going to butt heads with the guy.

Bad idea. Too dangerous. Before he could signal her, she bent her knees and pushed up hard, slamming into Minetti's nose with a hard thud.

"Ow. Shit!" Sal sagged, releasing Chloe to clutch his nose. Riley grabbed Sal's gun, then spun him and forced him to the ground.

Mickey ran to his daughter.

"I'm okay, Dad," she said, charging to where Sal lay on the floor. "You are a creep and a monster and an asshole," she yelled. "And your cologne smells like poison and—" She sagged, starting to cry, shaking violently.

"Get her to the couch, Mickey. She's about to faint. Chloe, put your head between your knees. Slow your breathing so you don't hyperventilate."

He wanted to go to her, but he had Sal to handle. A patrol officer entered and cuffed him. Riley followed them outside, where patrol cars crowded around. Crime scene tape blocked the yard. A crime scene technician stepped from her mobile unit. And he could hear the whap of media helicopters overhead.

He wanted to check on Chloe, but he spotted a couple of guys from another detective squad headed his way. The suspects had already been placed in separate patrol cars for questioning. He briefed the detectives quickly, then left them to start on Sal and his crew, so he could check on Chloe.

He found her on the couch, patting her father on the back—comforting the man who'd nearly gotten her killed. "It's okay, Dad," she was saying. "It'll be okay now."

Outrage flooded Riley's brain. "The hell it will!" he snapped. "He's been driving for Sal, Chloe. Did you know that? What the hell did you think you were doing? If you think they won't charge you, you're crazy."

The man just looked at him.

"He was learning more about Sal's operation," Chloe said, chin up, ready to defend her weak father to the death.

"Bullshit. He's done nothing but protect his own hide since this started." He looked down at Mickey. "Look at the pain you caused your daughter. She risked her life for you. Do you realize that? Do you?"

"Stop bullying him!" Chloe's voice cracked. "He risked his life to save me. You risked both our lives." She seemed to catch herself. "We both were stupid. We know that. I should have called you." She stopped, suspicion in her eyes. "Where were you, anyway? Dad said you were way out of town when he called."

"I was doing surveillance."

"On another case?"

Guilt washed through him. "I tailed Enzo out to a ranch."

"Where he plays poker? I don't believe you. You're still hounding the man?" Her words were bitter and her eyes angry.

"We just haven't caught him yet." It was a stupid thing to say, but he had to justify being so far away when she needed him.

"You're hopeless," she said. "Why did I ever think that you— Just forget it."

"Can we talk?" He nodded down the hall. "Detectives will be in for your preliminary statements soon."

"Will you be okay, Dad?"

"He's right, Chloe." Mickey raised wet eyes to his daughter. "This is all my fault."

"Don't answer one question, Dad. I'll get you an attorney. I didn't think we needed one, but obviously we do. The police don't give a damn about us." She glared at Riley.

"The law is the law, Chloe."

"The law is supposed to serve the people, Riley. But you don't seem to get that part."

This was going downhill fast. "Would you come with me?" He tried to take her arm, but she marched off down the hall.

He paused in the bathroom to wet a cloth for her injuries. He found her in the bedroom, arms folded.

He came toward her with the cloth.

"It's nothing," she said, taking the cloth and rubbing it brusquely over her mouth and cheek. "Stop acting like you care."

"I do care. I care a lot." With a jolt, he realized just how much. He loved her. And they were breaking apart, like ice floes in the spring, helplessly sailing apart on the current, never to be joined again. He took the cloth and wiped gently at her arm.

She watched him, her expression bleak. "You won't really charge him, will you? He was helping the case."

"No, he wasn't. And it's up to the D.A. what he'll be charged with. And the FBI." The woman had barely escaped death and she was agonizing about her father's screwup. "He was working with Minetti. For pay, Chloe."

"Sal forced him. And it was just deliveries. He quit when he knew it was drugs. He hates that he let me down." Her voice broke. She had such a big, foolish heart.

"He broke the law, even after the deal we cut to save him. He made his own bed, but he got you to lie in it. Can't you see that?" He had to get through to her. He had to save her from the Sals and Enzos of the world. And from her own father.

"You're pretty quick to point out everyone else's mistakes, Riley. What about your own? Even if I had called you, you were out chasing Enzo. Where were the police who were supposed to watch Sal's place? If Carlo hadn't been delayed at the bar, you'd have been too late and I'd be dead. My father, too."

The words hit like a shotgun blast into Kevlar and the breath went right out of him. "You're right. I haven't used good judgment."

"Neither of us has. Not since the beginning." Her anger softened to sadness. "You did what you thought best. So did I and so did my father. We made mistakes. Some of them whoppers." A tear slipped down her cheek. She brushed it away angrily.

"Chloe, I—" What was he going to say? How could he fix this when he felt her slipping away?

She held up her hands. "Don't apologize. We tried, but we're from different planets. I believe in my family—and in people—and you don't. Maybe I do too much for my family, maybe I'm too soft, but you're too damn hard."

He just looked at her. She'd figured him out at last. He was too damn hard. He felt a sharp pain behind his ribs. If he wasn't mistaken, whatever heart he had had snapped in two.

He stuck with the facts, with his job, with what he could do. "I'll do what I can for your father. My report will emphasize what he did to help the case. I'll talk to London and the D.A. Maybe they'll be lenient. It depends on what Sal does and what happens with the case."

"I appreciate that," she said stiffly.

"If there's anything else I can do—"

"There's one thing." She took a shaky breath. "Is there any way to keep Enzo and Natalie from finding out what I did?"

He shook his head. "This'll make the papers. Ronnie will be arrested. I don't see how they wouldn't know."

"I hate this," she said, breaking into a sob. "I hate what we've done to them." She swallowed, her eyes full of despair.

"We did what had to be done." He tried to be gentle. "You have to let go of the Sylvestri fairy tale. They were kind to you, but when push comes to shove, their loyalties lie with each other. You worked for them." Her innocence made him ache.

"Don't try to poison me against them."

"I want you to see people for who they are. You let people use you. You let love confuse you."

"And you never do, do you, Riley?" she snapped, her words deadly cold now. He'd said the wrong thing. "Love doesn't confuse you because you never let it touch you."

Chloe couldn't stop the harsh words, even though Riley looked like she'd slapped him. Because of him, she'd betrayed the Sylvestris and now, innocent though they were, they would be dragged through the mud because of her, because of this heartless, stubborn man with no mercy in his soul.

She felt like sobbing and she felt like punching him. "You got a raw deal in life, Riley, and so you expect everyone to hurt you. You're so busy protecting yourself, you miss all the good parts. You have no loyalty except to the law and I doubt that will keep you warm at night."

He stood there, taking in her attack, his dark eyes troubled, but accepting. She felt a pang. He always listened to her. Always. She remembered how he'd welcomed her first kiss, laughed when she set off that car alarm, told her she was the birthday girl. She couldn't stand this pain and she grabbed at her chest, tightening her fingers in her still sweaty shirt.

"Sometimes the people you love hurt you," she continued. "But if you love them, you don't give up. You forgive, you encourage, you help where you can. And you hang on to the love, you let it heal you in the end. Because it will, Riley, it will. I know you don't believe that. Maybe you can't believe it."

Her heart filled abruptly with despair. What had existed between them had been killed by all that had happened. Tears spilled down her cheeks. She cared for Riley more than she wanted to admit to either of them.

"Don't cry, Chloe." He took her by her upper arms and looked at her so softly. Here was Birthday Riley, warm and tender and loving. For a second, she wanted to say, *Never mind, let's try again, maybe I can help you change.*

"Ms. Baxter? May we have a word?" The voice from the hallway startled her. The police wanted her statement.

She turned to call out, "I'll be right there."

By the time she looked back, Riley's soft look was gone, replaced by Detective Connelly's tough-guy exterior. What was she thinking? That she could save the man? That was the old Chloe, who rescued everyone she could get her hands on. She couldn't rescue Riley. He didn't want it.

It was time for the new Chloe to move on. Except the last time she'd felt like the new Chloe had been in bed with Riley. And that was over. This time for good.

A FEW DAYS LATER, Chloe and her father arrived at the police station to learn what charges would be filed against Mickey. Their attorney was already here. Nervous sweat trickled down Chloe's sides, she'd bitten her lip raw and she could not catch a solid breath.

She was startled to see Riley waiting for them in the lobby, just as he had the first time they were here. "Hello, Chloe... Mickey." Again he wore his stern cop face as he let them through the security door and into the same interview room.

Three men rose to greet them—Agent London, Paul Adams, the assistant district attorney, and their attorney, the only one who smiled.

"Shall we get started?" Agent London said, sitting.

"Please," her attorney said.

"I'll get right to the point," London said. "You're very fortunate that Sal Minetti has chosen to help us make a case against those above him." He looked at them as if they were misbehaving children who'd been given an unearned break.

"What does that mean for us?" she asked, aware that Riley had moved. She glanced at him. He gave her a look. *Take it easy. Listen first.* Okay, she would try to stay calm.

"He's not acting out of remorse, mind you," London continued, again ignoring her question. "He's in big trouble for freelancing beyond the Chicago connections. He has named the guy at the security firm working on the fencing scheme, as well as his drug source."

"And…?" This time it was her attorney losing patience.

"Because of Ms. Baxter's and Mr. Baxter's help, the FBI has no interest in pursuing federal charges. As to the state of Arizona…" He motioned to the assistant D.A., who cleared his throat.

"On that matter, there are numerous counts at question—accessory to burglary, transporting illegal substances, aiding and abetting criminal activity, on and on. I won't enumerate them all." He leveled his gaze at her father. "That said, we have examined your testimony, considered your earlier cooperation, have talked to the officers involved in the case, and have decided to offer two years' imprisonment, with the option of alternative incarceration."

"Two years?" Chloe demanded, horrified by the thought of her father behind bars. "That's terrible. We can't accept—"

Her attorney touched her hand to stop her. "May I have a moment with my client?" he said to the attorney. Everyone cleared the room.

"It's good, Chloe," their attorney said. "We're talking a halfway house and electronic monitoring. With good behavior, it could be cut in half. It's the best outcome we could hope for."

She looked at her father. "It's good, Chloe. It'll be fine." In a strange way, he seemed relieved, so in the end, she said yes.

When the men had returned, she asked what would happen to Ronnie.

"He was selling ecstasy to kids," London said, "but he's a minor with a top attorney. He'll likely to get off with probation." The agent sounded disgusted. Chloe hoped Ronnie would learn his lesson. She knew his parents must be sick with worry. She'd left a dozen phone messages, but neither Enzo nor Natalie had returned her calls. The thought of them made her physically ill. What were they thinking about her? It had to be the worst.

"And Enzo? What about him?"

"We have no proof he had knowledge of any of this." London shook his head. "Sal confirms this. The man had his head in the sand or has lost his touch. Hard to say."

She shot a look at Riley. *I told you so.* His expression remained neutral. His cop face was firmly in place. The distance between them made her ache.

They finalized the deal, talked through some details and finally were finished. They all stood and shook hands. This time the men managed fleeting smiles. She tried to be happy. This was a decent decision, though thinking of her father imprisoned made tears sting her eyes.

They were in the parking lot when she heard her name. Riley was calling to them again. Despite everything, her name on his lips made her melt. What a fool she was, still in love with an impossible man.

She waited for him to reach them.

"I wanted to thank you again," he said. "You were a tremendous help. Seeing the drug packet in the truck's engine compartment made you an eyewitness to the drug distribution system, which convinced Sal to give it up."

"That's good, I guess."

"Very good. Remember all the white trucks? They used that make and model because the manufacturer had altered the shape of the engine, but retained the chassis, leaving an empty space they covered with a metal plate. Sal's crew didn't have to tamper with the trucks to stash their packets."

"I'm glad I could help," she said, avoiding his eyes. She didn't want to see the hard cop or the loving man. Both made her too sad for words.

"I want to thank you, too, Riley," her father said. "I know you spoke up for me. And you kept your promise—you watched over my daughter." His voice cracked.

"I did my best."

She raised her eyes to his and found Birthday Riley's dark eyes full of tender concern. And sorrow. He missed her, she could see, and that made it so much worse. Her heart knotted in her chest. She missed him, too. More each day.

"I'll meet you in the car," her father said, moving away.

"Are you okay?" Riley's eyes searched her face.

"As good as can be expected. You?"

"Same." He gave a rueful smile.

"How's Idle?"

"He misses you," he said softly. *So do I.* But he had the sense not to say the words.

If only they could fix this, try again. *Stop it,* she told herself. *What's done is done.* "Enzo knew nothing about what Sal was doing. I was right."

"He closed his eyes to what his son was up to with Sal."

"When you love someone, you don't want to see their flaws." Which was exactly what she and Riley had done.

"Have you talked to Natalie?" he asked gently.

She shook her head. "She won't take my calls."

"She'll come around. You kept her son from digging himself into deeper trouble. They're grateful to you. Give them time."

"Do you really believe that?" she asked, startled by the optimism in his words.

"It's what I hope. For your sake. I want the best for you."

"I know you do." She longed to rest her head on his chest, tuck herself into the cave of his body, pretend it was enough.

"I just wish—" She stopped herself. What did it matter what she wished? A birthday wish had started this and look how it had ended. No more wishes for her. Not for a long, long time.

"You'll still go to cooking school, right?"

"Eventually. For now I have to make sure my father's okay. I quit Enzo's so they wouldn't have to fire me. I'll get a new job, maybe two, and save my money." Nothing good came easily, no matter what wishes or promises you made.

"Take care of yourself, Riley," she said and hurried away before he could see her cry.

15

RILEY FOUGHT THE URGE to chase Chloe down and pull her into his arms. Better to remember who he was: a cop—and cops were tough on relationships—and a solitary guy who kept his distance from people.

Except he wasn't quite that guy anymore and it was all her fault. He couldn't stop missing her. Her body, her smell, her touch, the steady, serious way she looked at him, even how stubborn she was.

She'd changed him and now she was gone, and he couldn't get back to his old ways. He'd been happy before. Now he was miserable. Somehow, even with the spring sun so bright it hurt, the world seemed gray with gloom.

He'd liked it better when his heart thumped along evenly—no banging into his chest or jumping into his throat, making it hard to make a sensible decision or keep his emotions in check, or even be the kind of cop he'd always been—direct, clear, devoted to the job, content with a social life limited to barbecues and beers and sports events with squad mates.

That had been plenty for him and he counted himself lucky.

Now he couldn't stop wanting more.

Neither could Idle, it seemed. The dog hadn't stopped moping since Chloe left. He kept giving Riley accusatory looks. *What did you do to chase her away?* That was another way Chloe had messed him up. She had him reading his dog's mind.

IN THE END, Chloe drove to the Sylvestris' house, determined to talk to someone. Natalie seemed startled to hear her voice through the intercom. "This isn't a good time," she said grimly.

"I'll wait here until it is," she said, tears stinging her eyes. "I have to explain."

Natalie sighed. The gate clicked, the fence parted and Chloe drove in to face the music.

Natalie opened the door to her, her face pale, dark circles under red-rimmed eyes. "Come in," she said and led Chloe through the house where she'd made so many lovely meals, enjoyed the praise and pride of the family before she'd ruined everything. Now the air smelled of disappointment… or was it…?

Burnt cookies. That was what the air smelled of. A plate of black-bottomed snickerdoodles rested on the counter.

"Is Enzo home?" she asked tentatively.

"He won't come down. You have to understand how hurt he was. He thought of you as a daughter."

"And I thought of you both as second parents. You were always so kind to me."

"We took you into our home, like family, and you did this, this *spying?* I couldn't believe it. Our Chloe? I couldn't accept it at first."

"I felt so awful, I can't tell you how awful." Shame and guilt washed through her, bitter and hot as burnt espresso. "A million times I wanted to tell you, but the police wouldn't let me say a word. Not if I wanted to save my father. You understand, don't you? I had to help my dad?"

"Have a cookie." Natalie pushed forward the plate, then hesitated and pulled it back. "They're pretty nasty. I'm no Chloe in the kitchen." A tiny smile peeked through the sadness.

"If I could change it all, I would."

Natalie waved a hand. "It wasn't just Enzo. I was angry, too. Maybe more than Enzo. But then I thought about Ronnie. Sal and his creepy friends dragged him down a bad path and we looked away. When I think about all the kids who took the drugs he got from Sal…I feel so ill. Ronnie wants to change, thank God. It could have been so much worse. I guess we should thank you."

Then she threw up her hands. "No, no. Too soon for that."

"Again, I'm so sorry. If there's anything I can do—"

"Please, you've done enough!" She shook her head, trying to joke, but it clearly hurt. "You know, your boyfriend, the policeman, came by. What nerve, but he wouldn't leave until we heard him out."

"Riley came here?" Chloe was startled.

"To defend you. He told us the FBI and the D.A. forced you, that it tore you up what you had to do, that you swore by Enzo's innocence with every breath."

"He said all that?"

"Not in so many words. He's not a big talker, Riley."

"No, he's not." But she was touched by what he'd done.

"I offered him some lasagna and when I said you made it, I thought he would melt right in my kitchen. So, you broke up? Over this?"

"Over this and because we're not well suited."

"You give up too soon, Chloe."

She didn't want to talk about Riley. She wanted to make things right with Natalie and Enzo. "What he said is true. I wanted only to help your family. Do you think Enzo can ever forgive me?"

"He's bruised and grumpy right now, striking out at everyone. This is a lesson to him to never turn a blind eye. Give him time."

"Thanks, Natalie, for telling me."

"Now what about you? What will you do about your schooling? You quit the restaurant, I hear."

"I thought it was best. I'll get another job, save my money like before."

"I could put in a word with my sister-in-law Olivia. Her

Dream A Little Dream Foundation gives grants to worthy ideas. You'd have to write an application. Would that help?"

"You've done so much for me, Natalie. Too much. I can't accept." Her throat closed and tears blurred her vision.

"With family, you forgive." Natalie wrapped Chloe in a bruising hug. "Here's a thought, Chloe. You're always doing for others. Maybe because your own life scares you? Think about it." She leaned in to whisper, "That's from Oprah, by the way."

Natalie's words rang in her head for the rest of the day, and the weeks she struggled through, missing Riley and worrying about her father. The good news was that he'd have eighteen months of house arrest at a halfway house.

On the morning he was to report to the house, Chloe went into his room to see if she could help him pack. He was gathering books from a shelf. His sock drawer was open so she grabbed a handful and carried them to his open suitcase.

Her father took the socks from her. "This is for me to do," he said in a tone more sober than she'd ever heard. "I've asked my sponsor to drive me. We'll say goodbye here."

"But I want to help and I can easily drive you."

"It's time I helped myself. I told myself a fairy tale about how to be a good father. I always said I let you down, but I didn't really see how badly I had until Sal attacked you."

"That wasn't your fault."

"Yes, it was. I feel like someone's ripped off my skin and the air singes what's been exposed. It hurts like hell, but at least I'm finally being honest."

"You don't have to do this alone."

"Some things you do. You've been my angel, Chloe, and now I need to find my own wings."

What had Riley said about her father? *Maybe if you didn't always jump to his rescue, he'd stand on his own two feet.*

Evidently he was right. "It's your decision, Dad," she said. "I'll let you finish up."

She sat at the kitchen table, feeling oddly lost. She didn't know what to do with herself, so she was grateful when the doorbell rang.

She answered to find an impossibly huge basket of gourmet foods. She signed for it and read the card.

With Dad away, we know you'll be lost. This should keep you busy cooking. I'll keep calling.
Love, Clarissa and Ryan.
P.S. Ryan got a job and I'm back in school!

Clarissa. In all the mess with her father and Riley, Chloe realized she'd completely neglected her sister. She'd left her request for money hanging in thin air. Meanwhile, Clarissa had called more than once to talk with their father or to leave messages of encouragement and love for Chloe. Clarissa had been taking care of her own life and helping Chloe, too. Her sister had grown up and Chloe hadn't noticed.

Natalie was definitely right. She'd looked after her father and Clarissa partly to keep from looking after herself. Delaying cooking school had almost been a relief and she'd turned down Natalie's help with a grant flat out.

What was she afraid of? That she would fail? That she would be disappointed? That she'd disappoint herself?

No. She was afraid to be different. She'd felt useful as her father's keeper and her sister's parent. Without that role, who was she? Old Chloe fit her like a glove. New Chloe was uncertain, a wish and a hope. A work in progress.

Except when she was with Riley.

With Riley, the new Chloe felt real and free. She'd felt so good with him, like she could rest or go wild or be however she wanted to be. With him she felt safe and cared for. With him she felt like herself.

Maybe that scared her. Riley believed he didn't have the heart for a relationship. But she didn't believe that. Not really.

Just because he didn't recognize his warmth and tenderness didn't mean it wasn't there or couldn't be nurtured into fuller display.

If she could see herself in a new way, then Riley could, too. She could help him. Not change him, not take over his life, just help him see all that he was and could be.

Her heart lifted like a balloon and she was dancing on her feet. She had to talk to him. They needed each other. To sort it out, to grow, to become fully who they were meant to be. And wasn't that what love was?

WHEN THE HELL would this stop hurting? Riley asked himself, parking on a bench in the dog park. Again. Poor Idle just sat beside him, tongue lolling a yard long, almost touching the grass, exhausted. Riley shouldn't have dragged him out simply because he couldn't stand the ache in his chest.

Dammit. Where the hell was his old contentment? He figured all he needed was a couple weeks, maybe a month, but no. He was still wrecked.

Giving up, he brought Idle home to collapse for a nap and headed to the station to catch up on paperwork.

He was proud of the case, at least. That had been good. And he'd decided to request additional training, give himself another challenge. SWAT, hostage negotiations, maybe FBI training. Something to keep him busy.

It was funny, but Chloe had changed his views a little. He didn't see suspects quite the same. Enzo's face when he saw his son in cuffs had affected Riley. There was rage and frustration and deep sorrow and desperate love. Riley actually felt sorry for the guy. That was new.

Would seeing the humanity of the bad guys make Riley a better cop? He had to hope so. The fence between good citizens and criminals wobbled and sagged here and there. There were well-meaning bunglers like Chloe's father to consider and maybe Enzo really was retired.

"Got something for you."

He looked up to see Marie holding out a mini tape recorder. "What is it?"

"Something the crime lab sent over." She wiggled the recorder. "From the Minetti case. Your informant had it. They're finished with it. There's something for you on it." She looked at him curiously.

He took the tape player. Chloe had recorded a message while she'd been in that trunk. His heart kicked hard.

He plugged in the earbuds from his iPod and hit Play. *This message is for Detective Riley Connelly.* Chloe's voice, shaky and scared, woke up every nerve in his body. He could hear the hum of tires on the road and engine noise in the background. *Riley. In case we don't see each other again…* She hesitated, then cleared her throat. She'd believed she was being driven to her death at that moment.

She continued, her voice steady. *Here's what you have to believe, Riley. You have a heart bigger than you know. Find a woman who makes that clear to you.*

She took an unsteady breath. *You'll be a great husband and a father. Overprotective maybe, but you're a cop, so you can't help that. You'll be great exactly for the reasons you think you won't be—you know what a messed-up childhood feels like. You know what you needed and you'll give that to your kids.*

You can say I'm a Pollyanna or a dreamer or that I have rose-colored glasses, but I know you, Riley. I know you.

He looked up, realizing his vision was fuzzy. His eyes had filled with water.

Find a woman who won't let you get away with less than all you have to give. She was crying a little, which made him blink back the sting in his eyes.

He needed privacy, so he stopped the tape, left the station for a bench that faced a patch of desert wildflowers.

He pushed Play again. *While I'm at it, call your mother.*

Give her a chance to ask for your forgiveness. Yeah, she blew it, but she's family. Forgive her. Help her forgive herself.

She paused again. He couldn't believe her last thoughts were of him and his estranged mother.

I guess that's all the orders I'm giving out, Riley. Tell my sister—my father, too, if he survives—that it was fast and I didn't feel a thing.

Her voice went more urgent, she spoke more quickly now.

Riley, listen...I wish that we'd... I wanted us to— I love you, Riley. We're different, but what is it they say? The heart wants what it wants? I wish I could cook one last big meal for you. Something special I'd invent just for you. An early birthday dinner. And I'd dream up a new cake. Something with caramel. Take care of yourself, Riley. Make a life with your arms wide open, okay? For me. For yourself. For the family you'll have if you're not too stubborn to give yourself that gift.

I'm thinking of you now and somehow I don't think I'll ever stop.

The tape squealed abruptly, as if she'd started to cry and didn't want it to show up on the tape.

Her words grabbed him and wouldn't let go. She knew him. She knew how he felt about family and himself. Chloe, of all people, had plenty of reason to give up on family. But she hadn't. She never would. Her father had nearly gotten her killed. Yet she loved him, forgave him, stuck with him. Did that make her naive, blind or a saint?

Maybe it made her brave.

Willing to get disappointed, but still to believe, to hope, to push for more, to be there to be counted on.

Find someone to love... Open your heart... You're better than you think you are. What if he was? And if so, the woman he wanted was the one who'd whispered into this tape, believing she was about to be killed.

Stubborn, cheerful, hopelessly optimistic Chloe, who

laughed like a song and smelled like spring rain. Who loved like there was no tomorrow.

Maybe he could be a husband, a father and a cop all at once. With Chloe beside him, maybe he could try.

She'd rescued her father, her sister and a feral cat. Maybe, just maybe, she'd rescue him.

She'd made that tape thinking those were her last words. She'd lived, though, and maybe that had changed how she felt. Maybe she'd given up on him.

He wouldn't let her get away that easily. If she'd given up on him, he'd win her back. He knew just how because he knew her, too.

"WHAT ARE YOU DOING HERE?" Chloe said, her heart beating so fast and happily she could hardly speak.

"What does it look like?" Riley stood on her porch in the rain, no umbrella, with two grocery sacks from the gourmet store. Idle, dripping wet, woofed in greeting.

"You want to cook something?" she asked.

"You got it." His eyes had a peculiar light in them. Like Birthday Riley but more solid, more sure. There was tenderness and attention and desire and, deep in his eyes, the low flame of hope.

"Come in out of the rain," she said, opening to him and his dog, tears in her eyes. She had so much she needed to say.

He brought in the smell of spring and wet desert, like the night they'd made love with the window open and her heart jumped in her chest. She breathed in the moment and the man.

Idle shook himself, spraying them both with water.

They laughed, the sound blending into lovely music.

A meow made them turn. Pepper Spray was looking straight at Idle, who lowered his ears and body and belly-walked over to the cat in pure adoration. She sniffed delicately at him, then put her paws on either side of his muzzle and began grooming away the water on his head.

"Those two seem happy to meet again," Riley said.

She kept her eyes on him. "What's on the menu?"

Riley set the grocery sack on the floor, keeping his eyes on her. "I listened to the tape you made. In the trunk."

"The tape? Oh. I forgot about that. Everything was so terrible that night."

"Did you mean what you said? About me being better than I think I am, that I could be a good husband and father because I know what I missed as a kid?"

"Every word," she said, tears filling her eyes. "From the bottom of my heart."

"You make me want that, Chloe. I want to be one of the people you won't give up on no matter what—the ones you forgive and encourage and help where you can. I want you to have faith in me and I want to be worthy of that faith. I love you, Chloe, with all the heart I've got." She saw water gleam in his eyes.

"You have plenty of heart, Riley. I've felt it."

"Me, too, I guess. Without you my chest hurt so bad, I figured there must be something more in there than muscle and blood."

She laughed, loving him so much she thought she'd burst. "I gave up too soon. I was afraid to trust how we were together, afraid to be the Chloe I want to be. The Chloe I can be with you."

He kissed her forehead, then looked hard at her. "I'm still a cop to my bones. When they call, I'll be there. I love you, but I'm there for the job."

"I respect that. Don't forget I'll be pretty intense about cooking school…once I get there." She'd already started an application to Olivia's foundation. "I'll always worry about my father and sister. But you were right. If I don't jump in to rescue them, they can stand on their own two feet."

"I'm glad I was right about something."

"For the first time in my life, what *I* want comes first. And what I want is you."

He pulled her into his arms. "I missed you so much," he said, crushing her against him, then leaning back. "I called my mom, too."

"You did?"

"It was your dying request. I had no choice."

"What did she say?"

"She cried, Chloe. She said she wished she'd had the courage I had to make the call."

"I'm glad, Riley."

"We'll get together. The three of us. Maybe you could cook us something nice? Help me say what I need to say."

"I'd be honored. I'll come up with something new. Reconciliation Stew?"

"Good idea." He dipped to kiss her and her entire body rose to take the love he offered, to meet him halfway. Afterward, he cupped her face. "Thank you for making me your birthday wish."

"It was more than a wish. It was a promise."

"Be careful what you wish for," he said, cupping her backside in that possessive way he had, his smile wry. "You've got me now—for better for worse."

"Mmm," she said, wondering how much better it could get.

They would struggle, she knew. They were both stubborn as hell and they had plenty of lessons to learn, Birthday Riley and new Chloe, but she had a feeling they would do just fine.

"I wanted to work up that new cake you mentioned on the tape," Riley murmured in her ear. "That'll have to wait."

"Mmm," she said, liking where he was headed. "Just one question…"

"Do you have to ask? Of course I brought the caramel sauce."

"Sounds like heaven."

He swept her into his arms and carried her away, the dog and cat trotting close behind.

* * * * *

Here is a sneak preview of
A STONE CREEK CHRISTMAS,
the latest in Linda Lael Miller's acclaimed
MCKETTRICK *series.*

A lonely horse brought vet Olivia O'Ballivan to
Tanner Quinn's farm, but it's the rancher's love
that might cause her to stay.
A STONE CREEK CHRISTMAS
Available December 2008
from Silhouette Special Edition

Tanner heard the rig roll in around sunset. Smiling, he wandered to the window. Watched as Olivia O'Ballivan climbed out of her Suburban, flung one defiant glance toward the house and started for the barn, the golden retriever trotting along behind her.

Taking his coat and hat down from the peg next to the back door, he put them on and went outside. He was used to being alone, even liked it, but keeping company with Doc O'Ballivan, bristly though she sometimes was, would provide a welcome diversion.

He gave her time to reach the horse Butterpie's stall, then walked into the barn.

The golden retriever came to greet him, all wagging tail and melting brown eyes, and he bent to stroke her soft, sturdy back. "Hey, there, dog," he said.

Sure enough, Olivia was in the stall, brushing Butterpie down and talking to her in a soft, soothing voice that touched something private inside Tanner and made him want to turn on one heel and beat it back to the house.

He'd be damned if he'd do it, though.

This was *his* ranch, *his* barn. Well-intentioned as she was, *Olivia* was the trespasser here, not him.

"She's still very upset," Olivia told him, without turning to look at him or slowing down with the brush.

Shiloh, always an easy horse to get along with, stood contentedly in his own stall, munching away on the feed Tanner had given him earlier. Butterpie, he noted, hadn't touched her supper as far as he could tell.

"Do you know anything at all about horses, Mr. Quinn?" Olivia asked.

He leaned against the stall door, the way he had the day before, and grinned. He'd practically been raised on horseback; he and Tessa had grown up on their grandmother's farm in the Texas hill country, after their folks divorced and went their separate ways, both of them too busy to bother with a couple of kids. "A few things," he said. "And I mean to call you Olivia, so you might as well return the favor and address me by my first name."

He watched as she took that in, dealt with it, decided on an approach. He'd have to wait and see what that turned out to be, but he didn't mind. It was a pleasure just watching Olivia O'Ballivan grooming a horse.

"All right, *Tanner,*" she said. "This barn is a disgrace. When are you going to have the roof fixed? If it snows again, the hay will get wet and probably mold…"

He chuckled, shifted a little. He'd have a crew out there the following Monday morning to replace the roof and shore up the walls—he'd made the arrangements over a week before— but he felt no particular compunction to explain that. He was enjoying her ire too much; it made her color rise and her hair fly when she turned her head, and the faster breathing made her perfect breasts go up and down in an enticing rhythm. "What makes you so sure I'm a greenhorn?" he asked mildly, still leaning on the gate.

At last she looked straight at him, but she didn't move from Butterpie's side. "Your hat, your boots—that fancy red truck you drive. I'll bet it's customized."

Tanner grinned. Adjusted his hat. "Are you telling me real cowboys don't drive red trucks?"

"There are lots of trucks around here," she said. "Some of them are red, and some of them are new. And *all* of them are splattered with mud or manure or both."

"Maybe I ought to put in a car wash, then," he teased. "Sounds like there's a market for one. Might be a good investment."

She softened, though not significantly, and spared him a cautious half smile, full of questions she probably wouldn't ask. "There's a good car wash in Indian Rock," she informed him. "People go there. It's only forty miles."

"Oh," he said with just a hint of mockery. "*Only* forty miles. Well, then. Guess I'd better dirty up my truck if I want to be taken seriously in these here parts. Scuff up my boots a bit, too, and maybe stomp on my hat a couple of times."

Her cheeks went a fetching shade of pink. "You are twisting what I said," she told him, brushing Butterpie again, her touch gentle but sure. "I meant…"

Tanner envied that little horse. Wished he had a furry hide, so he'd need brushing, too.

"You *meant* that I'm not a real cowboy," he said. "And you could be right. I've spent a lot of time on construction sites over the last few years, or in meetings where a hat and boots wouldn't be appropriate. Instead of digging out my old gear, once I decided to take this job, I just bought new."

"I bet you don't even *have* any old gear," she challenged, but she was smiling, albeit cautiously, as though she might withdraw into a disapproving frown at any second.

He took off his hat, extended it to her. "Here," he teased. "Rub that around in the muck until it suits you."

She laughed, and the sound—well, it caused a powerful and wholly unexpected shift inside him. Scared the hell out of him and, paradoxically, made him yearn to hear it again.

* * * * *

Discover how this rugged rancher's wanderlust
is tamed in time for a merry Christmas, in
A STONE CREEK CHRISTMAS.
In stores December 2008.

Silhouette

SPECIAL EDITION™

**FROM *NEW YORK TIMES*
BESTSELLING AUTHOR**

LINDA LAEL MILLER

A STONE CREEK CHRISTMAS

Veterinarian Olivia O'Ballivan finds the animals
in Stone Creek playing Cupid between her and
Tanner Quinn. Even Tanner's daughter, Sophie,
is eager to play matchmaker. With everyone
conspiring against them and the holiday season
fast approaching, Tanner and Olivia may just get
everything they want for Christmas after all!

*Available December 2008
wherever books are sold.*

Visit Silhouette Books at www.eHarlequin.com LLMNYTBPA

HARLEQUIN *Presents*

EXTRA

THE ITALIAN'S BRIDE
Commanded—to be his wife!

Used to the finest food, clothes and women,
these immensely powerful, incredibly
good-looking and undeniably charismatic
men have only one last need: a wife!

They've chosen their bride-to-be and they'll
have her—willing or not!

Enjoy all our fantastic stories in December:

THE ITALIAN BILLIONAIRE'S SECRET LOVE-CHILD
by CATHY WILLIAMS (Book #33)

SICILIAN MILLIONAIRE, BOUGHT BRIDE
by CATHERINE SPENCER (Book #34)

BEDDED AND WEDDED FOR REVENGE
by MELANIE MILBURNE (Book #35)

THE ITALIAN'S UNWILLING WIFE
by KATHRYN ROSS (Book #36)

nocturne™

New York Times bestselling author

MERLINE LOVELACE

LORI DEVOTI

HOLIDAY WITH A VAMPIRE II

**CELEBRATE THE HOLIDAYS WITH TWO
BREATHTAKING STORIES FROM
NEW YORK TIMES BESTSELLING AUTHOR
MERLINE LOVELACE AND LORI DEVOTI.**

Two vampires, each wary of human relationships,
are put to the test when holiday encounters blur
the boundaries of passion and hunger.

Available December wherever books are sold.

REQUEST YOUR FREE BOOKS!

2 FREE NOVELS
PLUS 2
FREE GIFTS!

HARLEQUIN®

Blaze™

Red-hot reads!

YES! Please send me 2 FREE Harlequin® Blaze™ novels and my 2 FREE gifts (gifts are worth about $10). After receiving them, if I don't wish to receive any more books, I can return the shipping statement marked "cancel". If I don't cancel, I will receive 6 brand-new novels every month and be billed just $4.24 per book in the U.S. or $4.71 per book in Canada, plus 25¢ shipping and handling per book and applicable taxes, if any*. That's a savings of 15% or more off the cover price! I understand that accepting the 2 free books and gifts places me under no obligation to buy anything. I can always return a shipment and cancel at any time. Even if I never buy another book, the two free books and gifts are mine to keep forever.

151 HDN ERVA   351 HDN ERUX

Name	(PLEASE PRINT)
Address	Apt. #
City	State/Prov. Zip/Postal Code

Signature (if under 18, a parent or guardian must sign)

Mail to the **Harlequin Reader Service:**
IN U.S.A.: P.O. Box 1867, Buffalo, NY 14240-1867
IN CANADA: P.O. Box 609, Fort Erie, Ontario L2A 5X3

Not valid to current subscribers of Harlequin Blaze books.

Want to try two free books from another line?
Call 1-800-873-8635 or visit www.morefreebooks.com.

* Terms and prices subject to change without notice. N.Y. residents add applicable sales tax. Canadian residents will be charged applicable provincial taxes and GST. Offer not valid in Quebec. This offer is limited to one order per household. All orders subject to approval. Credit or debit balances in a customer's account(s) may be offset by any other outstanding balance owed by or to the customer. Please allow 4 to 6 weeks for delivery. Offer available while quantities last.

Your Privacy: Harlequin Books is committed to protecting your privacy. Our Privacy Policy is available online at www.eHarlequin.com or upon request from the Reader Service. From time to time we make our lists of customers available to reputable third parties who may have a product or service of interest to you. If you would prefer we not share your name and address, please check here. ☐

HB08R

Harlequin® Historical
Historical Romantic Adventure!

THE MISTLETOE WAGER
Christine Merrill

Harry Pennyngton, Earl of Anneslea,
is surprised when his estranged wife,
Helena, arrives home for Christmas.
Especially when she's intent on
divorce! A festive house party
is in full swing when the guests
are snowed in, and Harry and
Helena find they are together
under the mistletoe....

*Available December 2008
wherever books are sold.*

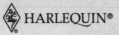 HARLEQUIN®

 *Blaze*™

COMING NEXT MONTH

#435 HEATING UP THE HOLIDAYS
Jill Shalvis, Jacquie D'Alessandro, Jamie Sobrato
A Hunky Holiday Collection

Santa's finally figured out what women want—hot guys! And these three lucky ladies unwrap three of the hottest men around. Don't miss this Christmas anthology, guaranteed to live up to its title!

#436 YULE BE MINE Jennifer LaBrecque
Forbidden Fantasies

Journalist Giselle Randolph is looking forward to her upcoming assignment in Sedona…until she learns that her photographer is Sam McKendrick—the man she's lusted after for most of her life, the man she used to call her brother.…

#437 COME TOY WITH ME Cara Summers

Navy captain Dino Angelis might share a bit of his family's "sight," but even he never dreamed he'd be spending the holidays playing protector to sexy toy-store owner Cat McGuire. Or that he'd be fighting his desire to play with her himself…

#438 WHO NEEDS MISTLETOE? Kate Hoffmann
24 Hours: Lost, Bk. 1

Sophie Madigan hadn't intended to spend Christmas Eve flying rich boy Trey Shelton III around the South Pacific…or to make a crash landing. Still, now that she's got seriously sexy Trey all to herself for twenty-four hours, why not make it a Christmas to remember?

#439 RESTLESS Tori Carrington
Indecent Proposals, Bk. 2

Lawyer Lizzie Gilbred has always been a little too proper…until she meets hot guitarist Patrick Gauge. But even mind-blowing sex may not be enough for Lizzie to permanently let down her guard—or for Gauge to stick around.…

#440 NO PEEKING… Stephanie Bond
Sex for Beginners, Bk. 3

An old letter reminds Violet Summerlin that she'd dreamed about sex that was exciting, all-consuming, *dangerous!* And dreams were all they were…until her letter finds its way to sexy Dominick Burns…